WHISPERS
of
SHADOWBROOK HOUSE

OTHER PROPER ROMANCES

As Rebecca Anderson
Isabelle and Alexander
The Art of Love and Lies
The Orchids of Ashthorne Hall

As Becca Wilhite
Check Me Out

PROPER ROMANCE

WHISPERS
of
SHADOWBROOK HOUSE

REBECCA ANDERSON

SHADOW
MOUNTAIN
PUBLISHING

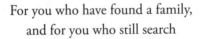

For you who have found a family,
and for you who still search

© 2025 Becca Wilhite

All rights reserved. No part of this book may be reproduced in any form or by any means without permission in writing from the publisher, Shadow Mountain®, at permissions@shadowmountain.com. The views expressed herein are the responsibility of the author and do not necessarily represent the position of Shadow Mountain.

This is a work of fiction. Characters and events in this book are products of the author's imagination or are represented fictitiously.

PROPER ROMANCE is a registered trademark.

Visit us at ShadowMountain.com

Library of Congress Cataloging-in-Publication Data
Names: Anderson, Rebecca, 1973– author
Title: Whispers of Shadowbrook House / Rebecca Anderson.
Description: [Salt Lake City] : Shadow Mountain Publishing, 2025. | Series: Proper romance | Summary: "In the crumbling Shadowbrook House, governess Pearl Ellicott and heir Oliver Waverley unravel a haunting mystery while confronting their growing forbidden love"—Provided by publisher.
Identifiers: LCCN 2024057323 (print) | LCCN 2024057324 (ebook) | ISBN 9781639933884 trade paperback | ISBN 9781649333599 ebook
Subjects: LCGFT: Fiction | Romance fiction | Novels
Classification: LCC PS3623.I545 W45 2025 (print) | LCC PS3623.I545 (ebook) | DDC 813/.6—dc23/eng/20250131
LC record available at https://lccn.loc.gov/2024057323
LC ebook record available at https://lccn.loc.gov/2024057324

Printed in the United States of America
PubLitho

10 9 8 7 6 5 4 3 2 1

PROLOGUE

1880, Hampshire, the New Forest

The rolling River Hamble weaves through land grown thick with trees. Old houses of all origins and sizes hug riverbanks, sinking their feet into the earth and its history even as the world looks forward toward the coming century.

In a crumbling manor of red brick, a lonesome man clings to the memory of all those he's lost. Whispers echo through walls and down staircases, voices of the dead clinging to this ruin of a house that once was a home. Clenching his teeth against the murmurs, he nevertheless breathes in the sound with all his senses, desperate to keep any connection with those who have deserted him in life as well as in death.

The old man grips most fiercely to the child who remains. Fingers clamped as tightly as jaw and heart, he cannot allow himself any release, for he knows to relax his hold would be to lose the only person left he might still—in his flawed, desperate way—remember how to love.

CHAPTER 1

Going home shouldn't feel like walking into a nightmare. Not that Shadowbrook had ever felt much like a home.

When he requested a visit with his uncle Arthur, his letter went unanswered. In a different situation, Oliver might have waited.

Waiting was no longer a possibility.

The driver took the sharp left turn faster than Oliver would have, and he winced as his shoulder slammed into the carriage wall. This journey would have been more comfortable on the back of a horse. Seats with springs and walls to keep out wind and rain were all very well, but Oliver wished he'd opted for a mode of travel where he was the one driving. Being unable to see the road gave him the feeling he wasn't as in control of his arrival as he wished.

He knocked at the carriage wall and called out, "Stop here, please."

The driver reined in the horses, and as soon as they'd stopped, Oliver opened the door and jumped out.

"I'll walk the rest of the way, thank you." Pulling his cases from the rack at the back of the carriage, Oliver looked ahead. The lane to Shadowbrook twisted through the darkness, overrun with trees and wild branches.

"There's no place for me to turn about," the driver said. "I've got to go ahead to the house. May as well stay in for the ride."

Oliver shook his head. "I'd rather not." There were quite a few things about this visit he'd rather not do. Walking the lane was one element he could choose.

The horses pulled the carriage away toward the house, their hoofbeats and the jangle of tack quickly swallowed up in the edges of the New Forest. Soon, nothing more than the hush of wind through autumn leaves joined the sound of Oliver's feet on the lane.

Before many minutes had passed, the carriage returned to view, the horses snorting. The driver raised a hand in farewell, no hint of a smile on his face as he hurried away. The man must have noticed the tumbledown state of the house. Oliver understood his eagerness to be gone as quickly as possible.

Occasional flickers of movement in the trees on either side of the lane would have made a younger Oliver shudder with a perfect combination of fear and delight, but he was far too old to believe in haunted forests now. The woods held no specters. No monsters. No fairies. Only possibilities for improvement and a path forward into the future.

At the lane's final turning, the house came into view. Once a magnificent family home, Shadowbrook now resembled a storybook ruin, and if buildings had feelings, this house would be weeping. More than simply neglected, Shadowbrook leaned and shuddered, its very foundations seemingly unable to support the crumbling red stones.

Oliver turned toward the western border of the property where a slope led to the river's edge. How many hours had he spent there as a boy, watching ships sail past and hoping for a miraculous future that would carry him away from this place?

He was no longer that wishful boy. He made his own fate now.

Readjusting his grip on the handles of his cases, he turned to the house. He took one look at the imposing front door and opted for the kitchen entry. Much better to walk in as though he belonged here than to chance an encounter with his uncle's butler. If he did happen to bump into Jenkinson, Oliver planned to make eye contact and nod at the man. Maybe even smile. He knew that didn't seem like much of a plan, but it was more than he'd ever managed before. Not that Oliver was afraid of the butler; he'd simply rather give himself time to be prepared for their meeting.

The butler's large stature had a way of making Oliver feel small, even though Oliver himself was quite tall. The way Jenkinson looked at him, though, always reduced Oliver to being ten years old again, late for something, and in trouble.

As far as Oliver knew, Jenkinson had never smiled, but now that Oliver was a man himself, it couldn't hurt him to extend a bit of friendliness. Perhaps he could warm the butler's icy heart and bring him around to seeing the wisdom in Oliver's proposal for the future of the property.

Maybe, in turn, Uncle Arthur would listen to his most trusted servant.

It was possible, if not likely.

As he opened the door to the kitchen, the house seemed to sigh. When he was a boy, Oliver had heard such sounds as voices. Murmurs and whispers. Now he understood a building's tendency to breathe in and out as doors opened and closed, to creak as stairs and walls shifted and settled.

Everything in the kitchen looked smaller than he remembered it: tables, work surfaces, cupboards. Had he truly grown so much taller in his time away at school and Cambridge and the subsequent years in London?

Though the kitchen fire was banked, the aromas of a meaty stew hung about the room, reminding him of the occasional silent dinners he and his uncle had shared many years ago.

With no sign of a cook or a serving maid in the kitchen, Oliver moved through to the main floor's maze of hallways leading to rooms of questionable structural integrity and far more questionable original intent. Whatever they'd been meant for, Uncle Arthur had left his mark on many of the rooms. The room to Oliver's right housed a collection of human figures sculpted in white marble, many of them covered in draperies as if several ghosts had gathered. There was more space between the figures than there used to be. Perhaps Uncle Arthur had begun selling off his collections. All the better, as that meant less for Oliver to get rid of when he took over the house.

He closed his eyes for a moment and imagined Shadowbrook completely empty. Echoing halls. Cleared corners. No rooms full of centuries of ignored collections, no crates and trunks piled against walls, no stacks of unused serving platters that wouldn't fit in the kitchen. It was hard to imagine it, but the vision was rather pleasant. Clean. Unburdened. Oliver smiled at the impossible thought.

With the wind whispering through cracks and seams, Shadowbrook was never silent, but now it came close. There was no sound of movement or household conversation as Oliver made his way past a few more rooms with boarded windows and draped furnishings. The echo of his quiet footfalls and creaking beams followed him. He refused to slow his steps enough to hear the music.

Not that he believed in the music.

It was a childish ghost story he'd shared with his friends. Now that he'd returned after so many years, it was easy to believe he'd invented the strains of violin music floating through the halls of Shadowbrook on dark nights. He focused on the shushing of his own shoes' soles against the floor.

Finally, he arrived at the entry hall, his arms protesting the weight of his bags.

Shadowbrook's main staircase was a showpiece, lovely even to Oliver's jaded eyes. Majestic gray marble stairs rose from the entryway up to a high-ceilinged upper floor, each wide step covered with a thick, velvety carpet. Even after all these years, Oliver could remember sinking his toes into the soft warmth of that rich carpet.

At the top of the first landing, he turned right, heading toward his childhood bedroom. He hoped he'd be allowed to take that same room for the duration of his visit.

Before he arrived at the bedroom door, he set his bags down and felt along a blank stretch of wall. His fingers acted by memory alone, locating the small gap in the paneled wall. He pressed his finger into it, and the hinge opened silently.

Oliver smiled at the memory of many solitary hours spent drawing pictures in this secret, hidden space. Before he was able to pull the door fully open and step inside, a flurry of arms and skirts and hair tumbled from the cupboard, and a laughing voice exclaimed, "Well done, young explorer! You've found me far earlier than I expected you to."

Her hands gripped his elbows, and he stared down into a sweet, smiling face that quickly shifted into astonishment.

A woman who did not appear much younger than Oliver's own twenty-six years blinked at him from beneath a fan of eyelashes as black as her hair, her lips parted.

His voice, rusty from disuse, cracked as he replied, "Yes, I've found you. And I didn't even know I was looking." He smiled in natural amusement at the situation.

"How very fortunate for us both," the angel with a mane of black curls said, the startled look melting into a smile of what Oliver hoped was true pleasure.

He felt his smile grow even larger. "Indeed. Although I think it only fair to confess, I'm not at all sure what I've found. A sprite? A specter?"

The woman laughed, a sound like the tolling of bright silver bells. And was that a dimple in her porcelain cheek?

"Nothing quite so interesting, I assure you. A governess and nothing more. Hardly the stuff of fairy stories." She looked down at her hands, still pressed to his arms.

Oliver had no complaints about the way she held on to him. He noticed her unpretentious gray-blue dress, clearly made more for function than fashion, though the simplicity of her uniform didn't dim the sparkle in her eyes nor the brightness of her smile.

She seemed to notice they were standing very near to each other, and she removed her hands from his arms, taking a small step backward. Oliver forced his legs to hold still and not close the distance between them immediately. He didn't want to appear as though he was chasing her.

"Are you Mr. Waverley, then? The heir?" She pronounced each syllable distinctly, as if his name was an important word.

Someone had mentioned his name to this woman. Perhaps that was a good omen. Perhaps he was welcome and expected after all.

With a smile, he asked, "Are you not sure? Perhaps you're expecting additional guests today?" It wasn't really an answer, but finding such a vibrant woman in the maddening gloom of Shadowbrook House made him lose his head for a moment.

Her dimple reappeared as she grinned at him. "If you know Mr. Ravenscroft at all, you know he doesn't entertain guests."

Oliver nodded. "I suppose he's required to make an exception for me, since I'm family."

The woman's smile slipped. "I'm not accustomed to seeing Mr. Ravenscroft make exceptions." She gave a small shake of her head and put on a polite expression. "But, of course, you know him better than I do."

"I'd imagine not, as you live here, while I've not seen him for years." Oliver realized he didn't know this woman's name. He continued, "You do live here, don't you? You said you're the governess?"

She nodded. "I do, and I am. Pearl Ellicott." She held out her hand and they shook.

Oliver had the strangest urge to hold her hand and not let go. "Pearl. That is a lovely name. And very appropriate for a woman of your..."

Oliver trailed off. Was he really going to say "beauty" and mention he'd noticed the radiant luminosity of her skin? Not if he wanted to ever face her again without feeling a complete fool. And he did want to face her again. Maybe she hadn't heard him.

"My what?" she asked, her dark eyebrow arched.

He tried for many seconds to come up with a reasonable ending to his sentence without any luck at all.

Her smile teased him. "No, really. Do go on. How am I like a pearl? Do you refer to my granularity? My roundness? My ability to grow inside an oyster's shell?"

Oliver laughed. Her banter was an excellent way to repair his foolishness.

"Your name is appropriate for a woman of your age."

There. That wasn't so bad.

But she was not about to let such silliness pass unremarked.

"And do you presume to know what my age is?"

He laughed again. Unbelievable. Engaging in simple small talk in a city ballroom was never as risky as this conversation with this young woman had become. How did Pearl Ellicott manage to confuse his brain so much that his mouth released words without consulting him?

"Miss Ellicott, would you allow me to begin again?"

She tucked her hands around her elbows and nodded with a polite smile. Unless he was much mistaken, she knew exactly what effect she had on him, and she was enjoying his discomfort. He was quite glad to see her enjoyment, and willing to play the part of the fool if she kept smiling at him.

"I'm pleased to make your acquaintance." He took her offered hand and held on perhaps a moment too long before letting it go. "And I hope to meet little Max soon. He was a newborn baby when I was here last."

When I was sent away, Oliver thought but did not say.

Miss Ellicott's eyes flicked past Oliver and down the hall. Some of the light receded from her eyes, and she offered a small sigh.

"He's no baby now, but you ought to prepare yourself. He's not strong. He's rather small for his age, and often ill and tired."

Oliver wished they were sitting. She looked as though the admission had tired her. "It's true, then, what people say? He's unwell?"

The rumors were far stronger than the word "unwell" suggested, but Oliver didn't want to repeat any of the things he'd heard. Village gossip, even far from the surroundings of Shadowbrook, spun stories of a reclusive old man and a child wasting away in a sadly neglected house. Such stories always seemed to reach Oliver when people learned of his connection with Shadowbrook House.

As soon as his question passed his lips, Miss Ellicott stepped back and her posture grew rigid. Her hands curled into fists at her sides and any joy he'd seen in her expression was replaced with fire.

"Maxwell Ravenscroft is a perfect child. Brilliant and kind. Beautiful. All that he should be. No matter what *people* may say."

The force of her tone suggested this young woman had something to prove. To him? To herself?

Had he asked about the child with too much pity? Was there an unintended hint of delight at Maxwell's misfortune?

Oliver nodded. "I apologize if I offended you. I admit, I'm curious about my cousin, but I'm certain he is everything you say. One hears things, you understand." The words felt weak, somehow both too apologetic and not an apology at all. He tried again. "I am looking forward to meeting him, and I hope we will be friends."

Oliver did not specify which "we" he meant, but he certainly hoped his careless reference to the gossip about Shadowbrook had not ruined his chances to see Miss Ellicott's smile again, and soon.

He also understood Pearl Ellicott was not a woman who would answer any of the idle questions that filled his mind. That was unlucky, as she would be the best source for information about the house and especially about his uncle. But her apparent insult regarding the whispered gossip proved to Oliver that she was not likely to sit at evening firesides and share details of life within the crumbling walls of the manor.

Miss Ellicott watched him, one eyebrow arched and her head turned slightly. She was searching for something, but Oliver couldn't tell if it was a quality she hoped to discover or one she'd rather not find.

He knew himself well enough to know he'd prefer her to see only the best side of him. There was too much of his uncle within the darker parts of his mind, elements he attempted to keep hidden even from himself.

He forced a reflection of his previous smile. "Would this be a good moment for you to introduce me to my cousin?"

She continued to watch him from beneath that arched eyebrow for another uncomfortable moment, but then her smile returned. "I imagine you have time to put your bags away before he discovers me. And speaking of discovery, I must make his search worth the reveal."

Without another word, she spun back to the hidden panel in the wall, pressed her fingers to the secret latch, and stepped inside, pulling the door tight with an almost inaudible snick. Only a second before, she'd stood in front of him, and now she was gone. The architectural alchemy of Shadowbrook House could make a person believe in ghosts.

When Oliver realized he was alone in the hallway staring at the wall, he picked up his cases and hurried to the room he'd once called his own. If Miss Ellicott was so interested in hiding, he probably ought to get out of the way of whatever game he'd walked into.

If the kitchen had seemed smaller upon his entry this evening, the bedroom seemed to loom. Had the ceiling always risen so high? And the windows, although curtained with thick winter ivy—had they always been so vast? Something was different. The room not only looked bigger, it felt more solitary. Even lonely.

He turned and faced the wall beside the door.

The painting. It was gone.

The only thing about this house he'd ever truly loved—a portrait of his mother prepared for her wedding day—used to hang there on the wall. As a boy, he'd wake each morning to the sight of it. He'd kneel beside his bed at night for the prayers his nanny demanded, but although his lips spoke words to God, he'd crack one eye to watch the painting and imagine his mother was there listening.

And now she was gone, both from his life and from the room.

Perhaps the painting had simply moved to a different wall. It was his painting, after all, and it couldn't be gone. Portraits didn't disappear.

But he thought of the life-sized white sculptures missing from the gallery downstairs. If a marble statue could be sold, how much easier to relocate a framed portrait?

Against the east wall was the alcove he used to hide in. He strode to the other side of the bed, but space there had been furnished as a dressing room, complete with wardrobe, mirror, and shaving table. No sign of the painting.

He pulled the curtains from the darkened windows, but he found nothing.

An unexpected wave of sadness crashed over him, and he felt his fists clench. Who would remove his mother's portrait from his room? And why?

The sorrow passed as quickly as the answer came. Shadowbrook wasn't his home. Not until he inherited. The painting didn't belong to him until the house did. If Uncle Arthur wanted to move it, he had every right to do so. But even still, Oliver regretted the picture's loss. Would it be strange for him to ask for it back, if only for the days he stayed?

He knew he was here on very shaky agreement. Even with Oliver's pleading correspondence, Uncle Arthur had not actually consented to this visit. He couldn't ask more of the old man. At least not yet.

Once he accepted the painting was gone and he wouldn't find it, he allowed himself a moment to grieve. Had the portrait always been what connected him to this place? Perhaps it had. And now that it was gone, he felt less attached than ever to Shadowbrook. Surely Uncle Arthur would understand it was time to rid themselves of the house. Oliver found himself justifying his hopes of selling the property. He pictured sitting across from his uncle at a desk or a table, leaning forward and speaking clearly, compassionately. He'd be gentle with Uncle Arthur; after all, this run-down place had been the old man's shelter for decades. But the days of the grand houses were passing. Within twenty years, the world would cross the threshold of a new century. Old things must pass away and make room for the new.

Oliver realized he was muttering his practiced arguments aloud to himself and shook his head. "I've got to get out of this room."

CHAPTER 2

"Mr. Oliver Waverley," Pearl whispered to herself, smiling at the thought of him.

She'd heard of Mr. Waverley, but he'd never visited the house in the six years she'd been at Shadowbrook. Six years was a long time to stay away from home, even if it was home in name only. Had he chosen not to come, or had Mr. Ravenscroft made him feel unwelcome? Pearl couldn't imagine avoiding any house that held an uncle or a cousin. She'd give anything for a family connection.

Having never met him before today, she'd assumed several things about his character, most of them befitting a villain from one of Maxwell's adventure stories, complete with an oiled black mustache, a swirling black cape, and a matching black heart.

The truth was much brighter.

Oliver Waverley smiled a lot for a villain. And his easy laugh held no malice. He looked quite nice in his neatly cut suit and waistcoat instead of an imagined billowing cloak. What was she supposed to do with this new information? She'd never considered Oliver Waverley might be charming. Nor had she thought about the possibility he'd be terribly handsome.

As she stood in the dark cupboard, she wondered if he was, in fact, particularly good-looking, or if her reaction was simply to seeing someone new in this house, someone near her age.

But then she remembered that smile. His deep brown eyes, wide shoulders, and narrow waist. His hands, large and gentle. His hair that appeared freshly cut, as if he'd taken care to look his best for this unusual visit to Shadowbrook.

Pearl resolved to seek out further information about Shadowbrook's heir and felt her smile growing larger at the thought of how such information might be gathered.

She'd been quick to assume the gossip Mr. Waverley had heard about Maxwell was cruel, and far too quick in assuming he believed it. But maybe Mr. Waverley's question about Max was more kindly explained. Perhaps he was simply looking for information about his cousin.

He'd asked her to make an introduction, which had to be a good thing. If he didn't care about the boy, he'd hardly seek him out. Oliver Waverley seemed to take at least a passing interest in Maxwell, and nothing mattered to Pearl more than Max's well-being.

Probably not a villain after all.

Pearl replayed the memory of their unexpected meeting. Oliver Waverley had known about this room. He'd pressed the hidden latch. He'd found her here. She tried not to dwell on the fact that she'd thrown herself at him and embraced him as he opened the door. How could she justify such an action? She had been expecting Max, but what accounted for her continuing to hold on to Mr. Waverley's arms for several shocked moments after it became clear he was not the small boy in her charge?

Such thoughts might make a governess question her state of mind.

Perhaps, she thought with a smile, it was best to pretend it hadn't happened.

Pearl shook herself from the admittedly pleasant wanderings in her mind. She had work to do.

With her back to the secret door leading out to the hallway,

Pearl stretched her arms toward the ceiling. She couldn't reach all the way to the top of the wall, but, standing on her tiptoes, she managed to touch the squares of the decorative molding. She pressed on one and felt it click, twisted the next block to the right a quarter turn, then flipped open the third square of wood. A door in the molding above her released with a quiet squeak of its hinges.

She'd been here before, naturally. One didn't simply unlatch trapdoors in secret cupboards by accident. But she'd never opened this one while trying to remain so quiet. Nor had she ever before attempted doing so without a lamp. The ambient light from the hallway cast little glow in the dark cupboard.

Luckily, she'd cleared out the debris of the years on a previous exploration, so when the flap in the ceiling opened this time, she wasn't covered with dust and leaves and crunchy, desiccated shells of many-legged creatures. Now she made a leap and reached for the exposed area. This, too, she'd done before, but it took a few tries to jump high enough to reach the stick of wood she'd placed at the ledge.

She gave it a tug and a rope ladder unrolled down the wall.

Seeing Pearl's utter inelegance and silliness in this moment would have delighted Maxwell. However, knowing there was a man in the house, a stranger, Pearl didn't think her remaining pride would allow her to leap up and down when there was the slightest chance Oliver Waverley might see. She'd save any further acrobatics for when she and Maxwell were alone. After all, she and Maxwell were alone nearly all the time.

She gave the rope ladder a final tug, making sure it would bear Maxwell's weight.

She felt a tickle across her shoulder and reached up to brush her hand across her dress. A large spider crept onto her finger, and she shook her hand to toss it to the ground. After all, it was only a spider. But the feeling of crawling along the neckline of her dress persisted, and she brushed her shoulder again. Two more spiders crept across her hand.

One spider was nothing to panic about, but more than one was distressing, to say the least.

She shivered and began brushing at her dress in earnest, pushing against the fabric to rid herself of the deeply uncomfortable sensation of spindly legs on her skin. The sensation was accompanied by a murmur of fear—not words, exactly, but something more like audible shudders. Whispers she often heard in the darker corners of the house.

Pearl forced herself to take a deep breath and think clearly. She was alone in the cupboard. No one stood here whispering. The spiders were statistically unlikely to hurt her. They were only spiders, not bats, or rats, or worse.

Stop, she told herself. Thinking of rats was not helpful.

She forced herself to consider her reaction. Why was her breath coming fast, her skin crawling, and her face heating? Was it the darkness? The whispers? Being confined here for the sake of the game? The sheer number of spiders that might be hiding in any of the secret rooms in this house? And was her discomfort enough to ruin Maxwell's game?

The last question was easiest to answer. She would suffer far worse than the shudder of tiny legs on her skin to give Maxwell a few moments of delight at discovering this secret room.

But she couldn't get the memory of spider legs out of her mind. Pearl knew what to do—think of something pleasant. Like Oliver Waverley's sudden appearance in Shadowbrook House.

CHAPTER 3

Oliver wondered what was keeping Miss Ellicott so long. He thought she'd come knock for him when she and Maxwell finished playing their game. Could she still be in the secret cupboard? Perhaps now was a good time to introduce himself to his cousin. If the governess happened to be in the child's room, even better.

As Oliver opened his bedroom door, he saw a small boy taking careful giant steps—one leg extended at a time—and counting aloud. "Thirteen steps north-northeast from the last stop."

The boy stopped outside the hidden panel in the wall and studied something in his hand. He spun in a slow circle. When he faced the direction of the bedrooms, Oliver saw the boy looked quite a bit like himself, or at least as he had as a child. Large dark eyes, the same squared-off chin, and unruly brown curls. This must be Maxwell.

"All right, Pearl. Where are you?" Oliver heard a laugh in the boy's voice. "Don't cheat. If I've found you, you have to let me see you."

She did not appear, and Oliver felt the child's regret at her failure to arrive. It couldn't be stronger than his own regret. He wondered why she didn't show herself.

Maxwell turned in another slow circle, and this time he looked up at Oliver standing in the doorway, watching him.

With no obvious surprise at seeing a stranger in the hallway, he raised a small, pale hand and gave a short wave. "I haven't seen you before."

It wasn't a question, and his voice was more serious now than when he'd called for Miss Ellicott.

Oliver raised his own hand in greeting. "I'm Oliver."

The boy inspected him with a frank stare. "Are you a ghost?"

No one had ever asked him a question like that before.

"Not that I'm aware."

Another moment of consideration was followed by a serious nod. "I think you'd know." Maxwell tilted his head as if listening for a quiet sound. After a moment, he added, "Not a ghost. Just a visitor." Still standing in the hallway, the boy seemed to reconcile himself to something. "Hello. I'm Max. I'd come over there and shake your hand, but I'm sure I'd spoil the game."

It was almost an invitation, and Oliver would take it. "I'd never want your game spoiled. What is it you're playing?"

"Explorer's Search."

Oliver stepped away from the door and closed it behind him, shutting out the memories of the empty bedroom.

"I don't know the game. How does it work?"

Maxwell shrugged. "Pearl sets me a map. Well, not exactly *a* map. Many maps, I suppose. One movement at a time." He waved a scrap of paper and then held up a compass on a chain. "I follow the compass directions and calculate the number of steps, and when I reach the end, there's another clue." He squinted up at Oliver. "She calls it playing, but she's really trying to sneak in teaching me things. Sums and reading compass directions and such. Sometimes she writes the clues in German or French, but I'm not so good at reading French."

He looked too young to be able to read anything at all, but Oliver was no expert at assessing a child's age.

Maxwell studied the small piece of paper in his hand again. "Now I'm at the end, and there are no more clues."

An urge to help the child battled with a desire to stay and watch him puzzle out the challenge.

"Is there any chance you've taken a wrong turn?"

The little shoulders raised up and then drooped. "There is always a chance. This house was built for wrong turns. But if I did, this clue will have been the only one I failed. All the others led to new ones."

Oliver wondered if his arrival had somehow prevented Miss Ellicott from leaving Maxwell his final clue. He glanced around the hallway, and what he saw made it difficult not to smile.

He rubbed his jaw and tried to look wise. "Perhaps you need to look at things a different way."

Maxwell's expression nearly made Oliver laugh aloud. It wasn't a pout, exactly, but it was certainly related. "That sounds like something Pearl would say."

"Does it? Seems like your friend Pearl is very wise."

Maxwell gave a dismissive shrug. "She's not my friend. She lives here."

"Lucky you have a friend who lives in the house with you. I once lived here. Did you know that?"

Maxwell shook his head. "Are your parents dead?"

Oliver's eyebrows lifted in surprise at Maxwell's bluntness.

The boy ducked his head. "Sorry if that was rude. I was just wondering."

"Why do you wonder about that?"

Another shrug of the thin, small shoulders. "My parents are dead. Pearl's, too. And my grandfather's parents are, or they'd be hundreds of years old. I think people come here to live when they've got no one left."

Oliver was stunned into silence at both the surprising maturity and wisdom in the words, but also the great sadness. He studied the little boy. Maxwell didn't seem sad, but perhaps his seriousness was an effect of lifelong sorrow.

Finally, he managed to string a few words together. "How lucky Shadowbrook is here, then. I'm glad I've found you at my return."

Maxwell nodded. "I think we should be friends. When I thought you were a ghost, I didn't know if we could manage it. We might have done. But I've never made friends with a ghost before. You would have been the first."

"And if you had been the ghost, you'd have been my first ghost friend as well. For the time being, we'll simply have to be the usual kind."

"All friends are unusual to me," Maxwell said. "I never leave the house, and no one comes here. At least, not until you."

Oliver wondered if Miss Ellicott heard Maxwell's quiet statement from behind the wall. Could she hear the somber acceptance in the words?

Then, with impressive mental agility, Maxwell reverted to a previous topic. "I wonder if I *have* taken a wrong path on my Explorer's Search. Pearl should be here, or at least a note should."

Right, Oliver thought. The boy was looking for his governess and a clue, not a conversation about the possibility of being ghost-friends with a near stranger.

"I find," Oliver said, "that a change of perspective helps me see things a new way." He folded his legs and sat on the floor in the middle of the hall.

Maxwell looked at Oliver with a question in his eyes, but upon Oliver's offering of a smile, the boy nodded and followed suit. Oliver placed both hands on his knees, and Maxwell did the same. Oliver leaned back, looking toward the ceiling, where a scrap of torn brown paper was pinned near the top of the wall.

"It's my next clue," Maxwell said, somehow both cheerful and calm.

Oliver was happy he'd followed his instinct not to simply

point out the paper to the child. There was something satisfying about letting him make the discovery. "And what does it tell you?"

Maxwell got up from the floor with more effort than Oliver was prepared for. After he caught his breath, he stood with his hands clasped behind his back, staring up at the paper high above his head.

"It doesn't say anything."

Oliver wondered if the boy's illness affected his eyesight. Surely Miss Ellicott wouldn't place a wordless clue at the end of the game.

He stood behind Maxwell and looked at the paper. The boy was right—no words at all. Oliver reached up to take the paper from the wall, but Maxwell stopped him, a calculated look on his face. "Wait a moment."

After staring at the wall for a few seconds, Maxwell turned and grinned. "She's here."

"How can you tell?"

"Look," the boy said, but instead of directing Oliver's attention to the hidden latch, he pulled a small pile of paper scraps from his trousers pocket. "These are the clues. What do they have in common?" He handed the lot to Oliver, who looked at each in turn.

"They're all written in the same hand," Oliver said.

Maxwell nodded. "Yes, of course. Pearl did them all. What else?"

Oliver stifled a chuckle at the boy's lecturing tone, as if Maxwell was a tutor and Oliver his student.

"Each has a compass direction and a mathematical equation to solve." Some of the calculations were quite complicated. Oliver wondered at the governess pushing the sick boy quite so hard.

Maxwell sighed. "I already told you that. Look at the paper."

Each piece in Oliver's hand was folded neatly, and the edges matched exactly. Perfect squares. He held them up and pointed at the angles.

Maxwell nodded. "And that paper," he said, pointing at the torn scrap on the wall, "is the clue."

He moved to stand directly beneath the note. "It's in the shape of an arrow, you see. Well, not a very good one. It's pointing me to the next move."

Oliver knew it was true, but he didn't want to give Miss Ellicott's hiding place away, so he carefully stared at the brown paper as Maxwell ran his palm from side to side across the wall, starting as high as he could reach and feeling every inch of painted plaster. After a minute or two, Maxwell had traveled far from the hidden catch in the wall.

Should Oliver stop him? Show the boy how to get inside? He recognized a strong urge to protect Maxwell from wasted effort, but knew it would be wrong for him to step in. Better to let the child solve the puzzle, even if it took some time.

Maxwell dropped his arms and stared at the wall. Oliver wondered if he'd ask for help, but he hadn't so far. Perhaps he would shout in anger or frustration. Oliver wouldn't blame him. He was feeling a hint of frustration himself. Watching the boy's back, Oliver saw the thin arms come up and cross in front of his chest. Was he giving up? He tried to remember being a small child trying to do a difficult task. Before he could arrive at any idea, Maxwell turned to face him, a smile stretching wide and showing a missing tooth.

He knelt and placed his hands against the base of the wall, this time moving with more confidence. "She showed me where to look, but if she'd made it more obvious, I wouldn't have needed to stretch my mind."

What eight-year-old spoke this way? Oliver watched, feeling his heartbeat increase as Maxwell's fingers inched closer to the hidden catch in the wall.

When his fingers found the knot, Maxwell grinned over his

shoulder at Oliver. "This house is full of secret rooms and passages."

Oliver nodded but did not tell Maxwell he already knew all about Shadowbrook's secrets, including this room. It was too much fun to watch the boy discover it.

He pushed a finger into the divot, and the door swung open. Oliver realized he was holding his breath in anticipation of Miss Ellicott's second arrival in the hallway. But she did not rush out to embrace Maxwell the way she'd embraced Oliver. Had he somehow ruined the finale?

With another glance over his shoulder and a cheeky grin, Maxwell nodded at the open door. "Coming?"

"I wouldn't miss it."

They stepped into the empty cupboard and waited for their eyes to adjust.

Maxwell clapped his hands. "I've never seen this one before."

Where was Miss Ellicott? Had she come back out of hiding before Oliver left his room? Was there another clue placed somewhere inside this cupboard?

"You play in the secret rooms often, then?" Oliver tried to sound unconcerned as he stared into dark corners, wondering where Miss Ellicott had gone.

"Of course. This is my house. I can go wherever I wish. And right now, I wish to go up." Maxwell pointed to a rope ladder dangling from a hatch in the top of the wall.

Oliver hadn't known about the hatch, regardless of the many hours he'd spent hiding here with a candle stub and his drawing papers. He remembered the way his feet would fall asleep as he dangled his legs over the edge of the small bench built into the wall, his head bent over a notebook.

"Help me?" Maxwell's half-request, half-command brought Oliver into the present. Oliver pulled on the ladder to make sure it was fastened securely and would hold the boy, then beckoned him forward.

Maxwell gripped the wooden bar at his eye level and stepped onto the lowest rung. Oliver came around behind him, his hands on either side of the ladder, holding it as steady as he could.

"Will you climb with me? I don't want to slip." For the first time, the boy's voice hinted at his nerves.

"Of course. I wouldn't want to miss your discoveries now that we're friends."

Maxwell looked at Oliver over his shoulder, his fists still gripping tightly to the ropes. "Are we friends already?"

"Absolutely. I have very good instincts. We're suited to be good friends for the rest of our lives. It doesn't hurt that we're already cousins. Now, up you go. I'm right behind you."

Maxwell nodded but did not move.

"Everything all right?"

Maxwell nodded again and spoke to the wall in front of him. "I don't have many friends. Or any, really. I didn't know it could happen so quickly."

Oliver's heart gave a painful lurch at the boy's words. He wanted to wrap his arms around him, but he thought it might be a shock. If living here was anything like Oliver remembered, Maxwell could not be used to much physical affection.

Maxwell put one foot on the next rung of the ladder, pulling himself up a few inches. "I mean, there's Pearl, but it's like I told you. She lives here. She's staff. That means she gets paid to play with me. Friends come because they want to. Pearl hasn't got a choice."

"Did she say that to you?" Maybe Miss Ellicott wasn't as gentle and lovely as Oliver thought. If she could tell this child she only spent time with him because it was her responsibility . . .

"Oh, no. She would never. Pearl loves me. But sometimes

it would be nice to have someone else to talk to." He moved up another rung. "So I'm very glad you've come."

"I'm glad as well." Oliver heard the quiver in his voice and wondered that this conversation with this child could affect him so strongly.

Maxwell continued his careful climb, and when he reached the opening at the top of the wall, he called for Pearl. "Are you up here? Oliver and I are coming in. You should put on a light for us. It's more welcoming that way."

Before the last words were fully out of his mouth, Maxwell tipped forward through the trapdoor.

A muffled cough floated down to Oliver, and he took the ladder two rungs at a time, the ropes swinging beneath his feet.

"Are you hurt?" he said, hardly pausing to put his head into the opening. He caught sight of Maxwell's back as he moved around a corner, the floor beneath his feet almost level with Oliver's head.

He pulled himself up through the strange doorway and made his way to his feet, noticing the ceiling soaring above him. Following Maxwell around a corner, he was relieved and delighted to see Miss Ellicott sitting at a small round table, candles alight in small tin holders, and a tea party prepared for her guests. His heart thudded when he noticed there was a place set for him.

"Well done, Pearl." Maxwell's voice was gleeful, his words punctuated with a few short coughs. "You've discovered completely new rooms. I've never seen this place before."

The rooms were very obviously not new, but Oliver knew what Maxwell meant. The thrill of discovery had always delighted Oliver as well—both as a child and today. "Nor I," Oliver added. "It's wonderful."

Maxwell glanced back as if he'd forgotten about Oliver in the excitement of finding Pearl.

"Oh, Oliver, this is Pearl. Pearl, Mr. Oliver Waverley, my cousin and my new friend."

"A pleasure." Oliver made a small bow.

"Pleasure's all mine, I assure you," she said.

What would it take to bring that smile to her face regularly? He was certain he could trade it for air, and it would keep him alive.

She gestured to the table. "Do take a seat, gentlemen."

Maxwell scrambled into a chair, looked around the table at his companions, and placed his hands against the smooth, worn wood on either side of his plate. He gave his governess a very serious look.

"Did you carry a table and three chairs up a rope ladder? That seems dangerous."

Pearl placed her hand atop the boy's. "Thank you for looking out for my safety. And no, I did not. The entrance we used today is not the only way into this space." She grinned at him, and Oliver could see these two likely shared many happy secrets.

He'd like to share a few secrets with Miss Pearl Ellicott himself.

CHAPTER 4

Pearl loved when her games had such successful outcomes. As she sat and waited for Maxwell to join her, she hoped he'd appear with Mr. Waverley. More than that, she realized now: She counted on it. Maxwell couldn't climb the rope ladder without the man's help.

She'd heard the boy's cough when he'd dropped into the strange loft. If he'd been cross or overtired, that cough might have gone on much longer. Not that he would ever give in to his illness, but there was an element of will in recovering from some of his more troubling episodes. And when he was in the middle of exploring, Maxwell had quite a strong will to be able to breathe through the fit.

Pearl served tea that was no longer hot and lemonade that was no longer cold, but there were no complaints from the gentlemen at the table. Even though he rarely stopped talking, Maxwell managed a few bites of his favorite lemon cake.

"The rope ladder is a good one. Can I have it in my room? We can attach it to the ceiling, and I can practice climbing it every day for exercise. Dr. Dunning says exercise is good for me."

"Pearl, did you know Oliver lived here at Shadowbrook when he was a boy? But he's never been in this room. You discovered it because you're an adventurer like me."

"These custard tarts are just like the ones we had for my birthday."

"Oliver, are you married? Before you inherit this house, you probably need a wife."

"Is there more lemonade for me?"

Whenever Pearl dared a look at Mr. Waverley, he was watching Maxwell with as much interest as she was. Why, then, did she feel his eyes on her? Maybe he was doing the same thing she was—sneaking glances when no one was watching.

Oliver Waverley was a mystery. Mr. Ravenscroft never spoke to Pearl about his heir. Not that he spoke to Pearl about much of anything that wasn't Maxwell. Her employer was a quiet man, uninterested in the dealings of his household staff as long as everyone kept Shadowbrook running in its way. He never entertained, and only the village doctor ever visited. Even Pearl's employment had been arranged without a personal meeting via a few letters exchanged with the housekeeper, Mrs. Randle.

After a few more minutes of Maxwell's constant talking, Pearl was sure the boy's energy was dimming. His voice grew softer, and his words slowed. It was time to move him to his bedroom before exhaustion overtook him and caused him pain.

"I believe it's time for us to say good night, Max. Come, help me gather up the dishes."

Maxwell gave a breathy chuckle. "You'll have to show me the alternate exit. I can't go down the ladder with a plate in my hands."

Pearl shook her head. "I'm afraid you're right. We must leave behind the adventure and go out through the door like the rest of the world. We can't be explorers all the time." She pointed to the far wall, where a tapestry hung.

After reaching for one of the small glass lamps on the table, Max scrambled out of his chair and tugged aside the tapestry. When he gripped the doorknob, he turned back and grinned at Pearl. "This was a wonderful game. I'm so glad you're here, Oliver."

Maxwell pulled the door open and walked through, the mystery of what lay beyond causing him to forget he was supposed to help clear up.

Pearl caught Oliver's eye. "Will you go with him?"

"Oh, no. I'll help you carry these things."

With a shake of her head, Pearl gestured after Maxwell. "One of us ought to be with him. It's not entirely safe here."

Oliver looked at her in surprise.

She lowered her voice. "He's not strong. And this part of the house has far more dangers than the sections in daily use. Walls crumble. Floorboards might not hold."

With a nod, Oliver moved toward the tapestry-draped door. Before he crossed the threshold, he turned and grinned at her. "I hope I don't get us both hopelessly lost."

Pearl attempted to tamp down her returning smile. She gave what she hoped was a serious nod. "I believe I'll be able to find you. But just in case, there are three connected rooms to walk through before you arrive at the west hallway stairs."

Oliver glanced from Pearl through the door and back again, clearly torn between leaving her alone and leaving Maxwell alone.

A good sign, she thought. *For inheritance reasons.*

After Oliver had trotted off after Maxwell, Pearl reassured herself that her fascination with Mr. Ravenscroft's heir was strictly due to the pending state of affairs at Shadowbrook. How the transfer of ownership would affect Max. Nothing more.

But as she collected the serving plates from the small table and placed them in the basket, she smiled at the memory of Oliver's laugh. At the way he'd watched Maxwell with real interest. Listened to his funny statements and answered questions that were far too personal.

Pearl had never before considered the way a young child took so much of the awkwardness out of making a new acquaintance.

Maxwell asked things Pearl would never dare, even though she was as interested in the answers as anyone could be.

When Maxwell had asked about Oliver's marriage prospects, Oliver had responded with a shrug. "I've had no luck. Maybe I've been looking in the wrong places."

Maxwell's answer, quick and confident, was to tell his cousin—a man who was practically a stranger—he'd be happy to help him secure a wife. The fact that Maxwell knew exactly four single women, and two of them were employees of the house, didn't seem to factor into their consideration. They'd shaken hands on the bargain.

Of course it was all silliness. Just a game within a game. But Pearl couldn't hide her smile now that no one was there to see it nor ask her to explain it.

With the basket of serving plates and blown-out candles over her arm, she made her way through the dim rooms beyond the door. Each of the connected bedchambers held a bed, a small table, and a chair. From these rooms, she'd borrowed furnishings for the evening's tea. She could return the table and chairs at any time. No one used these rooms now; they had been functional many years ago, when a full complement of servants lived and worked in Shadowbrook. Now the serving staff stayed in the rooms off the kitchen. Pearl imagined they rarely, if ever, had reason to come here.

Showing Maxwell this part of the house gave her the feeling of waking it up again, if only for an evening of tea and cakes. There was something healing and comforting about lighting a lamp in a room that had been years in darkness.

In the third of the connected bedchambers, Pearl found Maxwell lying atop the bed's bare mattress, his hands under his head.

She swallowed away her inclination to rush to his side, ask if he was well, check for fever. And a moment later, she was glad she had refrained, because Oliver Waverley was stretched out on the floor beside the bed, one hand beneath his head and the other arm pointing to the ceiling.

"This one is Ceres. That's Pallas. Vesta's here, and there's Juno. They were discovered in the early years of this century, so whoever painted them here probably did so in the last seventy-five years."

"I thought the painting was much older."

Pearl followed Maxwell's gaze to the ceiling of the small room, where a painted star chart covered nearly the entire surface. Swirls and lines surrounded white circles, suggesting movement through the night sky.

"You know," Maxwell mused, "you could be inventing all these names, and I'd never know."

Oliver chuckled, and Pearl stifled a laugh of her own.

"I'm not terribly clever when it comes to naming things. There was a dog that came around my mother's house when I was small. I called it Oliver. It was the only name I could think of."

"But that's your name." Maxwell laughed and then coughed, bringing one arm over his face as his chest heaved with the effort to suck in a breath.

Pearl held herself back from running to him. He'd proven already today that he could settle himself. When his lungs calmed, he pointed to the ceiling again.

"Those last four you pointed out. Are they stars? Or planets?"

Pearl hovered in the doorway, reluctant to interrupt the conversation or miss a word of it.

"I'm not sure. Maybe neither. How about this? You grow up to travel through the skies and come back to tell us all about them."

Maxwell hummed. "No. I won't. I'll never be an adult, and I'm not well enough to travel. But it's a lovely painting, and I'm glad we found it."

Pearl's heart tore in two. Poor Maxwell.

Mr. Ravenscroft insisted on being honest, though careful, in discussing the boy's condition, and Maxwell seemed to understand his prognosis. But on a day of play and relative strength, Pearl allowed herself to forget that Max wouldn't grow up. That he didn't have the privilege to dream about his future like other children did.

If his response to Oliver's comment was any indication, the fact of his mortality was never far from Maxwell's mind.

Oliver turned on his side, an arm propped beneath his head. "Does it hurt you to speak of your illness?"

Would he have dared ask such a deeply personal question if he knew Pearl was listening?

Maxwell mirrored Oliver's movement, and the lamplight caught the planes of his face, casting shadows and making his eyes look even larger than they were. "No, but I think it makes my grandfather sad. And Pearl."

"I'd never want to bring sadness to either of them, but if you want to speak about it, you can always talk to me."

"Always?" Maxwell's eyes widened. "Do you mean you're going to stay with us from now on?"

Oliver's shoulders drooped, and Pearl wished she could see his expression. Hiding in doorways had both benefits and drawbacks.

"I've only come for a short time. I don't have permission to stay. Your grandfather wouldn't like having me here always. I meant you can speak to me when I'm here, and you can write to me when I'm back in the city."

"And I can talk to the voices in the walls." Max gave a slow nod and rolled onto his back again. Pearl thought she could see a shine in his eyes, though it could be a reflection of the lamplight.

Pearl did not like to hear him speak of voices she couldn't hear. She knocked at the open doorframe and put her head inside the small room. "Did the walk back tire you both out?"

Maxwell sat up, swiping at his nose with his shirtsleeve. Under any other circumstance, Pearl would have commented on such lack of manners, but she'd seen enough of the boy's vulnerability.

He did not need a scolding or a reminder to use a handkerchief tonight.

Oliver also sat up, moving so his back was against the wall. "I was exhausted. Max agreed to rest with me so I wouldn't accidentally fall into an enchanted sleep and never be found."

"He's only teasing, Pearl." Max scooted off the bed and reached for Oliver's hand to help him off the floor. "We saw the painted ceiling and wanted to explore it."

She looked up at the star chart again, seeing it more clearly in the lamplight. "Oh, it's lovely."

Maxwell snuggled beside her and put his arm around her waist. "Maybe you could paint one like it in my room? I'd want you to make sure you include Ceres and Juno and the others I can't remember."

Oliver came to stand beside Maxwell, and the two shared a look over the boy's head.

"Is your governess a painter, then?" Oliver asked.

"Pearl can do everything." The uncomplicated trust Max had in her made Pearl feel maybe she could, in fact, do anything.

"Is this true?" Oliver looked at Pearl, but Max answered.

"She can do a lot of things a little bit. It's how they train a woman to be a governess."

Pearl held Oliver's glance for a moment longer. "It's not a very flattering picture of my skills, but he's not wrong. It is good training to know a bit about a great many things."

Oliver nodded. "I would be a dreadful governess, then. I know very little about only a few things."

"Like what?" Maxwell took Oliver's hand, and the three of them stepped into a hallway that was not quite wide enough for them to walk together. They continued anyway, Maxwell tucked snugly between Pearl and Oliver.

"Architecture. I love buildings, and I spent my university years studying design."

"What else?"

"I'm a very proficient cook. I know at least twenty ways to prepare an egg."

Maxwell wrinkled his nose. "Are you joking? Eggs are just eggs."

"Not in my kitchen, they're not."

Pearl smiled at Oliver again. He was taking care not to speak to Maxwell as though he were a baby, and she appreciated his efforts.

They arrived at a staircase, and Maxwell looked up into the murky darkness of the ascending stairs before pointing down. "This way?"

With a nod, Pearl lifted the small lantern in her hand to light the steps before them. There were no windows on either side of the staircase, and the sconces, likely once flickering with candles, were dusty and cobwebby with disuse.

The boy chattered as he walked. "You did a good job finding this place. I'll come here again from the secret door in the wall. I'm not so sure about walking back this way."

"Never alone, however," Pearl warned him. "Too many turns on your own and you could get lost in Shadowbrook's passageways."

Maxwell's sigh was heavy and aggrieved. "I know. I mustn't go anywhere alone. I must stay near my room. I must have no fun whatsoever."

Pearl chuckled and patted his arm as he walked down the stairs beside her. "No fun whatsoever is the first rule you ever learned."

"I've learned it too well," Maxwell grumbled.

Oliver spoke up. "But your Explorer's Search game was fun. I enjoyed our adventure tonight."

Maxwell shrugged. "It was acceptable."

Oliver laughed loud and strong. "You must be a very difficult young man to please. I'm sure if I had a companion such as your Miss Ellicott, I'd never complain of anything ever again."

A sigh preceded Max's next words. "Yes, but you think eggs and buildings are exciting. You're not a very good judge of fun."

Pearl spoke the words she knew she must—reminding Maxwell of his manners. But in her heart, she repeated Oliver's last statement over and over, hoping it had been true.

CHAPTER 5

Oliver wasn't sure how long he stood outside Maxwell's room, but when he realized he was leaning quite near the door hoping to overhear Pearl and Maxwell discussing their game, possibly discussing him, he made himself move away. He didn't want to go back to his own bedroom and its soulless walls, but neither did he have any wish to cross paths with his uncle unprepared. There was no place within this old house Oliver felt he belonged.

He'd planned for months how to discuss the future of Shadowbrook with Uncle Arthur, and now he needed to make sure his presentation was solid enough to withstand any possible argument. His uncle would ask many questions. Oliver would be ready with answers. Arthur Ravenscroft clutched jealously to his land, but Oliver had no intention of being the same kind of landowner. No, he was not interested in the building or its property at all. What Oliver wished for was a way to leave a lasting mark on the world. To make a change that would benefit someone.

His idea of selling Shadowbrook to the Campbell Clothing Company was a nearly perfect plan. The opportunity would employ many of the families around the New Forest. The clothing the Campbell Company produced would see more children dressed with far less inconvenience to their parents. He'd noticed women, including his mother and her serving girl, sewing late into the night. Imagine their leisure hours if they did not need to sew their own clothes—what they might do with so much extra time.

Additionally, bringing industry to the area offered prospects for many young people coming into their majority to be employed by a successful local business. He'd enjoyed his time at Cambridge, but that was an opportunity not everyone could embrace or afford. He recognized his privilege in receiving such an education.

Now he could be part of offering a viable alternative to many others. And if he did, *when* he did, someone might remember him as more than the disappointing, awkward orphaned nephew of Arthur Ravenscroft.

Lingering in the shadowed hallway outside Maxwell's room reminded Oliver of his childhood, of those evenings he'd lurk outside rooms where his uncle sat, hoping the man would come out and speak with him or invite him inside. Even the imagined conversation would have been optional; Oliver was a child who could sit in quiet. If only his uncle had ever extended him the invitation.

But he was no longer a child, and tonight he wasn't waiting outside a closed door for his uncle.

How long would Miss Ellicott stay in Maxwell's room? She must leave when the boy was no longer awake, mustn't she? Surely she didn't sleep in the nursemaid's closet attached to the bedroom. Maxwell was far too old for such babying. Given the vast hallways full of unused rooms, Uncle Arthur must have offered her a place of her own in the house.

Oliver checked the time on his pocket watch. He told himself he'd wait no more than five more minutes for her to appear. He wanted to speak with her, but he didn't want to appear to be the kind of man who lurked in hallways all night.

A draft whistled down the hall, the contours of Shadowbrook's strange angles lending it a familiar musical note. When he was a boy, he imagined the ghostly violin was accompanied by singing and whispering, in turns comforting and frightening. He was grateful not to imagine such silly things anymore.

Each moment waiting for Miss Ellicott lasted half an hour, but every time Oliver pulled his watch from its pocket, the reliable timepiece showed him less than half a minute had gone by.

Four minutes passed this way, and Oliver decided perhaps he could wait ten minutes for her.

It would never do for him to stand and stare at the door, so he moved between two of the hallway's gaslight sconces to study the painting hanging there.

It was a village scene in a strange and slightly spooky primitive style, and each figure seemed to have a bit of demon in them. The smiles were too toothy, the postures loose-jointed as if the people would, at any moment, join together in a midnight dance. Oliver thought each hat pictured must be covering a set of horns.

He stared at the young woman painted in the middle of the scene, the only figure not smiling. Her golden hair framed a face so pale it practically glowed from the twilight scene, her eyes wide and as blue as Dutch-painted saucers.

Oliver felt a surprising sense of worry for her, though she was not even the painting's primary subject; the girl was smaller than the grinning peasants surrounding her. What would happen to her? And why did he feel he could prevent something disastrous if he stayed here and kept watch?

He didn't hear the door open behind him, but suddenly Pearl was standing beside him.

Without turning from the painting, he asked, "Why would anyone paint such a horror as this? And why hang it near a child's bedroom? This must terrify Maxwell."

Pearl gave a whisper of a laugh. "On the contrary. He loves it. He chose it to put here."

"But it's so disturbing."

Her hum of assent didn't sound disturbed.

"What will happen to her?" Oliver pointed at the golden-haired girl.

Pearl looked at Oliver. "Don't you know?"

"Why would I know?"

"It's the 'Goblin Market.'"

Oliver heard her matter-of-fact tone, but the words meant nothing to him. He shook his head.

"The poem by Christina Rosetti."

As if that was any kind of explanation. He gestured toward the picture, still feeling like he needed to keep his eye on the frightened girl near the center of the chaos. "This is supposed to be a poem?"

Only a patient teacher could have heard his sarcastic question without a sign of annoyance. "Obviously not. This is a painting. Of a story. A story told in a poem."

"Looks a bit of a horror."

When he glanced at Pearl, he saw her gazing at the painting, a small smile playing at the corner of her mouth. "Indeed. A delightful one."

"I don't understand. What's pleasant about it?"

Pearl turned fully to face Oliver. "Perhaps you should read it."

He suddenly wished he was a man who had ever willingly read a poem.

"I don't dare turn away from her," he said, pointing to the girl in the painting. "She seems to need my protection."

"Lizzie is the strongest and bravest person in the story. She'll be fine."

"You call her Lizzie?"

"The poet calls her Lizzie, and she's here to save her sister."

"She doesn't look capable of fighting off these people."

Pearl shook her head and dropped her arms from where they'd been crossed over her stomach. "Her fight isn't against them. It's within herself. But she must travel into the danger to prove she can best it."

Oliver dared a look at Pearl's face. She seemed filled with patience when the opportunity to teach presented itself.

"Will you tell it to me?"

She glanced from the painting to his face. "The poem? It's quite long."

"The story, then? I'd like to understand."

The way her forehead softened suggested he'd said exactly the right words.

"Two sisters, doing their chores, hear the call of the goblin men at nightfall. Of course, they resist as good girls must. One night, brave Laura follows the invitation and tastes the most delicious fruits the goblins offer. When she returns home, a change overtakes her. She grows old and gray and sad and never hears the goblins call again. Frightened Lizzie still hears the goblins hawking their perfect fruits, and chooses to wander into the night when she's sure it's the only way to save her beloved sister. She makes a dangerous sacrifice, and Laura is saved by her sister's uncharacteristic bravery. It's a tale of love and resistance, of daring and withholding. Mostly it's an exploration of the dangerous world and an inevitable homecoming."

"So everyone is all right in the end?"

Pearl tilted her head. "Everyone is changed in the end. But both sisters survive, if that's what you're asking."

"Survival is good. The story's still frightening. And it doesn't make the painting any less gruesome. But now I can see the fruit I didn't notice before." He pointed at the baskets in the painting.

Pearl hummed in agreement. "Some would argue that all of life is frightening. And that we don't always notice certain elements surrounding us until someone points them out."

Oliver thought if he'd ever had a teacher like Pearl, he might have been a far better student. He'd like to listen to her speak for hours. "Which sister are you? The brave or the frightened?"

Pearl's eyes met his again. "Both sisters are brave. And both are frightened. And this may be what appeals most about the poem, as bravery stronger than fear is required of all of us who dare to love someone."

"Do you have sisters to protect, then?" Oliver asked.

She gave a small shake of her head, her voice low. "Once I had a brother. I didn't protect him. He's passed on."

Oliver wished to lighten the sudden sadness in her face but worried anything he might say would worsen her renewed grief. Instead, he faced the painting again, giving her a moment to collect her thoughts.

"I can see how the story would appeal to an ill boy," he said in a gentle voice.

From the corner of his eye, he saw her nod. "And to anyone who must stay at home, the goblin's cry will always be tempting. Tempting, but no less dangerous."

"But the point of the story, if I understand it, is that both girls did leave their home. They faced the danger and survived."

Pearl turned to him with a half smile on her face. "And do you suppose one writes a story only as a means of instruction? The characters in a novel did a thing, so you, reader, ought to do it as well? That theory doesn't hold up for many of the novels I've read."

"Perhaps only the Bible," Oliver assented.

A ringing laugh escaped Pearl's lips. "Have you ever actually read the Bible, Mr. Waverley? It's far more often a warning than it is a suggestion."

Oliver joined in her laugh. "I seem to have entered this battle of wits unarmed."

"Sir, I assure you, we have not been doing battle. You would be in far worse shape if I'd been on the attack." Pearl's lips pressed together in a visible effort to suppress her smile.

Oliver nodded. "I surrender. I bow to your superior knowledge in all matters of art, literature, language, and history."

"And in all matters of what's best for Maxwell." It was not a question. She was simply adding his cousin to the list of what she understood better than he ever would.

Pearl Ellicott undoubtedly had gained significant knowledge in her years working at Shadowbrook, teaching Maxwell and caring for him. But Oliver was the boy's family. They shared history. Relatives. This house, and all they both learned here by growing up beneath the alternately watchful and neglectful eyes of Arthur Ravenscroft. Pearl may know many things about teaching children, but Oliver knew what it was to be a male member of the Ravenscroft family. He was confident he knew a thing or two that might surprise her.

Not that he'd say any of that to her tonight.

He could disagree without being disagreeable. He inclined his head in a bow.

"Are you at all interested in a cup of tea and a piece of toast, Miss Ellicott?"

She tilted her head up toward his in the most charming way. "Almost always. And you?"

"I think it would be a perfect way to change the topic of our conversation. I feel I've been behindhand too much since I arrived this evening. With a visit to the kitchen, perhaps I can regain my confidence. I am, you might be surprised to know, an expert on the topic of toast."

He extended his arm, and Pearl placed a hand near his elbow. As they walked down the dark staircase, Oliver hoped he could turn their discussion toward far more pleasant paths.

CHAPTER 6

The housemaids had retired for the night in preparation for an early morning, but when Pearl and Oliver made their way to the kitchen, Mrs. Randle sat on a tall stool at the long worktable, polishing silver.

"Good evening, Mrs. Randle. How nice to see you. It's been a long time." Oliver pointed his smile directly at the woman. It had not taken Pearl long to learn the power of that smile, but she had no doubt how Mrs. Randle would receive it.

The housekeeper glanced at Oliver, then over at Pearl, then back to the serving fork in her hand. "You've returned, I see."

His blank look suggested he'd hoped for a warmer welcome.

Pearl removed her hand from Oliver's arm. "Mrs. Randle, would you care for a cup of tea? Mr. Waverley and I would be happy for you to join us."

Pearl caught Oliver's sudden look of alarm. He was clearly unaware of the trick of removing Mrs. Randle from one's company.

Without looking up from her polishing, she spoke a single word. "No."

"Very well. We'll have this prepared and be out of your way directly."

As there was nearly always a pot of hot water in the Shadowbrook kitchen, Pearl made quick work of preparing the tea things, laying out a few slices of toast, and collecting a small pitcher of milk.

Oliver stood with his hands dangling at his sides, looking unsure how to handle Mrs. Randle's cold rejection of his greeting, so Pearl handed him a lantern and a candle, then she picked up the tea tray and told him to lead the way to the blue drawing room.

They were a few steps out of the kitchen when Oliver whispered to her over his shoulder. "I have no idea which is the blue drawing room. You better lead the way, or I might accidentally take us to the pink morning room or, heaven forbid, the green afternoon room."

Pearl shook her head. "You'd have a time getting to the green afternoon room. It's up three flights of stairs and behind a bricked-in doorway."

Oliver stopped and turned to face her, his eyes wide. "Is it, really?"

She shook her head. "No. Turn left here."

Oliver obeyed, and Pearl followed him into a dark and twisting hallway. "Keep making every left, and we'll arrive in the blue drawing room when you run out of turns."

Oliver's steps became more confident, and Pearl focused on the way the lamp's glow outlined his broad shoulders. Mr. Waverley did not move like a soldier, which was perfectly understandable, since he'd attended university instead of serving in the army, but his gait swayed as he walked, as if he might break into a run at any time. It was a youthful walk, and one that Pearl enjoyed watching.

It did not take many left turns for her to decide the man was an excellent walker.

At the door to the blue drawing room, he stopped, raising his elegant eyebrows in a silent question. Pearl nodded that this was the correct room, and he turned the knob.

Nothing happened.

"Try it again," she said.

Oliver rattled the doorknob. "It isn't locked. The handle is turning. The door simply won't open." He turned the knob again and shoved his shoulder into the door. Nothing.

This was not an unusual occurrence, but Pearl wasn't certain if Oliver Waverley was the kind of man who would understand that, sometimes, Shadowbrook House didn't want to open its doors.

Instead of asking him to try again, Pearl moved in front of the door. Balancing the tea tray in one hand, she laid her palm flat against the door and whispered, "May we please come in?" She ran her hand down the door as she might caress Maxwell's back, a single sweep. Then she reached for the knob, turned it, and opened the door.

She was several steps into the room before she realized Oliver still stood in the open doorway, mouth agape, the lantern flame shuddering with the shaking of his hand.

"I'm going to need you to explain that."

She nodded. "Very well, but come in first. You could use a cup of tea."

"If the house continues to behave this way, I'll need something stronger than tea."

Pearl laughed softly. "I can't help you there, but the tea is hot. Come inside and put the lantern on this table."

Oliver took a tentative step into the room, holding the lamp high to look around the room. In a slow turn, he inspected what his light allowed him to see. Pearl didn't rush him.

When he turned back to her, she gestured again to the table holding the tea tray. She took the chair on one side.

"Do I need to ask permission before I sit down?" He pointed to the other chair, his face giving a fair attempt at amusement, though Pearl saw his lingering discomfort.

She couldn't help herself. She leaned in and whispered, "It can't hurt."

He'd already begun to sit, but at her comment, he straightened back up in a quick hop. Both feet left the floor at the same time.

Oliver looked up toward the ceiling. "May I take a seat?"

Pearl was tempted to push on his chair with her foot while his eyes were averted, but she didn't know how much the poor man could handle in one evening, so she simply focused on pouring his tea.

Oliver hesitated another moment before he sat slowly at the very edge of the chair.

He lifted the cup to his lips and sipped before looking at her again. "So. Haunted?"

His tone was so carefully casual she knew he'd tried for this note of nonchalance exactly. She wondered how much effort it cost him to hold his voice and fingers steady.

With a shake of her head, Pearl drank from her own cup. After swallowing, setting down the cup, and tapping a napkin to the corners of her lips, she said, "Particular."

"Particular how?" Oliver asked.

Pearl brushed a hand along her skirts. "You know how old houses are."

Oliver made a quiet sound of exasperation. "Well, obviously *you* know how old houses are, or at least how this old house is. You requested entry of a locked door, and it opened for you. I used to think this place was full of ghosts, but I hoped it was a childish fancy."

At that moment, with Oliver's brow furrowed in frustrated puzzlement, Pearl could see the greatest connection yet between him and Maxwell. Something of the boy Oliver once was showed through the man he had become.

Pearl couldn't hold in her smile. "It's rather amazing, isn't it?"

"Practically unbelievable," he muttered.

She could feel his irritation, and she took only a small amount of pleasure in it.

"Things are not always what they seem, Mr. Waverley." She realized she kept using his name and that she probably ought to stop, as it seemed terribly familiar. But she loved the sound of it, the shape of the syllables. At least she wasn't calling him *Oliver* the way Maxwell did. It had been so easy for the boy to become immediate friends with this stranger.

Of course, as they had sat together around the small table in the hidden room, she'd felt herself becoming rather immediately friendly as well.

"Are you saying you tricked me, Miss Ellicott?"

There was enough smile in his voice to take away any accusation in the question.

"It's possible you were deceived, but that was not my intent. I assure you, there was no malice in my actions."

"No malice, but was there magic?"

She wished she knew him well enough to tell if his question was a joke, but since she didn't, she decided to answer him plainly.

"No magic either."

"So, in theory, I could learn the trick of entering the—what was this place called? The blue drawing room?"

Pearl spread some golden peach jam onto a triangle of toast and passed it across the table. She was unwilling to admit just how much she enjoyed keeping him in suspense. Finally, he ate the toast in two large bites and brushed the crumbs from his fingers. Steepling his hands in front of him, he tilted his head as if listening closely for an answer to his question.

Pearl obliged. "The wood of the door has a bow in its center that affects its unlatching mechanism. Pressure at the base of the bowed section will align everything within, and at the turning of the knob, the door will open. No amount of pressure in a different part of the door seems to suffice."

"And the request you made?"

"Oh, that's just a game I play."

She couldn't tell him the truth. Couldn't simply ask him, *"Have you ever been so lonely you make conversation with the walls surrounding you?"*

"Quite a good game. I'm glad I was here to witness it. And is this game generally for your enjoyment alone? Or is it one you subject all the house's visitors to?"

If he'd asked the question with any sense of being offended, Pearl would have known his charm extended only to situations in which he held an upper hand. But here, in a dark, unfamiliar space with only her for company, feeling himself rather foolish, he could laugh. A man who could laugh at himself seemed a rare treasure indeed.

"As you know, we don't get visitors here."

"But surely there are some?"

Pearl gestured in Oliver's direction. "Aside from Dr. Dunning, you are the only exception in six years. I suppose Mr. Ravenscroft might have a host of guests secreted through the house in rooms I've never come across, but I've never run into anyone in hallways."

Was he remembering the way she'd leaped into his arms at his arrival? The way she clung to the sleeves of his coat as if she'd never seen anyone so fascinating and absolutely must not let him go?

She hoped not. Or at least, she hoped he couldn't see the memory replaying itself on her face.

"So my uncle goes out when he wants to visit?"

"Mr. Waverley, I think you misunderstand. It's possible that Mr. Ravenscroft leaves Shadowbrook, but in the time I've been employed here, I've never seen it happen. Perhaps things have changed since you lived here."

Oliver gave a calm, serious nod. "A great many things have changed. And now I think of it, the only people who visited here when I was a boy were other boys, and they were not exactly invited. Not that they required an invitation. All three of us would simply appear at each other's houses."

Pearl wondered at the simple magic of children finding each other. Poor Maxwell might never know such a childlike enchantment. There were no children in any of the nearby houses, and even if there were, she was sure Mr. Ravenscroft would not welcome them into Shadowbrook.

"Please, tell me more about your friends."

"George Yates was from the village. His father worked as head gardener over at Hastings House. George was a crack shot with a sling and a stone, but he only ever aimed at walls. I wondered how that could be fun until I saw how he selected tiny targets for himself—this notch in the wall's stone, that edge of the kitchen door—and he rarely missed. Russell Trowbridge lived in the house next door, but to call it a house doesn't do it justice. Oakdell Manor was built before Shadowbrook, and it used to tower over the surrounding trees. I think it cast the shadow that gave this house its name. Its builders mimicked the Tudor style, and most of the house was made of wood. A few drier-than-usual years followed by a terrible accident left it a smoking ruin. That happened the last year I lived here. Trowbridge and I left for school not long after the fire, and he and his father determined the best thing to do would be to tear the place down and sell the land. Only recently has a decent offering been made, and they've sold their property to the Campbell Clothing Company."

"And you? What were you like as a boy?"

Oliver shook his head. "I don't want to tell you."

She laughed, but when he looked up at her, she saw his face was serious.

"I won't hold your childhood sins against you."

Oliver breathed out a long sigh. "I don't know how you could help it. I was a dismal child, sullen and miserable. When I made it out of my bed, it was only to wander around with a scowl on my face. It's a wonder anyone ever gave me a chance to grow up and prove myself anything but a complete grouser. Coming to Shadowbrook offered me a new way to see the world. At first, it was even more difficult here, because my uncle was not interested in entertaining a sad little boy. The walls felt heavy with sorrow. I thought I heard voices telling me to lie in bed and never get up. Isn't that a state? But before too much time passed, I took myself outdoors and met the lads. It's the miracle of my childhood that George and Russell found me. They brought a sense of wonder back into my life, and it's never gone fully away."

"How lovely for you to have had such good friends."

Oliver nodded. "And to keep them into adulthood. I know good luck and good fortune are nothing to be proud of, but I consider holding onto these friendships to be one of the great accomplishments of my life."

Pearl swallowed away the lump in her throat. Hearing Oliver speak of his boyhood friends reminded her strongly of her relationship with her brother, Edgar. Even some of the words Oliver used brought to her mind a few of his traits. She imagined Eddie working toward a goal with the same precision that George Yates practiced hitting his targets.

"I'm rather inclined to like them both," Pearl said, hoping if she continued in the small talk, she could shake off the feeling of sadness that overcame her whenever she considered what her brother's life might have been had he survived.

I'm rather inclined to like you too, she added to herself. Mr. Waverley had not even been here a whole day, and he'd managed to turn everything upside down. She knew Mr. Ravenscroft would not be pleased with a new occupant at Shadowbrook House, but as Pearl settled into both her chair and conversation with Oliver, she couldn't help but be intrigued by what else might change because of Oliver's arrival.

CHAPTER 7

Admittedly, Oliver had very little experience with women, but Pearl Ellicott was driving him mad.

When he'd arrived—was it only hours ago?—she had literally thrown herself into his arms. He understood that had been a mistake, but he wouldn't mind if it happened again. And again. They'd had such a nice time exploring the house. And Maxwell was a delight. Watching Pearl care for the boy gave Oliver a sense of what future happiness might look like. He wasn't ready to consider too deeply what that might mean, but he knew there was a seed planted in his mind.

When they'd had tea together, he couldn't deny his attraction to her. But did she have any interest in him? Or might she be like one of those city girls who found out he had an inheritance coming and drew around him like birds to a dropped piece of bread? None of those bird-girls kept up their interest longer than one dance or one evening at a party. But perhaps that wasn't a completely fair assessment. Maybe it was Oliver who lost interest. He couldn't think of any young woman he'd met in the last two years who captured his attention like Pearl had.

Was it possible that all along, what he hoped to find was more than a pretty face and a charming smile? Could it be he was truly looking for an active mind as well?

Oliver attempted to prepare for bed, but his thoughts wouldn't settle. He paced his room a while, but the blank walls seemed to loom above him a bit taller each time he passed, so he stepped into his shoes and set out among the hallways and passages of Shadowbrook House. He'd learned quite early to never walk through the house without a source of light, so he brought a candle that had been set on a table in his room.

He stopped for a minute outside Maxwell's room, wishing he could go inside and see if the boy was sleeping peacefully. That was a strange urge, one he'd never felt before. Of course, he'd never lived in a house with a child, sick or otherwise, so maybe it was simply a natural effect of having someone young and vulnerable under the same roof.

At the next room, he stopped again. Light leaked into the hall from under the closed door. This must be Miss Ellicott's bedroom.

He wondered what the room looked like. Did paintings hang on each wall? Had she chosen the decor? Were the decisions made to help her feel most at home? Or, like Oliver, did she feel a stranger there?

A soft hum came from Miss Ellicott's room. Singing?

What was she doing in there? The light was bright enough to work by. Did she sit in her room at night and plan the ways she'd teach Maxwell the next morning? Write out sentences in Spanish or Italian for him to read? Make sketches of the house, marking each newly discovered room and passageway? Might she be, even now, drawing a pirate map to guide Maxwell on his next adventure?

Did the boy know how lucky he was?

The thought took Oliver by surprise. Maxwell Ravenscroft would never grow into a man. He wouldn't live long enough to attend school or find enjoyable employment or fall in love. He'd never have a home of his own, but Oliver thought him lucky.

Because the boy had Pearl Ellicott. Her company, her undivided attention, her affection.

Lucky indeed.

Oliver soon recognized the impropriety of standing outside the governess's door while the rest of the house slept. He turned toward the main staircase and looked both up and down the steps.

Where to begin? What part of the house should he visit?

He took the main staircase up one level, forcing himself to tread confidently, although silently, on territory that had been forbidden him as a child. Uncle Arthur's study was along this hallway, and when Oliver was a boy, Mrs. Randle made it clear Oliver was not to go anywhere near the room.

Without question, he'd complied. Having no wish to disturb his uncle while he was at his work, whatever work that might have been, he'd been perfectly satisfied to explore as many of the other parts of the house as he could.

Now he moved ever closer to the forbidden section, his candle throwing a trembling shadow down the hall. All was darkness and silence but for the ever-present shushing sounds of wind against the building and the scurrying of tiny feet inside the walls. Another thing Oliver preferred not to consider.

The study's door was massive, a double pane of wood so dark it was almost black. The doorknobs, twin brass globes that stared from the dark wood like a pair of yellow eyes, were surely fastened tight. Whatever his uncle protected in the mysterious study must be locked away at night.

Look inside.

Oliver heard the words as if they were whispered in his ear. He knew it was only in his mind, but such whispers used to come to him just this way, years ago in this house.

Oliver reached for a knob, and to his surprise, it turned silently in his hand. He pulled the door, but nothing happened. A small remnant of his childhood fear whispered it was just as well; entering the study was forbidden and he should walk away.

But Oliver couldn't be ruled by juvenile fears forever. He

pushed. The door swung away from him, opening into a cavernous and shadowy room, empty except for the massive desk in the center.

Not a single side table stood ready to hold his candle, not a curtain on the walls or a window to open. There was nothing hung or displayed to beautify the room. No bookshelves lined the walls. No chair placed by the yawning, empty hearth, and not even a rack of fireplace tools. A layer of dust covered everything like a depressing snowfall.

Like the other disused, empty rooms, this one smelled of nesting birds, rodents, and abandonment.

This was the room that had been forbidden to him? This empty space? Had his uncle ever actually occupied it?

And if he had, what had made him abandon it?

Oliver had thought his bedroom spartan, but this was desolate. Not even the memory of a once-comfortable space lingered here. He thought the desk must still stand in the center of the room only because it was too large for anyone on the staff to remove it.

With a glance over his shoulder, he stepped into the room and pushed the door closed behind him.

Placing the candle on the enormous, empty desk, he walked around the whole room, his shadow pacing the walls beside him.

What was so special about this room? Why had his uncle kept it to himself for all those years? And why was it now sitting empty?

Oliver wondered if there was a passageway from the study to one of the other rooms on this level. Perhaps even to Uncle Arthur's own bedchamber. He stepped closer to the walls, watching his shadow diminish a few inches for each step he took away from the candle's light. The walls were plastered and painted, and aside from the usual cracks and darkened patches, there was nothing to suggest a hidden hinge within the wall. No secret doors. Not even a window.

If the room lacked a passage to somewhere else, it must have been nothing more than what it seemed: a private sanctuary. It was possible that for all those years, Uncle Arthur spent his hours in this study simply to be alone. To be away from Oliver?

He circled the room again, this time with a hand on the wall, feeling for any change in texture, any give. Nothing but the small cloud of dust he kicked up as he walked the dirty floor. He stifled a sneeze, then another.

Remembering the hatch inside the hidden cupboard, he looked up. He had no idea how Pearl had discovered its existence, and understood even less how she had activated its opening, but knowing this house had doorways at ceiling height made him want to investigate more closely.

The ceiling was out of his reach, but even if he could touch it, was there any way Uncle Arthur could? His uncle wasn't ancient, but some people seemed to lean into aging, and Uncle Arthur had been an old man for twenty years at least. Maybe once there had been a ladder here, a hidden staircase that would help Arthur access a high, secret panel.

Oliver sat on the edge of the desk, placed his hands behind him, and leaned back, staring at the flickering candlelight dancing on the ceiling.

The disappointment he felt at not discovering a secret passageway cloaked him in a strange sadness. Why, he wondered, did his failure to find what was certainly not there distress him?

Had he convinced himself he'd really heard a voice telling him to look inside?

That was impossible.

As a boy, he was used to finding paths and passages in and around Shadowbrook, but he'd never felt sad when his explorations weren't fruitful. Why was tonight different? As soon as he had the thought, he also knew the answer. His time with Miss Ellicott and Maxwell had given him a feeling he rarely experienced in Shadowbrook House: hope. And he'd been hopeful for a successful adventure here.

The unfamiliarity of the emotion caused him to consider its effect on his actions tonight. Walking into an adventure armed with hope was a far different experience than trudging along, certain of a middling outcome.

Maybe hope was a dangerous indulgence.

He brushed the dust from his hands and picked up the candle stub that was sputtering as the wick drew close to the end.

He pictured Pearl's smile and thought the experience of bringing it back to her face might be worth the disappointment of a few failed explorations.

Pulling the huge wooden door open, he stepped out into the hallway and nearly crashed into a figure standing outside the door. Scrambling for balance, he wheeled his arms in small circles until his equilibrium allowed him to bring his feet back under him. The guttering candle extinguished itself, and Oliver stood in shadow.

But not alone. Even in the oppressive darkness, he sensed a presence. Too large to be Pearl. Too solid to be Mrs. Randle; the housekeeper was practically transparent.

"Uncle?" he whispered.

The figure gave a short, quiet grunt. The syllable was small but heavy with displeasure.

The tone was as much a giveaway as if all the gaslights in the house had come on at once.

Jenkinson.

As Oliver's eyes adjusted to the heavy darkness of the midnight hall, he saw large shoulders and a head held perfectly straight. He knew well the shape of Shadowbrook's intimidating butler.

Jenkinson had served in the house before Oliver had arrived at Shadowbrook. Mostly silent, the butler managed to project an air of protectiveness, but Oliver knew better than to think it was the butler's job to protect *him*. No, Jenkinson's work was to protect the house. And, by extension, Uncle Arthur.

He would show the butler he was no longer afraid of him. He'd speak to him like a master of the house spoke to his serving staff.

"Good evening, Jenkinson," Oliver said, hoping his voice would carry a hint of confidence, even if he didn't feel it. "I didn't expect to find you here."

"No. I suppose you did not." That was more words than Jenkinson usually spoke to Oliver in an entire conversation.

"Have you got a candle, by chance? Not that I mind the dark."

Oliver minded the dark far more when Jenkinson lurked so close to him. He'd rather be able to see the man's expression than wonder how much trouble he might be in.

Jenkinson said nothing, which was to be expected.

Oliver tried for a chummy laugh. "What brings you to this hallway tonight?" Could the butler hear the tremble in his voice?

"I might ask you the same."

Oliver wanted to be bold enough to laugh at Jenkinson or possibly to remind him that soon, Oliver would own this house and therefore be Jenkinson's employer. He couldn't make himself say anything at all. Every bit of the self-assurance he'd tried to gather up in the past few seconds deserted him. He may as well be nine years old again.

Come on, old boy, Oliver told himself. *You're a man. He's a man. There's no reason for you to fear him. Just think of something to say. Make conversation.*

Nothing came to his mind. Not a word.

He stood in the dark hallway, wishing his brain worked faster. A moment that felt like an hour passed before Jenkinson spoke again. "It's time for you to find your way back to your room."

Oliver wanted to say he wasn't a child. He wanted to argue against being sent to his room. He wanted to behave like a Ravenscroft.

But the problem was, Oliver wasn't a Ravenscroft. His mother had been, but Uncle Arthur had made it clear she had not passed any of the important family traits down to her son.

What if Oliver refused to move? What if he decided to be a person who could not be intimidated by his uncle's butler?

Would Jenkinson simply continue to stand here, threatening without speaking?

All the combined emotions of the day left Oliver unable to try to be someone else. He barely had the energy to behave like himself.

"Right you are, Mr. Jenkinson. Shall we?" He began to walk down the hall, heading for the staircase. Hearing the snick of metal on metal, he turned to see Jenkinson holding a key to the door's lock.

As Oliver went down the stairs toward his room, he heard the echo of a memory, a floating melody that sounded exactly like a mournful tune played on a violin. The sound used to frighten him when he was a boy, but those days were long past. With everything he felt now, there was no time to indulge in childish fantasies of ghostly voices and phantom violins.

CHAPTER 8

The next morning dawned crisp and brittle. Winter settled gently in the New Forest, but it always seemed to last too long.

Pearl readied herself for a trip into the village, as she did every Tuesday morning. It was her half day, a request she'd been granted during employment negotiations with Mrs. Randle for the governess position at Shadowbrook. Mrs. Randle had grumbled that she didn't know of anyone nearby who gave any of their household help a half day, but she supposed it would be allowed. Pearl was glad for the concession.

When Pearl first arrived at Shadowbrook, she discovered why none of the neighbors gave half days. Situated almost midway between Portsmouth and Southampton, the houses on the River Hamble were not near enough either city to make an easy trip.

The village of Riverwood was tucked almost a mile upriver from Shadowbrook, and the walk through the forested lanes became a weekly delight for Pearl. Even if the town didn't have much to offer, there were some lovely lanes. And it had Nanette's Treasure Trove, a small bookshop where Pearl was happy to spend an hour and a bit of money each week.

Entering the shop, Pearl was met by the familiar, delicious smell of musty, dusty paper. Nothing in the world could ever be as wonderful as a shop full of books—the old, peeling leather of secondhand stories, the crisp crackle of new-pressed pages, the lingering feeling of possibility in the air.

A small bell announced her entry into the shop, and Nanette called out in a muffled voice, "Welcome to the Treasure Trove." Her voice floated past a column of crates piled high on the shop's main counter. Pearl made her way around the pile and found her friend. More precisely, she found her friend's hair.

Nanette's hair was an explosion of golden curls, the kind that everyone born with straight hair was sure they'd love, while everyone born with the curls resented them and spent their lives trying to tame them. Nanette rarely succeeded at taming hers, and she told Pearl she'd decided upon turning twenty-five to give up the fight. "I embrace the madness," she was fond of saying. That attitude was one of the things Pearl had loved first about her friend.

In the years they'd known each other, Pearl had come to admire many things about Nanette. She was incredibly well-read, she gossiped freely and without malice, she had interesting opinions about history and philosophy, she laughed with abandon, and she was unerring in her book recommendations for Maxwell.

If she chose a book for Max, he loved it.

Pearl knelt behind the shop counter beside her friend, who had her arms full of fabric and ribbons. She squeezed Nanette's shoulders in a hug and gestured to the pile. "Are you selling dressmaking materials now? I don't know where you'll find the space for them."

One of the delights of the Treasure Trove was how packed full it always seemed. Piles of books tottered atop crammed shelves. Every surface had stacks of stories, sometimes organized by topic or color or binding size. Sometimes not organized at all. But Nanette knew where each book could be found. The map resided in her head along with fantastical stories and ideas about the people who came into her shop.

With a flick of her wrists, Nanette shook out the fabric in

her hands to unfurl a dress of such magnificence, Pearl thought it ought to be in a museum. Layers of hand-tatted lace cascaded down a slim skirt of golden silk. It looked like something a lady would have worn to a ball at court seventy years ago.

"It was donated with a huge box of three-volume novels after the death of a customer's favorite aunt. What do you think?" Nanette asked as she gazed at the gown.

"Delicious." Being in this store always brought the romantic parts of Pearl to the surface.

"It is, isn't it? I'm going to drape it from a display shelf and absolutely bury it in Regency romances. I have a small but fierce band of women who can't get enough of Miss Austen's stories." She grinned as if such a thing was a strange but charming quirk in her customers.

Nanette folded the dress in half and placed it on the corner of the desk. She turned away from the glorious gown and gave Pearl her full attention.

"How are you today? What's been happening in the silent and mysterious Shadowbrook House since last we met?" Nanette generally asked Pearl such questions, and Pearl generally responded with a tale about finding a new secret passage or Maxwell's delight in one of the books she'd brought home for him.

Today she had something truly interesting to share.

"Dreadful news." Pearl worked to hide her smile.

Nanette's eyes gleamed with excitement. She gasped, but her grin softened the sound into a new kind of laugh. "A vampire in the attics? Soldiers storming the riverbank? One of the portraits began to speak to you?"

Pearl lowered her voice and spoke in a mournful tone. "The heir has returned."

Her friend gave a joyful clap. "And he's horrible and angry?" Before Pearl could disagree, Nanette shook her head. "No, no. Wait. I know. Even better. He's handsome and stares at you with the soul-weary eyes of a man who has seen far too much. You fear being alone in a room with him, for at any moment he may lose control and ravish you."

Pearl laughed. "Has anyone ever mentioned you read too many novels?"

Nanette grinned back. "It's a particular hazard of the work I do, I suppose. Well? The heir?"

A piece of Pearl wanted to keep the game going, with Nanette adding in more fantastic plot points she'd read in books, but another piece of her simply wanted to say the truth aloud. To see if the story was as interesting as it felt in her heart. "He wasn't invited. He announced he was coming and threw the staff into chaos. Apparently, he has *plans* for the sale of the house. But that's not the worst part. He's rather lovely."

"Oh dear."

They both laughed.

Pearl looked over her friend's shoulder at the folded golden gown to avoid Nanette's eyes. "I don't think we ought to form our final opinions about him yet."

Nanette tugged her hand, bringing her eyes up to meet her friend's. "You like him."

"No. Not at all."

Nanette's mouth drew down while her eyebrows rose into the mass of blonde curls that covered her forehead, changing her from a charming young woman full of spirit to a caricature of a disapproving matron.

Pearl couldn't lie to her friend. "Perhaps a bit."

Nanette shook her head. "You can't like him. He's the villain."

"Not necessarily." Pearl knew she sounded defensive.

"Everyone's heard he wants to sell Shadowbrook, which means you'd move far away from me. There's nothing else for it. Villain."

Pearl stifled an urge to point out that many of the books

they'd both read leaned heavily on the heroine falling for the villain, but she saw the look in Nanette's eye.

She was thinking the same thing and shaking her head. "That's not the kind of story you're in."

At that, Pearl laughed aloud. "I'm an orphaned governess living in a tumbledown Gothic mansion with a reclusive employer and ghosts in every room."

Nanette joined the laugh. "Don't forget the timid housekeeper, the silent butler, and the looming forest."

Neither mentioned the ill child central to the entire story, but Maxwell was on both of their minds, Pearl knew.

"No. That's only your story's setting. And possibly your plot. Your *story* is different."

Pearl loved when Nanette spoke to her like this—with depth of understanding about something they both prized.

"And what kind of story do you find me in?"

Nanette motioned to a pair of chairs flanking a tiny table wobbling under the weight of a huge basket full of penny dreadfuls. How appropriate.

As they sat, Nanette said, "You're in a grand adventure. An epic tale of mystery and discovery. Perhaps romance, but that comes later." A wave of her hand proved how Nanette felt about the romance part. "This story is the making of you. The unearthing of your inner strength, the depth of your mind, and the goodness of your soul."

How often had Pearl and Nanette given stories to the customers in the shop and the people in Riverwood village? It was a simple game to assign a role in a story to a casual acquaintance. To tell each other what Miss Morten must have been doing before she walked into the shop and marched straight to the travel guides of Italy, lifted one from the shelf, clutched it to her heart, and tossed payment on the counter without speaking a word to either of them. Not to mention what Miss Morten might have done after walking out of the shop.

Creating a backstory for the lonely vicar was the work of many delightful mornings together. The elderly twins Miss Lola and Miss Francie, who came into the shop to purchase religious tracts, often became the heroes of a pirate adventure.

A simple and delightful way to pass the time. But Pearl was unused to being the main character in these imaginings. She was always an observer. Nanette's direct attention unnerved her. She would much rather give stories to people she hardly knew.

"And what about your story?" she asked Nanette. Let her friend see how uncomfortable it was to be central to the telling.

Nanette shook her head. "Mine's a poetry collection. Not much plot at the moment, but many, many words. It's pretty to look at, and it makes you think." She put a finger to her chin and looked toward the ceiling, a simpering grin on her face.

Pearl laughed. "What if I want to be poetry too?"

"Oh, no. That wouldn't do at all. You've got far too much atmosphere over there at Shadowbrook. It would be wasted on anything but an adventure. How do you feel about a quest?"

The way she said the word made Pearl's mouth water. It was a delicious-sounding word, even though she knew better. A big story wasn't for her. She'd always been meant for a quiet life.

"Sounds wonderful. But I wouldn't know how to quest. You tell me what to do, and I'll follow your every suggestion."

Nanette's laugh carried up over the stacks of books and circled the ceiling. "That's called a play, and you'd only be an actor. No. You need to be the driving force. Although, I'll admit, there was a time I wondered if you'd come to Shadowbrook to fall in love with your employer."

Now it was Pearl's turn to laugh. "Mr. Ravenscroft?"

Nanette shrugged. "How was I supposed to know he's not a darkly handsome recluse, sitting home alone protecting his broken heart, just waiting for the governess of his dreams to carry him away from a lifetime of sadness and regret?"

"You've been reading the Brontës again, haven't you?" Pearl could laugh about the idea now, but she'd also wondered, when she was hired to care for a child at a large house, if the master of Shadowbrook might turn out to be a Mr. Rochester. Not that she was particularly attracted to brooding, angry men who kept silent about their very important secrets. She preferred men who smiled and laughed.

Her own orphaned state might have nudged her toward hope of finding a new family in her employment, but no one could replace her parents and her dear younger brother. Not even someone she adored as much as Maxwell.

Nanette interrupted Pearl's thoughts by pulling the basket crammed full of sensational little stories across the table and resettling them so they lay in a semblance of order.

"I sell more of these than anything else in the shop," Nanette mused. "People love thrilling stories."

Pearl gave an involuntary shudder as she remembered the spider in the cupboard. "I doubt they'd like it if they had to live inside one."

"But that's the pleasure of reading. You get all the thrill of excitement, the terror of monsters and frightening creatures, and then you put the book down and go back to your own boring life. But between the pages, you revel in the feeling of lurking danger."

"You've got quite an understanding of books and readers. Maybe you ought to do more than sell them. Maybe you should write them as well."

Nanette grinned. "How do you know I don't?"

"I would never assume any accomplishment is out of your reach."

"A perfect answer. We must both be allowed our secrets, even though we're such good friends." Nanette pushed the basket back to the center of the table. "But secrets aside, don't fall in love with your employer's nephew. It will end badly, and he'll break your heart, and I have neither enough feminine gentleness nor enough soppy novels to repair the damage."

"I appreciate your concern, but you don't need to worry about me. I'm armored against heartbreak." Pearl thumped her chest with her fist as they both laughed.

But even through the laughter, Pearl knew her jest was partly serious. She'd happily accept Mr. Waverley's casual attentions for the days he stayed at Shadowbrook. It was pleasant to be charmed and smiled at and flirted with, but her whole world revolved around Maxwell's health and safety.

If only Oliver Waverley didn't smile so easily or hold her eyes so confidently. If only he didn't look exactly like a novel hero with his carefully trimmed hair and his beautifully patterned waistcoat. But he'd arrived without invitation, and he'd be gone again too soon, back to the city and his life far from Shadowbrook. He'd leave and never give her another thought, taking with him any temptation for Pearl to act like a novel's swoony heroine.

Nanette might have seen something of Pearl's internal struggle, because she dropped the conversation. She stood and picked up a book tucked behind a small box on the floor. "I've been saving this one for your boy."

Pearl loved when Nanette called Maxwell *her boy*. She opened the book and flipped several of the pages. It was full of word games—rebuses and anagrams.

"Oh, this is perfect. With evenings getting darker, and the inevitable storms coming on, we can keep our minds sharp." Pearl tapped the side of her head.

Nanette passed her another book. "And this one is for you. A bit silly, but the lady, with her bold heart and her great talents, reminds me of you."

Pearl felt her eyes sting with the compliment. She glanced

away, but Nanette must have seen, because she went on in a playful tone. "Of course, she chooses the wrong man. Foolishly swayed by a layer of polish and a boatload of money. She should have married the farmer down the lane. He was perfect for her, and she was at her best when she was with him. But we can't expect everyone to make the right choices in every story, can we?"

The words were easy to say, but Pearl knew the truth. Only by carefully making the best decisions could anyone protect the ones they loved. And if they looked away at the wrong moment, a happy life could turn to disaster.

CHAPTER 9

Oliver knocked on Maxwell's bedroom door. It was so quiet in the hallway he could hear the trees scratching along the glass of the windows. Leaves and twigs dropped as fast as the raindrops might later in the afternoon if the heavy, dark clouds were any indication.

It was interesting that a visit with the boy was exactly what Oliver knew he needed. How could he tell? What was it about Maxwell that made Oliver feel this whole endeavor—the sale of the property, tearing down Shadowbrook and making it something positive—was worthwhile? He'd wakened from sleep that morning with an echoing suggestion in his head to seek out Maxwell. Almost as if the words had been spoken aloud.

The boy didn't answer Oliver's knock. Had Max gone looking for Pearl? Oliver had seen her leave the house, a small basket over her arm and a drab hat covering her raven-black hair. She was out, and Maxwell was presumably somewhere in the house. Oliver had no idea where Max might be exploring, so he made his way into a small parlor in the east corner of the main floor and sat facing the window. To wait.

He reminded himself several times he wasn't watching for Pearl's return. He simply looked out at the lane that approached the house. Not for anything in particular. If he kept thinking such thoughts, he might convince himself.

A young girl in a serving uniform stepped inside the room. She didn't look much older than eleven or twelve.

"Forgive me, sir. I was going to set a fire, but I'll come back later."

He shifted in his seat. "No, please stay. It's chilly here. I'd love a fire. Thank you."

He needed to stop speaking so fast. Why did he feel nervous talking to one of his uncle's maids? After a moment, he realized he was a bit afraid of her. Not the child moving to the fireplace, but the idea she represented. Servants. He couldn't imagine how he could ever manage workers the way his uncle had to. Oliver was sure he'd be terrible at directing a household staff. He couldn't even speak to Jenkinson without feeling like a small child who'd broken a priceless vase.

Not that it mattered. He wouldn't be living here. He wouldn't need to administer the work of the manor. Soon there would be no more Shadowbrook House to run.

That thought gave Oliver a thrill of both excitement and dread.

"Do you mind if I ask you a few questions while you work? It's much too quiet in this house, and all the silence makes me feel as though I'm underwater."

She gave him a quick smile. "Of course not, sir."

"Have you been here long?"

"Just over a year. My older sister worked in the kitchen until she married. I've taken her place, but I'm not much good at cooking. So I have other responsibilities." She indicated the fireplace and the iron bucket of wood in her arms.

"And what's your name?"

She glanced over her shoulder, trying for a curtsy as she hurried to lay the fire. "I'm Violet, sir."

"I'm Oliver."

She nodded at the fireplace. "Yes, sir."

"I'm here visiting my uncle."

Violet nodded again and laid a knot of old muslin on the freshly swept stone.

After a moment of awkward silence, Oliver spoke. "I wonder if you happen to know where the governess has gone today?"

"Into town, sir." She added a few small pieces of kindling across the muslin and paper.

"All the way to Portsmouth?"

The girl covered her mouth to hide a smile. "Oh, no. That's much too far. Just to Riverwood. She goes each week."

Oliver wondered if Maxwell missed his governess when she was away. "And you? Do you ever go with her?"

She shook her head and turned back to the fireplace, laying a midsized log on top of the others. "She doesn't take anyone with her."

"Not even Maxwell?"

Violet turned to look at him, confusion on her face. "I thought you were part of the family."

Oliver shifted in his seat. "I am." Could she hear the false note in his assertion? Impending inheritance aside, he didn't feel like a Ravenscroft.

"In that case, you know how ill Maxwell is. He must never go to town."

"He didn't seem ill at all when I was with him last night." He immediately regretted his defensive tone. Clearing his throat, he began again. "I don't know Max very well. I was happy to find him strong enough to play and explore."

Violet nodded. "He's doing quite well right now, thank goodness. But in winter, he must be cautious. We all must be. When illness strikes anyone in the house, as it always does, he can't leave his room. What shows up in one person as a chill could very likely kill him."

Oliver shook his head, thinking the girl was being dramatic. "Surely he's not so frail."

Violet struck a match and held it to the tinder. "We must all take care. The master couldn't live without young Max."

Fire lit, she stood and gave Oliver a short bow. "Good day, sir."

"Thank you, Violet." He spoke without looking at her, almost without thinking, as her last words echoed in his mind. Arthur Ravenscroft couldn't live without Maxwell.

Was it true? Did his uncle love the boy so much?

Oliver was uncomfortable with the very idea. Uncle Arthur had never loved Oliver, had barely tolerated him. But he adored his grandson enough to protect him, keep him safely in this house?

Not that Maxwell didn't deserve such adoration. He was a bright little chap, clever and funny. If Oliver had been more like Maxwell when he was a boy, would his uncle have liked him more? Would he have wanted to see him, to know him?

He couldn't imagine it. Not after years of living in this house, ignored and overlooked.

Sitting alone in the small room, Oliver stared into the fire, listening to the snap and clatter of twigs burning. Then he realized he was hearing something else, something soft and unfamiliar beneath the fireplace sounds.

Laughter. Light and high-pitched and free. Oliver had heard that laugh the day before, sitting at a laden tea table in a hidden room. The voice sounded like Maxwell's.

He stood from the chair and walked to the door, listening carefully. He tried to follow the sound, but as he crossed the hallway, the laughter died away. He walked back inside the empty room. The sound seemed to follow him, growing louder as he moved toward the outer wall of the room. There was no connecting room on this side because he'd been watching for Pearl's return through the south-facing window. Nevertheless, the sound of Maxwell's laugh seemed to grow stronger as Oliver approached the window.

Maybe what he heard wasn't Maxwell after all.

He stepped quietly from one side of the wall to the other, and there—the laughing was loudest directly in front of a portrait of a pair of young boys dressed in matching costumes. The older had his hand on the younger's shoulder, and both boys looked as if they were stifling their smiles. Like they were trying not to giggle. A prickling sensation crawled up Oliver's neck.

Maybe what he heard wasn't Maxwell's voice. Was the painting *laughing*?

He stepped away before he realized he was going to do it, bumping into the back of a chair placed near the fire. Stumbling while trying to right himself without touching either the chair or the wall, he kept his eyes on the portrait.

Another peal of childish laughter sent a shudder across Oliver's shoulders, but the sound that followed was even eerier than a laughing painting.

This sound was rusty and creaky and entirely unnatural. A wheeze accompanied each percussive beat. Oliver couldn't stand it. He reached out and pulled the frame as if to yank it from the wall. Instead, it swung open like a door on a hinge, exposing a narrow hallway where both the wheezing and the laughing blew toward him on an internal breeze. He paused only a moment before stepping inside.

The narrow hall bent and turned, and Oliver wondered what he might find at the end. The sounds he followed continued to float toward him, and he was even surer than before that he heard Maxwell's voice. Another turn in the passage and he stood facing a wall, but one with a series of slits in the wood. Light leaked through into his corridor, and he pressed his face close to the plaster-daubed surface.

Maxwell sat on a low couch, his feet tucked up beneath him, a book on his lap and a grin overspreading his face. And beside him, partially visible to Oliver from his hiding place, was a stooping, silver-haired figure who could only be Uncle Arthur.

He hadn't seen his uncle in years, but the curve of his neck and shoulders, the bend of grief, was the same.

Now Oliver saw where the terrible wheezing, crackling noise came from. The old man was trying to laugh.

It wasn't as if Oliver had believed his uncle was incapable of emotions other than frustration and exasperation. He'd simply never considered the man might enjoy . . . anything. In all the time Oliver spent within the walls of Shadowbrook, there had never been a hint of affection in the old man's treatment of Oliver. In fact, he'd been clear that Oliver was better off anywhere but Shadowbrook: school, Cambridge, the city, it didn't matter. He was unwilling to take young Oliver in and eager to see him off again. They'd never rested together on a couch, laughing over a story.

Yet here the old man sat, one arm draped over the thin, frail shoulders of little Maxwell. The old man smiling. Laughing. Embracing.

Such tender attention. Oliver would have paid any price to feel that arm across his shoulders in his youth. What had changed? How had Arthur Ravenscroft come to this?

It had to mean something, but all Oliver's assumptions made him feel alone and tired.

Oliver stood many minutes with his eye near the slit in the wall before retreating from the spot. So much guilt propelled him back through the twisting passages, he hardly noticed the sounds that followed him.

And how foolish he'd been to consider the painting as the source of the laughter. Nothing so mystical. Only another instance in which he was not the kind of person his uncle could love. On the day he left Shadowbrook to attend school, he'd made himself a promise. Oliver Waverley would become his own kind of man—one who didn't need to depend on his uncle for support.

He'd learn. He'd make connections. He'd discover the paths to independence and the new industry signaling England's future.

Shadowbrook was the past—and not only that, it was the worst echoes of every terrible time in Oliver's life. Despair and devastation had always hung like a fog within the walls of the house. But he was no longer the needy, terrified child he'd been at the death of his parents.

He'd show Uncle Arthur. He'd made something of himself, and now he could earn his uncle's respect. He'd make sound financial decisions and take this heap of stones and turn it into a prospect worthy of the future.

If he had to do it all behind his uncle's back, he would gladly do so. And there would be money enough to buy the best care possible for what ailed Maxwell, to see Uncle Arthur established in a house in which he could be comfortable, and for Oliver to walk away once and for all and never look back.

CHAPTER 10

The rain held off until Pearl was halfway back from Riverwood. She tucked the basket inside her cloak and watched the lane beneath her feet. Sometimes a chuckle snuck out of her as she pictured herself walking through a scene in one of the novels she and Nanette loved and laughed about, dripping wet and protecting her meager treasures with the tattered fabric of a generations-old wrap.

At least it wasn't stinging cold, and she wasn't walking away from the smoking ruin of her only chance for happiness. Such a fate was saved for the women in novels. The thought made her smile again.

At the gravel approach to Shadowbrook, she looked up to the top of the house the way she always did. A strange, wide turret, as out of place as many of the architectural choices thrust upon the house in the past two hundred years, caught her eye. The clouds framed it with a billow of deep gray. How might she make her way to that room, and what would she find inside? It would make a delightful endpoint for another game with Max. Unless, of course, the stairs had crumbled and the walls had caved in.

Always a possibility within Shadowbrook's passageways.

Several of the house's chimneys produced thin lines of smoke, the trails mingling in the air and meeting the clouds. She hoped little Violet had put a fire in whatever room Maxwell chose to spend his quiet hours in. It was growing cold, and the boy needed all the household to band together to protect him.

She wiped the rain from her face and rounded the side of the house. At the kitchen door, she shook herself and brushed down the sides of her sodden cape, hanging it on the peg outside the doorway.

Once in the house, she felt herself breathe easier. She was back. Safe.

It was a strange realization she'd made recently. Sometime in the last several months, she'd come to understand she was protected within Shadowbrook. Before then, it wouldn't have occurred to her that she needed to stay inside. Perhaps it was overhearing Mr. Ravenscroft as he spoke to Maxwell about the protections of the house. In any case, almost without knowing, she'd begun to consider herself shielded by the house.

Safeguarded.

A thought tickled the back of her mind: Once winter arrived in full, it would be better if she didn't walk into town for her half day. She ought to stay at home.

Home? The word was wrong. The feeling was wrong. This house was many things, but not her home. It was too strange, too formal, too unfamiliar. Too many hidden doors masked far too many secrets. She loved Maxwell nearly as much as she'd adored her own brother, but they weren't a family.

Pearl felt a jolt of sadness at the reminder. Family was in her past. Caring for Maxwell was the concern of the present. The future—a time when Maxwell would no longer need her—would show itself later. Hopefully years and years later.

After unpacking the small loaf cake she'd bought in the village and placing it on the kitchen worktable, she made her way out into the main part of the house, looking for Jenkinson.

The warren of drawing rooms and parlors and sitting rooms gave Mr. Ravenscroft ample opportunity to sit in a new space every day of the week, but she rarely saw him on the main level of the house before evening. He'd sit in one room or another and read by the fire until Max came in for his good night. It seemed a formal event to Pearl, who was unused to such planned attention. In her home growing up, the family had eaten together, read and played and sang around the piano together, sometimes wrestled and romped until the children were tired out, then her father would carry one or both of them up to their rooms for bed.

She didn't know if such familiarity and informality was rare, but it wasn't the habit at Shadowbrook. Maxwell seemed satisfied with her attentions throughout the day and his few moments with his grandfather before bed, but she wished more for him. She wished Mr. Ravenscroft would love the boy, not simply tolerate his nightly visits. How could anyone know Maxwell and do anything but fall in love with him? His cheeky, playful smile, his inquisitive mind, his beautiful eyes—each piece of him worked together to create a near-perfect child.

And while Mr. Ravenscroft accepted his visits, it seemed to Pearl he did no more than endure them. How sad for them both. Their relationship could be so much more if the old man allowed himself to love the boy.

But she understood the scope of her work. She was to care for Maxwell: teach him, play with him, and spend time with him. She was not hired to rebuild broken family bonds.

She turned a corner and found Jenkinson standing outside a closed door. She knew she must look a fright after the wet walk home, but she had no reason to smarten herself up for the butler. "Hello, Jenkinson. I have been to the postal office, and I have a letter for Mr. Ravenscroft."

Without even making eye contact, Jenkinson held out his hand.

Pearl knew he expected her to lay the paper in his palm, but she was disinclined to submit to his silence. "It was posted in

London. It's from someone named Madame Genevieve. Did you know Mr. Ravenscroft was communicating with a woman from London?"

Jenkinson said nothing. Jenkinson usually said nothing.

Pearl pointed at the paper's sides. "Her envelope is edged in black. It looks like a funeral announcement. Isn't that a strange form of communication?"

Again, nothing.

"Perhaps I'll take the letter inside and give it to Mr. Ravenscroft myself."

That did it. Jenkinson moved to block her as if Pearl might try to push past him to the door. She had no interest in a physical struggle; she only wanted to see if today was the day Jenkinson would engage in a conversation.

Apparently, it was not.

She handed the letter to Jenkinson. Before she could walk away, the door opened behind the butler, and Mr. Ravenscroft stepped into the hallway. With Jenkinson and Pearl already standing there, it felt crowded.

Mr. Ravenscroft spoke, his voice hushed and rusty. "Did I hear you mention Madame Genevieve?"

Pearl nodded. "I stopped for the post on the way back from Riverwood. There's a letter here for you."

She pointed awkwardly at Jenkinson's still-outstretched hand.

Mr. Ravenscroft immediately tore into the envelope right where he stood. He scanned each line of the note, and when he looked back at Pearl, he appeared to be smiling, or it might have been a grimace. It was difficult to tell. His eyes seemed to burn, and there was color in his cheeks.

"She's agreed to come."

Pearl had no idea if she was expected to understand who this woman was or what it meant that she planned a visit to

Shadowbrook. Was Pearl supposed to ask questions? Generally, the answer to that was no.

She chose to nod, as if her agreement had been requested.

"Maybe she can help us find some answers to our important concerns with Maxwell."

A doctor? But why would a doctor call herself Madame? She wouldn't. But who else would Mr. Ravenscroft call for help to answer his pressing questions about his grandson?

And what about Dr. Dunning, the man who had come to the house every week for longer than Pearl had lived at Shadowbrook? Mr. Ravenscroft followed every direction that came from Dunning's mouth carefully and exactly. The doctor's counsel had led to consistent bedtimes, an organized diet, and a regimen of gentle exercise. Pearl was quite sure Mr. Ravenscroft agreed to her weekly visits to Nanette's shop because Dr. Dunning recommended reading as a healthy activity for growing and stretching Maxwell's mind.

As ill as the boy was, he had good days as well as hours of more vigor, and Pearl attributed his improved health to Dr. Dunning's good care. She couldn't allow Mr. Ravenscroft to simply replace him. Although it was not her place to question the choices of her employer, it was her job to care for Maxwell.

"Sir, does this mean Dr. Dunning's visit tomorrow will be his last?"

Mr. Ravenscroft lowered the note slowly at her question. He didn't look angry, but there was a weariness to his expression.

He watched her face as if she might say more, but she'd already spoken too much.

"Miss Ellicott, you seem to be laboring under a delusion." His whisper was far more frightening than a shout would have been.

Oh, dear. Was this the moment Mr. Ravenscroft would tell Pearl her position as governess gave her no right to question his decisions or motives? Would he throw her out? The muscles in Pearl's throat thickened. She couldn't breathe.

"Dunning's care will continue as it always has. There is not a more capable physician in all of England. Neither you nor anyone else will convince me to stop bringing Dr. Dunning in to care for Maxwell."

Pearl wanted to deny her question had been a suggestion. She wanted to explain how much she appreciated the doctor's careful treatment of Maxwell. She wanted to breathe again, but Mr. Ravenscroft's eyes burned directly into her own, his gravelly voice pinning her feet to the floor.

She could not speak, but she managed a slight shake of her head, then worried it would seem she disagreed. She gave a nod.

"Madame Genevieve's gifts are different. What she offers is unlike anyone else's contributions. I have consulted with her for many years, and her work has been magnificent."

The fire in Mr. Ravenscroft's eyes softened. A strange expression settled over his face, and he lifted his eyes to the hallway's ceiling.

Pearl had no idea what that might signify, but she was ready for this interview to end. "Very good, sir. You have my full support for anything that will help Maxwell be happier and more comfortable."

Jenkinson broke his silence with a snort so quiet it could have been a breath.

Mr. Ravenscroft tucked Madame Genevieve's letter into his pocket and returned to the parlor he'd been sitting in. As Pearl began to walk away, Jenkinson's hand landed on her arm.

In a sharp-edged whisper, the butler said, "No one asked for your approval. You mind your place."

Pearl wanted to run, but she had no wish for Jenkinson to ever try such a tactic again. She reached up and pushed his hand away. "I know my place. It is with Maxwell, and it is both my responsibility and my pleasure to insist on the very best care for him."

Without waiting for a reply, she walked out of the maze of

hallways with her head held high. Only when she'd climbed the main stairway did she fully release her breath, and with the exhale, she felt her whole body shudder.

She'd rather have a dozen of those enormous wall spiders crawl down her dress than Jenkinson's hand on her arm.

Only a moment brought her back to control, and she put her basket away in her room before stepping up to Maxwell's door.

She gave her usual knock so he'd know it was her and waited for him to invite her inside. When he was well, she liked to give him the respect of choosing when to allow her entrance, although he'd never denied her. At the times of his most distressing illness, he was unable to even answer her knocks.

No word from inside the room.

She knocked again.

Nothing.

The third time, she rapped her knuckles quickly against the wood as she turned the knob, fear clawing at her throat about what she might find. Would he be pale and still against his pillow? Or red-faced and sweating, thrashing under his linen bedclothes?

She had no time for additional fears; the room was empty, the window in the far wall like a hole, damp gathering on the glass and sill.

Maxwell was not there.

At any other time, Pearl might have convinced herself not to panic, but her interaction with Jenkinson had left her unsettled. She ran from the room and began pushing open doors along the hallway. At least half of them were locked or jammed, but she threw her shoulder into each one, hope and fear spinning around her in almost equal measure.

Max must never be alone when he fell ill. His sickness—the horrible, lung-wrenching coughs—came so quickly, and sometimes so violently, he couldn't be on his own. Now he was in danger, and it was her fault. If she didn't insist on a half day away from the house, whatever terrible thing had befallen Maxwell wouldn't have happened. Just like if she'd been home when her brother Edgar took ill, he wouldn't have slipped into the darkness without seeing her face. Without hearing how she loved him.

Only when the pain in her throat matched that in her shoulder did she realize she was screaming for Maxwell. Footsteps clattered on the staircase. Pearl ran to the base of the upper stairs as Maxwell came flying down. He rushed at her, nearly bowling her over as he jumped from the last stair into her arms.

Close behind him, Oliver Waverley stuttered to a stop, but before she closed her eyes and pressed her face into Maxwell's hair, she saw Oliver's arms reach toward her as if to support her.

She did not need Oliver. All she required was Maxwell in her arms, squeezing her with all his meager strength.

Standing on the landing, rocking Maxwell in her arms, she felt her breathing calm and her heart regain its normal rhythm. She warred with the urge to hold Maxwell at arm's length and scold him—where had he been? Didn't he know how worried she would be?—but she released the impulse after a few quiet moments. She had no wish to shout at the boy, and certainly never wanted to frighten him.

He didn't need to be reminded of his illness. When the coughing fits overtook him, he gasped and wheezed. His throat grew sore and his ribs ached. Some effects lingered long after others, and no one knew them more intimately than Maxwell did.

Pearl satisfied herself with asking the simplest question: "Are you all right?"

He nodded.

"You know I worry when you're by yourself. But I'm here now, and I won't leave you on your own anymore."

Maxwell looked up into her face. "I wasn't on my own. Oliver's here."

Pearl pretended it wasn't a force of will that kept her from looking up at Oliver. Her conversation with Nanette echoed in her mind. Heroes and villains and literary love.

He couldn't possibly understand the dangers of Maxwell's condition, nor did he know how to help if something set the boy off. Such facts were easier to remember when she wasn't looking into his deep brown eyes.

"Come on. Let's get you back to your room."

Maxwell didn't move. "Don't you want to see what we found?" He grinned as if he already knew her answer.

She couldn't help it. She glanced up at Oliver, who still stood on the stairs. His smile held a hint of mischief, as if he dared her to come upstairs and join in their adventure.

"Wouldn't you like to see what Miss Nanette has found for you?"

Maxwell clapped his hands together, a sure sign he was pleased. "Oh, yes. First we explore, then we read my new book."

Then Maxwell began to cough. It wasn't a loud, thundering sound; he didn't have the strength for anything like that. It was a sharp gasp. A terrible wheeze. A squeezing of his poor, wretched lungs. Though it no longer surprised her, the sound broke Pearl's heart.

Maxwell tried to speak through the cough. "I'm fine. Just took in a bit of dust." He pressed a fist to his chest, but even before he could pound out the possible cause of the cough, he folded into a ball and crumpled onto the lowest step, curling in on himself and panting for breath. Puffing. Rasping. The fit went on and on.

Conflicting advice rushed into Pearl's mind like voices calling to her.

"Take him to his bed."
"Let him breathe outside air."
"He must rest."
"He needs to fight against his body."

She could almost believe the whispers were real. For a moment, she wondered which to obey, but then she remembered it was only her own thoughts crashing around in her head.

Pearl placed a hand on the boy's back and then lifted him into her arms. Oliver followed, asking how he could help, offering to carry Max, being attentive and generally in the way.

Pearl wanted to tell him to stay back, to remind him Max would have been fine if Oliver had left him alone to rest in his room instead of chasing him all around the house's deserted attics and dirty passageways. But she knew anything she said would land first on Maxwell's ears, and she needed to appear calm. Her worry would increase his, and that would only make the coughing fit worse.

"If you don't mind," she said to Oliver, forcing a calm into her voice that she did not feel, "you might open Max's bedroom door for me. He'll feel better after a rest."

"Of course," Oliver answered, matching her tone. He held the door open, and she carried Maxwell's shaking body to the bed.

The boy sucked in a thin breath between coughs. These fits wore him out so quickly, she wasn't surprised his muscles were rebelling. The twitching and convulsing might calm with a warm blanket and her gentle hands rubbing his back.

Pearl tucked Maxwell under the covers. He lay on his side, and she kissed his forehead before moving to the other side of the bed and sitting beside him, her hand against the curve of his back, drawing slow circles with her palm.

"Shh," she breathed. "You are stronger than this cough. You can find your breath. It hasn't really left you." She continued whispering soft words into his ear. Sometimes this treatment worked within a few minutes, but it was taking longer than she liked for Max to regain control of his breathing. She curled around him, his back against her stomach, and ran her hand up and down his arm, humming and soothing.

After a few long moments, the boy's breathing eased, and soon—but not soon enough for Pearl's comfort—he was able to take in an almost-normal breath.

Finally, he shuddered out a long exhale. In response, she felt her arm muscles loosen.

"There. Much better." She stroked Maxwell's hair away from his sweaty face and sat up, startled to see Oliver standing at the door. He hadn't moved since she carried Maxwell inside the room.

Pearl walked around the bed to look into Maxwell's face.

"Tight?" she asked. He often told her these coughing fits made him feel his chest was bound up with ropes.

He nodded and then shook his head. "I was. Not so bad now."

He was clearly exhausted, his eyes damp and his cheeks hollow. Such a fit used reserves of energy the poor boy didn't have. She brushed his hair away from his face with her fingers and kissed him on his forehead again. "Sleep now."

"I'm not tired," he said, but each word stretched longer than the last, and Pearl knew he'd be asleep in a moment.

She whispered in his ear, "I promise I won't have any fun without you."

He sighed and settled, a small smile making his pale face angelic. "I need to stay here in my bed."

Pearl nodded and stepped lightly to the door. Oliver followed her out into the hall.

After he pulled the door closed without a sound, he leaned against it and rested his head on the wood, his chin tilted up and his eyes closed.

"I had no idea," he began, but he seemed to run out of words.

"That was not a bad episode. He recovered quickly."

"He needs a proper doctor's care."

He stated it as if the thought hadn't occurred to her.

Pearl had never owned a cat, but she had seen plenty of them take a fighting stance, backs arched and spitting. Hearing Oliver's simple offer of a solution to a problem she faced almost daily made her feel feline and more than a bit feral.

"He is in the care of a very fine doctor." Her words held knives.

Oliver, his head still against the door, kept his eyes closed. "I hope it's not Dunning. He came to care for me once when I broke my arm. The man had no sympathy and no imagination."

She was in no humor to listen to anyone find fault with Maxwell's care, especially someone who knew nothing about the boy's history. Oliver's flippant, casual criticism stung her.

"I assure you, Maxwell's medical care is in hands far more capable and experienced than yours."

She turned on her heel and entered her room, closing the door in Oliver's face.

CHAPTER 11

Back in his gloomy room, Oliver removed his necktie and ran his finger beneath the collar of his shirt. An evening within these lonely walls might allow him some rest. With all the research, letter writing, and meetings he'd done in the past months, a quiet night was truly welcome.

He settled himself into the chair beside the fire but had barely placed his feet upon the footrest when there was a knock at the bedroom door.

Was it Pearl? He jumped from the chair to answer her knock. He hadn't made it more than two strides before he realized it couldn't possibly be her. He slowed his steps. Not only was she angry with him, but she was also a woman of education and breeding; she would not come to his bedroom door for a visit. Unless something had happened to Maxwell and she needed his help. He quickened his pace again. Or maybe it was Maxwell at the door, feeling stronger and wishing to continue their conversation.

He wrenched the knob in anticipation of a visit from either and found himself looking into the unsmiling face of Jenkinson.

"Mr. Waverley," Jenkinson said in a toneless voice. "Mr. Ravenscroft will see you in the west parlor."

Finally. This was welcome news.

"Of course. I'll be downstairs in ten minutes."

Jenkinson gave a single jerk of his head. "Now."

With a splutter of badly withheld frustration, Oliver gestured to his rumpled shirt and loosened collar. "I can be ready soon."

"You will come when you're called," Jenkinson said.

Oliver grabbed his small portfolio from the table and hurried after Jenkinson. Not that he was nervous to walk the halls of Shadowbrook alone, but Oliver wasn't sure which was the west parlor. Drawing room, sitting room, receiving room, morning room? Each wing of each floor held several.

He followed Jenkinson down the stairs, the butler standing as straight and tall as he always had. The man seemed not to have aged a day in all the years Oliver had known him. His hair was the same bristly thickness. No smile lines marred his face. He'd lost none of his rigidity. His shoulders widened to an almost impossible degree, a figure more like a boxer than a butler.

Oliver was very aware of his own posture, loose and flowing. He'd have considered the way he carried himself *comfortable*, except he'd once heard his uncle call him slovenly. A boy didn't forget something like that, even when he'd become a man.

With an effort, he lengthened his spine and held his trunk straight, not even allowing his chest to expand and contract with his breathing. Watching Jenkinson walk down the stairs, Oliver was sure if he tried to keep his own legs so stiff, he'd tumble directly into the butler's back.

Fine. The upper half of him was a good place to start. If the west parlor was in view of the main staircase, his uncle would see him in at least partial rigidity.

At the main entry, Jenkinson took a left into a hallway lit by gas lamps. The yellow light and steady hissing made Oliver shudder. There was something serpentine about the whole arrangement of twisting hallways lit by small golden orbs, as if the eyes of great snakes watched him in constant disapproval.

When Jenkinson finally stopped in front of a doorway, Oliver nearly bumped into the man's back. He stopped himself just before contact. Hurriedly, he checked that the buttons of his waistcoat were fastened and pushed the hair off his forehead.

"Mr. Waverley, sir."

Jenkinson moved aside, and Oliver stepped inside a room he was sure he'd never been in before. His uncle sat in a deep armchair, the soaring back rising above his balding head.

In this light, his uncle looked ghastly. If Jenkinson hadn't aged at all, Arthur Ravenscroft had done so in double time. Oliver attempted to hide his shock at the full view of the skeletal figure being swallowed by his chair.

He moved toward his uncle, holding out his hand. "Uncle Arthur, it is so good to see you. I am thankful to you for calling for me." Both statements were untrue in their way, but Oliver delivered his words with what he hoped was a confident smile.

Uncle Arthur didn't take Oliver's hand, didn't rise, didn't smile. Two spindly fingers gestured to a chair.

Under the scrutiny of a gaze that had only ever found him lacking, Oliver perched at the edge of the cushion and held his portfolio to his chest.

One or two stiff breaths were all it took for him to realize this would never do. He was not a naughty child. He'd done nothing for which he should be reprimanded or punished.

With that thought in mind, Oliver sat back into the chair and relaxed the muscles of his neck. He'd arrived at Shadowbrook as both heir and counselor, ready to help his uncle take the ancestral home into the twentieth century. Not that Uncle Arthur looked as if he'd make it that long. Twenty years seemed a great way into the future when a man appeared as frail and pitiful as Arthur did.

But when he spoke, there was nothing frail or pitiful in his voice.

"You asked to come here to bring me a plan for the future of my house. Let me see it."

The long-fingered hand, knuckles like pebbles beneath his skin, gestured impatiently for Oliver to hand over the portfolio.

That was not part of Oliver's practiced presentation.

"Indeed, I have a very exciting possibility to introduce to you. Tell me, what do you know of the garment industry?"

Oliver had rehearsed his speech many times, speaking the words aloud and imagining his uncle's reaction to his opening line. At no time had he expected his uncle would stare at him without the slightest hint of interest or curiosity. In his mind, this was when Uncle Arthur would say, "I know very little. Please, tell me more."

In reality, the man only continued to stare.

Oliver leaned forward, reasserting a physical confidence even if he felt none. "Over the past few years, manufacturing has moved from simply making cloth to producing ready-to-wear items. At first, these were mainly soldier's uniforms, but many merchants in the north are now selling ready-made pieces to shops."

Oliver swallowed but never took his eyes from his uncle.

"Mass clothing production is only a step away, and there is no reason it all needs to stay in the north. Here in Hampshire, we have an untapped workforce, a population ready for change, and a shipping lane that's not controlled by the Manchester mill owners."

Feeling himself getting excited, he watched his uncle's face for any sign he'd caught the vision.

Nothing.

"The Trowbridge family has already sold, as I'm sure you know, and their deal was incredibly lucrative."

Still his uncle did not respond.

"When the Campbell Clothing Company secures a sufficient sector of riverbank lands, they'll be able to convert the houses into factories. Offer employment to dozens, possibly hundreds of local families. The company will thrive, and so will the surrounding villages. Shadowbrook has been more than you can handle for years, and as time goes on, it's going to become harder to keep it from tumbling into the river. We can set you up in comfort. Looked at in any kind of logical light, this is the solution we've all been waiting for."

He continued talking, explaining, justifying. Words flowed from him.

Was he speaking too loudly? Too fast? He was sure he'd overlooked many of the descriptive phrases he'd planned. When Oliver finished, Uncle Arthur seemed to sink into his chair as if to escape Oliver's verbal onslaught.

"Well, Uncle? What do you think?"

The old man took a handkerchief from his waistcoat pocket and dabbed at the corner of his mouth. He lay the cloth across one knee, pressing it flat with both hands as if the conversation would go much more smoothly if his pocket square had no wrinkles.

Ravenscroft then removed a pocket watch on a chain, glanced at it, and compared the time to the clock on the mantel. He made a small adjustment to the pocket watch.

A tug to each sleeve, pulling his cuffs down his bony wrists seemed to take hours. Oliver was nearly jumping out of his skin—or at least out of his seat—when his uncle finally spoke.

"I am unconvinced."

Oliver steadied himself, took a bracing breath, and closed his eyes for a second. "I have significant further evidence. Allow me to show you some drawings—"

Was that a scoff? Did the dismissive sound mean what it had meant so many years ago? Uncle Arthur had never thought much of Oliver's drawings, once chiding him to put down the pencils and do something worth his time.

He pretended not to have heard the noise. It was better to ignore his uncle's reactions and continue the presentation as he'd rehearsed it, by assuming he was either alone or with a welcoming audience.

He opened his portfolio to a pen-and-ink drawing of Shadowbrook as it appeared on Oliver's last visit. The drawing was done from the dock at the river, the house looming atop the high bank. The moon lit the house from behind, highlighting each crumbling turret, each jagged angle where stones fell and chimneys tilted.

Oliver remembered sitting on the dock, his legs crossed beneath him, as he stared up the bank at the ruined corners and edges of the house. He remembered moving his pen across the paper, carefully following each line of deterioration. It was no masterpiece, but it was a faithful representation of Shadowbrook as he saw it. As it was, and as it had been.

Overgrown gardens and fallow fields added to the mood of decay in the drawing. Oliver didn't feel words were necessary to accompany this picture of devastation, so he turned to the next page of the portfolio.

This drawing, from the same perspective of the riverside, showed what might be: a clean, angular, modern brick building placed on the same site, solid and handsome, reaching toward a cloudless sky. Sunlight glinted off windows drawn at regular intervals, suggesting an interior full of bright light. A graveled road curved from the side of the building down to the dock, which filled the foreground. Drawings of wagons filled with textiles showed how busy an industry this could be, all in the space now wasted and rotting.

As Oliver explained the scope of the Campbell Company's plan, outlining their desired timeline, his uncle sat in silence. When he dared look up, he saw Uncle Arthur studying the drawing.

Was he preparing a criticism of the drawing, or of Oliver's presentation in general? Either possibility was likely. Not interested in waiting for his uncle's disapproval, he made his final statements.

"We have reason to believe the Campbell Company has made

their most generous offer. They are eager to move quickly, and the offer must be signed before the end of the month."

Oliver paused to collect his thoughts. What else did he need to say? He believed he'd touched on each relevant point in favor of selling—and doing so as soon as possible.

He looked up to meet his uncle's eye, but the old man was still staring at the drawing in Oliver's hand. Unfolding his spindly arms from around his waist, he held his hand out for the portfolio. Oliver slid it across the low table between them, watching anxiously for any sign of approval.

Uncle Arthur stared at the drawing for several long moments before turning the page back to the rendering of Shadowbrook as it now stood.

Seeing the picture from this angle, upside down and across the table, Oliver recognized he'd used a heavy hand in its execution. How dark the clouds. How tangled the encroaching woods. The house itself, which he thought he'd impartially represented, was in fact shown in its worst possible light. Oliver didn't regret such a decision; how could he? That was how the house lived in his memory, and nothing on the outside had improved in the time he'd been away.

Something tickled the corner of Oliver's mind, however. Something about candlelit tables and platters of lemon cake. Something about fires banked in bedrooms. Something about a smiling governess and a laughing child.

Uncle Arthur still said nothing, and Oliver could wait no longer. He fired his most likely shot. "This isn't only about you and the building you've lived in all your life. You need to think of the boy."

The old man's eyes snapped to Oliver's. A fire burned there, surprising in its ferocity.

When he responded, the words carried to Oliver in a hissed whisper. "I do nothing but think of the boy."

Oliver could not sit there and listen to such an expression of self-deception. "Obviously not, or you would take him to the city for treatment. His illness is clearly serious and only worsening, and keeping him locked up in this house another winter isn't going to heal him."

Another of Arthur Ravenscroft's sounds of contempt preceded his next command. "Do not speak of what you do not understand."

"What I understand is that this is no place to convalesce. There are many options in London for treating childhood illnesses. Sign the contract. Leave this horrible house. Take the boy to the city. Give him a chance to grow up strong."

Uncle Arthur stood from his chair, waving his arm in Oliver's face as though it was a saber. "You have been here only a few days. You know nothing of the care Maxwell receives."

"You are correct that I've been here only a few days, but it took me only minutes to recognize that this house is not safe for Maxwell. It's a terrible place to recuperate from an illness. But it's more than that, and you know it. His situation is dangerous, and having him here is doing you and the household no good. Shadowbrook is dying, and the only thing that could hasten the process is to keep a dying child imprisoned within its walls."

A crash and a gasp stopped Oliver's torrent of words, and he turned to the parlor's doorway. There stood Pearl, her face pale and angry, her hands covering Maxwell's ears, as if such a precaution might keep Oliver's outburst from being overheard. A large leatherbound book lay at the boy's feet, its spine stretched wide, pages splayed.

Oliver jumped from his seat and hurried toward Pearl and Maxwell. Before he could reach them, Pearl swept the boy into her arms and ran from the room.

CHAPTER 12

For as many excellent hiding places as Shadowbrook offered, there was little likelihood Pearl could keep Oliver from coming to find her and Maxwell. And as much as she hoped he'd simply stay away, she assumed he'd come looking for them so he could make an apology. It was the right thing to do, and she knew him well enough to know he'd try to do right.

Oh, but the cruelty of his words. She kept hearing them in her mind. *Having him here is doing you and the household no good. Shadowbrook is dying, and the only thing that could hasten the process is to keep a dying child imprisoned within its walls.*

Dying. *Dying.*

There was no chance Maxwell hadn't heard his cousin's forthright use of that word—a word she never used in front of the boy. A word that would never bring him anything but pain.

She regretted their decision to stand at the door and listen. She should never have breached propriety that way, and she certainly should not have done so with Maxwell beside her. They'd thought it a game, listening to Oliver's plans. Pearl became truly invested in Oliver's proposal when she realized he wasn't waiting until he inherited the property. He believed he had a right to sell Shadowbrook while his uncle still lived.

It was impossible to know how much longer Mr. Ravenscroft would survive, but the old man was stronger than Maxwell.

Oh, Maxwell. The poor child. He must have heard and understood every word.

She'd hurried Maxwell upstairs, practically pulling him by the hand. She couldn't even form sentences; all her effort was focused on not screaming or shouting or crying as she brought Maxwell to his room.

Now they sat, each in their favorite chair by Maxwell's fireplace. He stared into the flames, and Pearl placed a cedar plank in the fire, another attempt to mitigate the strange smell of the room. Flowers were easy to come by in warmer months, and pine boughs in pitchers often helped as well. As long as autumn, winter, and spring allowed, she made sure to keep a fire burning to mask the tangy, musty smells of this corner of Shadowbrook House.

She watched the boy while trying to appear she wasn't. Twice he'd opened his mouth, but no words had come out. The muscles in Pearl's back, arms, and legs were all tensed, keeping her in readiness to respond to whatever Maxwell needed.

When his words finally came, they were borne on a whisper.

"Is it true?"

She wanted to deny anything the man said, but before she could answer, she needed to know which part he was thinking of. The word "dying" echoed in her mind, in Oliver's voice.

How could a voice say such lovely and kind things and then turn to such thoughtlessness? What had Maxwell understood, and what did he assume from that understanding?

"Is what true?"

Maxwell's eyes flickered from the fire to Pearl's face, then back again. "Is it true I'm hurting Shadowbrook by living here?"

If she thought she knew what the boy would say, this wasn't it. She moved immediately from her chair and knelt at Maxwell's feet.

"Oh, dearest, no. You're nothing but joy and gladness. You bring every good thing to this house." Both his small hands fit inside her own, and she grasped and held them tight.

Maxwell continued to stare past her left shoulder, his eyes on the fire. "We shouldn't have gone down to say good night."

She shook her head. "Your grandfather looks forward to your bedtime visit. We could not deny him that."

He finally met her eye. "No, you're right. But I'm sorry we heard what Oliver said. It would have been better not to know how he feels about me. Do you know, though, even if we'd never heard the words, we wouldn't have stopped Oliver from saying them if that's what he thinks." An awful, joyless chuckle came out of Maxwell's mouth. It was a sound no child should ever make. "I must have made a terrible impression. I thought we got along so well. Imagine what he'll think when he sees me truly ill."

Blast Oliver Waverley and his pretty patterned waistcoat, his freshly cut hair, and his charming smile. None of it softened his cruelty. None at all.

As if she'd conjured him with her frustration, a knock at the door was followed by Oliver's voice.

"Maxwell? Miss Ellicott?"

Before she could rise from the floor in front of Maxwell, the boy said in the same toneless voice, "Come in."

A creaking accompanied the door's opening, and even though she wanted to ignore the very idea of him, Pearl watched Oliver enter the room. First his head, as if he needed to see he was welcome.

Welcome was a very generous term for it. Pearl patted Maxwell's knee and then stood. She would hardly sit in the chair and watch Oliver grovel for Max's forgiveness. No. She would stand near the wall and watch him grovel for Max's forgiveness.

Oliver stepped into the room, halted for a moment, and tilted his head. She saw his face contort as he tried not to wince from the smell. She slid another cedar board into the fire. No need to give this infuriating man another thing to find fault with.

She faced Oliver, ready to tell him exactly what she thought of his careless statement, her words backing up in her throat, prepared for the assault. Every angry thought she'd entertained in the last ten minutes lined up to make itself heard. But when he came over to Maxwell's chair and offered his hand as he would to greet a dear friend, she found she couldn't make a sound.

He handed Max the book he'd dropped.

She wanted to shout at Oliver. To show him his station here was beneath that of an invited guest, and that he would only be shown the most basic politeness for as long as he remained.

What gave Oliver the right to sit down in her chair? To lean across and put his hand on Maxwell's arm? To smile at the boy that way? And why did Max so easily forgive him when he offered a quick, albeit sincere, apology?

His current gentleness to Maxwell reminded her of their shared time together, and she would much rather forget any of that ever happened. Now she knew how Oliver felt about Max being in the way of his great and grand plans for his uncle's property. Now she understood the reasons behind his eagerness to befriend them both.

How dare he? What gave him the right to come into this room and act charming? She clamped her lips together, breathing like a winded horse through her nose.

Her pulse pounded so heavy in her ears, she heard nothing more of the conversation between the two cousins until Maxwell said, "You're sitting in Pearl's chair."

Oliver leaped out of the seat, a long apology to them both pouring out of him. Pearl wasn't sure whether to retake her seat or pretend she didn't hear.

She decided to walk to Maxwell's bed and straighten the already immaculate covers and cushions. She moved a pillow and then placed it back. Then she brushed a spot of invisible dust off the blue bedcover. A bit of light housework in a crisis. That would show him.

With her back to them, she felt herself calming down. Her heartbeat resettled in the neighborhood of its usual pace, and she heard Maxwell's explanation of his routine to say good night to his grandfather every evening before bed.

"Do you? Every night?" Oliver's voice held a note of surprise, even amazement. "I lived here for years, and I don't believe he ever called for me except to issue a punishment. I was forever getting in trouble just so I could be near him."

Pearl huffed softly in frustration. Would Oliver use his former bad behavior to try to build a bond with Maxwell? Maddening man.

And of course, Oliver couldn't be satisfied with simply confessing his past wrongs. He had to wiggle himself into Maxwell's heart by pretending to need the boy's advice.

"How did you manage it? I'll try anything to get him to want to see me again."

Was Oliver manipulating Maxwell's relationship with his grandfather for his own ends? Such maneuvering was horrible at any time, but to use a child? How could she have been so completely fooled about Oliver Waverley's character? She felt herself flush with shame that she was so easily swayed by a friendly smile and a stranger's willingness to climb a ladder.

She turned to see Max leaning far over the side of his chair, every muscle straining to be closer to Oliver. "It's been that way always. Every night."

Oliver nodded. "Except when he's busy."

A shake of Maxwell's head. "He's never busy. Not at bedtime."

Pearl felt a flush of pleasure that she'd managed this small miracle. When she'd been hired as Maxwell's governess, the process went through the housekeeper. It was Mrs. Randle who wrote to her, who answered her questions, who finalized their agreement, and who welcomed her to the house.

Pearl arrived at Shadowbrook in the throes of her private grief, but the routine of caring for little Maxwell was a perfect way for her to pass time until her broken heart began to heal.

When weeks of her employment had passed and she had not even laid eyes on her employer, she'd gone to Mrs. Randle for an explanation.

"He'd prefer it this way. You do your work of caring for the boy, and he'll do his work of managing the estate."

Pearl shook her head. "In our correspondence, we agreed Mr. Ravenscroft would spend some time with Maxwell every day. A growing child needs a connection to his family, and Maxwell is lucky to have his grandfather, especially since he has no parents."

A daily visit was a perfectly reasonable expectation, and she did not need to defend her reasons.

Mrs. Randle shook her head. "The master won't have you in his private rooms."

Pearl blew out a frustrated breath. "There are dozens of public rooms in this house. Or someone else can deliver Maxwell to his grandfather for a nightly visit. If it's me Mr. Ravenscroft objects to, there are plenty of solutions that will keep me out of his way."

Pearl spoke plainly, but in her heart, she felt the tug of separateness, the inevitability of being alone in this house. Of course, she had Maxwell, but as a child who'd not yet had his second birthday, he was hardly a replacement for daily conversation.

The very next evening, Mrs. Randle knocked on the nursery door and gathered Maxwell into her arms, telling Pearl they'd return when his grandfather decided he'd seen enough of the boy.

On every night since, Maxwell had spent at least a few minutes with Mr. Ravenscroft. In time, Pearl was allowed to bring Maxwell to the doorway of the meeting room, and after more than a year, she was occasionally invited to stay. Mr. Ravenscroft rarely spoke directly to her, but that was his prerogative. She understood these nightly visits were about Max and the time he was able to spend with his grandfather.

But tonight, their visit was abandoned, thanks to Oliver Waverley's thoughtlessness. Pearl only wished she'd been able to whisk Maxwell away sooner so he wouldn't have heard so much.

Maxwell seemed to have a gift for forgiveness. She knew he'd been hurt and angry at Oliver's words, but he didn't seem so now. If the worry he might be harming the house lingered, he made no sign of it.

Pearl turned away again, searching for something to do with her hands so it wouldn't be painfully obvious that she once again found herself in a room with people who didn't include her. Once again, she was the outsider.

When it was only Maxwell, she felt nothing of the kind.

Mr. Ravenscroft thought of her only as his grandson's caretaker, and that was completely appropriate; that's what she was hired to be.

The other staff seemed either too busy to be friendly or uninterested in forming relationships. The footmen looked past her as if she was invisible. Jenkinson certainly wasn't going to start smiling any time soon. And Mrs. Randle jumped out of her skin every time Pearl spoke to her.

As she shifted the water pitcher half an inch to the right, she wondered why these thoughts were crowding into her mind tonight.

When she heard Max and Oliver laugh, she realized it was a new wave of a familiar loneliness.

At Oliver Waverley's arrival, she thought she'd found a new friend. His easy conversation and willingness to go along with Maxwell's adventures promised a connection unlike any other in the household. But tonight, he'd spoken so matter-of-factly, so casually about taking Maxwell away. Sending the boy from his home for the convenience of some strangers in industry. Putting Max at serious risk for the slight possibility of decent care in the city.

It was too cold, too selfish an act for Pearl to forgive. Maxwell's care must be the first and highest priority at Shadowbrook. Nothing mattered as much as keeping the boy well.

Now that she better understood her feelings about her own solitude within the house, she put the sadness aside and turned to the reason for all her decisions: Maxwell's comfort and safety.

She stepped over to his chair and put her hand on his arm. "I believe it's time to say good night."

Maxwell made a sound of discontent, but Oliver jumped up again from his seat in Pearl's chair.

"Of course. I apologize if I've kept you too late. Thank you for the excellent conversation, and I do hope we can visit again tomorrow."

He said this all while facing Maxwell, but Pearl couldn't help but notice his eyes flicker to her no less than four times. Too many times to be accidental.

Oliver gave a low bow with a sweeping arm gesture, and Max laughed at the formality.

"Miss Ellicott, may I speak with you a moment? In the hallway?" Oliver gestured to the door, but Pearl was not interested in following him out of the room.

She shook her head and held out her hand to Maxwell, guiding him from his chair. "I will help Maxwell ready himself for sleep now. Good night."

Oliver did not seem to hear the *no* in her response. "It will only take a moment of your time."

Maxwell wrapped both his arms around Pearl's waist and turned to look at Oliver. "Once Pearl decides it's time to go to sleep, there's no talking her out of it. Believe me, I've tried everything."

Oliver grinned at Maxwell, but when he looked up to Pearl's face, his smile lost its confident, arrogant edge and turned itself into a wordless apology.

"Perhaps you can find some free time for me tomorrow, then."

Pearl refused to be softened by that admittedly humble expression on that admittedly handsome face. He may be attractive and attentive and charming and pleasant, but he was too frustrating to be borne. She turned away from Oliver and propelled Maxwell toward his bed. "Tomorrow is a very busy day for us."

She tried not to look at him again, but as it happened, her eyes followed Oliver as he turned toward the door. Another, shorter bow was followed by the quietest comment he'd yet made. "I'll be waiting if you find a moment."

He pulled the door closed gently.

"Pearl, what will keep us so busy tomorrow?" Maxwell shrugged out of his dressing gown, a miniature version of Mr. Ravenscroft's own wine-colored robe.

Instead of answering, she turned down the bedcovers. "Time for prayers."

Obediently, Maxwell knelt at his bedside and closed his eyes, his hands clasped at his chest. "Dear God, please bless Grandfather and Pearl and all the household. Help me to be strong. Bless the souls of my parents and Pearl's family that their spirits will be at peace. And thank you for bringing Oliver to us. Please make him and Pearl friends. Amen."

Pearl was not nearly as thankful for the arrival of Oliver Waverley as Maxwell was. Shadowbrook was an enormous house, but there wasn't room for him here. Not when Pearl couldn't decide how her heart should respond to him.

After a few moments, Maxwell's eyes closed. He breathed easily. Pearl moved through the room, finding nothing that needed her attention. After several moments of hushed stalking about the room, she turned the doorknob and stepped into the hall, closing the door silently behind her.

Oliver leaned against the wall, his eyelids lowered, one hand rubbing his neck and the other behind his back. He looked no more ready for a fight than Pearl felt.

But she could not, would not let him think he was right about Maxwell.

"Will you allow me to apologize?" His voice floated across the small space between them, gentle and soft.

She could simply answer no. Her frustration had wound itself into a knot of hurt and anger—a stone in her heart she'd happily hold onto for days or years. It was enough to keep her head turned away from this infuriating man.

But then she recalled his way with Maxwell. His gentleness and playfulness. Such a companion could only do the boy good—and if he was willing to apologize, maybe he realized he'd been wrong.

Could she listen to his apology? For Max?

Her small nod felt like a great effort. She didn't wish to argue, and there was no excuse Oliver could give that would make her think him right, but further tension in the house would only be difficult for everyone.

"If I could go back in time one hour," he said, his back still against the wall, "I'd say everything differently. The substance of my suggestion wouldn't change, but the words I used were inexcusable. I spoke in frustration and fear, and I wish to erase my comment about Maxwell from existence."

Pearl looked at him and rubbed at the corner of her eye. "It doesn't work that way."

"I know." With visible effort, Oliver peeled himself from the wall and stepped closer to her.

Her traitorous heart pounded at his nearness.

"And sometimes saying I'm sorry doesn't work, either. But I

am. So terribly sorry. I will spend my time and effort proving to you and Maxwell I can be a better friend."

She felt his sincerity, but she heard his excuses. He regretted Max hearing him say what he said, but he didn't seem to release his mistaken opinions about how to care for the boy. She knew this apology was no guarantee of a real, lasting change.

She watched him carefully, her heart warring with itself. This exasperating man: so sure of his flawed beliefs and so earnest in his care for the boy.

"Please, Pearl. Give me a chance to do better."

How often had Pearl's own heart wished an opportunity to say such words to her family? To offer such an apology, even though there was no chance for her to make new choices to change the course of their lives?

She wouldn't deny him that chance. She looked at him. "Yes. We can both try harder to do better."

His hands lifted to her shoulders, but she was not prepared for his touch. Too many feelings swirled around her, and being so close to Oliver only allowed her to focus on one or two. She needed to clear her mind and settle her heart.

She stepped back and shook her head.

He dropped his hands and put them behind his back again, almost as if he needed a barrier between his hands and her. "Thank you for accepting my apology."

The power of those words crashed over her. It was so easy to use the words "I'm sorry" for a justification or validation of an opinion, but Pearl had never considered what an acceptance would mean.

Pearl looked up at Oliver and saw nothing but sincerity in his eyes. She moved closer to him.

"You're so wrong about us, Oliver Waverley."

He lifted his hand and used a single gentle finger to smooth an escaped lock of hair away from her cheek before his hand disappeared behind him. "Am I?"

Eyes closing in a moment of rest or resignation, Pearl nodded. "Wrong about Maxwell and what he needs to grow healthy and strong. Wrong about your uncle's wishes."

"And you? Am I wrong about your needs and your wishes as well?"

She tried not to touch the curl he'd just moved back into place, but her fingers were drawn there. "You know nothing about either."

He no longer reached for her, but his eyes did not leave hers. "But I wish to know."

Shaking her head, Pearl smiled sadly. "All I could ever want is there behind that door."

Oliver watched her for a long moment. "It's possible you believe that is true. And I may be mistaken about you. But Pearl, you are mistaken as well. About me. About what's best for the boy. And about yourself."

She worried he might say more, speak aloud words that would crumble the foundation beneath her beliefs as easily as the stones of Shadowbrook House seemed to be disintegrating.

Her words left her mouth without much thought. "Maybe we're all wrong about everything." The echo of her words and truth of the statement followed her into her room and into her dreams that night.

CHAPTER 13

Oliver heard the huge clock in the upstairs hall toll the hour before he made his way to his room. Once there, he sat at the empty desk and stared into his portfolio. Even with a charcoal pencil in his hand, he couldn't make a mark on the blank page.

All he saw was Maxwell's sallow face, and then Pearl's exhausted, beautiful one.

The very air of Shadowbrook seemed to tell him he was making things worse by staying here. His visit, ill-timed and ill-conceived, was only hurting these people he had so quickly learned to care for.

He pressed the charcoal stick to the paper and made a few hasty lines. Before he fully realized what he was drawing, Maxwell's room took shape on the page. In simple lines, Oliver sketched the boy in his chair, firelight highlighting one side of his face. An attempt to draw Pearl ended in a shadowy blur. Oliver rubbed it away with his hand, knocking the charcoal pencil to the floor.

Pushing the chair back from his table, he knelt to retrieve it.

The floorboards in his room didn't have a speck of dust on them. Even though Oliver had invited himself to his uncle's house, someone was attending to this space and keeping the room in order. Someone had been in here recently, and possibly even during his years'-long absence, to sweep and dust. It seemed odd to Oliver, since so much of the house threatened to crumble to ruin.

Now that he thought of it, the rooms he'd spent most of his time in on this visit—Maxwell's room, several public parlors, his own blank page of a bedchamber—all felt clean and orderly. The front doorway dropped bricks like old men lose teeth, and the chimneys leaned at dangerous angles. Piles of crates and boxes lined the walls in several unused spaces, but the rooms that were in use were warm and comfortable.

Young Violet and the rest of the staff working with Mrs. Randle were doing a respectable job, even if at a glance the house looked like a stiff wind would knock it to the ground.

He stood staring at the blank wall for a few moments, trying to call to mind the portrait of his mother that used to hang there. Why had his uncle removed it?

There was no way to know how thoughts might form and develop in the old man's mind, so thinking about *why* Uncle Arthur did anything was a waste of time and mental effort.

But their conversation had ended without a signed contract. They'd failed to make a decision, either about the house or about the boy. He needed to speak with his uncle again. He closed the portfolio and took himself up the creaking, dark stairs. At the upper landing, he realized he had no idea where to find his uncle if he was no longer in the west parlor. Years ago, he would have been sure the old man sat in his study, but after his recent exploration, he knew the room was now unused.

To the left at the top of the stairs was the short hallway he and Maxwell had explored earlier that day. To the right, his uncle's personal wing.

The entire hallway carried the echo of warning from his childhood.

Off-limits. Forbidden. Private.

Which one of the doors was the entrance to Uncle Arthur's

bedroom? Would Oliver dare walk up to it and knock at the dark, heavy wood? Too many habits formed in childhood still lived in his muscle memory. Silence. Avoidance. Escape.

Approaching the massive double doors of the study, he reached for the knob again. Maybe he'd missed something when he'd explored the room earlier. A closer look might give him needed information about why his uncle was so angry, so cold toward him.

The doorknob didn't turn.

Violin music seemed to rise up the stairs, as if someone followed him, scraping a bow mournfully along strings.

He turned. There was no one else nearby.

The sound scampered up the bones of his spine, giving him a shiver.

He knew the reaction was foolish, but knowing didn't change the way his skin crawled.

How did a simple wind turn to ghostly mystery in mere moments? This house was the least peaceful place he knew. Every part of him—his thoughts, his feelings, even his pounding heart—was on high alert when he was here.

Turning from the locked study doors, he walked along the hallway. He had never been into Arthur Ravenscroft's private chambers nor entered any room in the wing, until he explored the empty study. One of these doors must be his uncle's bedroom. Oliver would try door after door until he discovered the right room.

You are no longer a child, he reminded himself. *You have business to manage, and the sooner you settle it, the sooner you can move on.* He lifted a hand to the door and tapped it with a knuckle. When there was no answer, he tried the knob, surprised when it turned beneath his touch.

The room was piled floor to ceiling with leather-strapped wooden crates. A forest smell, mildewed and slightly fungal, hung in the air. How long had these boxes been stored here?

He moved to the next door. Another rap of the knuckle,

another surprisingly easy twist of the knob. This room might once have been a library. Books lay in tottering, disordered piles growing up from the floor. The stacks reminded Oliver of cave formations he'd seen, pillars of sediment rising from years of slow, steady dripping.

Were his childhood books stored here? If he walked between the columns of volumes, would he find remembered stories he'd read beside his bedroom fire at night? Books that kept him company in this lonely house? The thought was almost temptation enough to stop and spend an hour exploring the piles.

But Oliver didn't have time to spare. Not tonight. There was too much to learn, and he could not make inquiries from here.

He tapped the next door and opened it, this time to a completely empty room. Not a box or a crate. Why was this room kept empty?

His mind was half excitement, half frustration. Why had he ignored this wing of the house when he'd had years living here to discover these treasures? No sooner did the question occur to him than the answer came as well. Entering this section of the house was against the rules, and indignant and resentful though he may have been about it, young Oliver had always obeyed his uncle's rules.

The next door might hold a dragon's hoard of treasure, while the next might be stacked floor to ceiling with firewood. There was no telling what ideas might have sprung from the irrationality of Mr. Arthur Ravenscroft's mind. Oliver's frustration was only partly about the unexplored possibilities. The rest was for the insistence of his uncle and his employees that young Oliver be kept separate and alone.

Where was his uncle hiding? Oliver threw open the next door without bothering to rap on the wood, and he nearly knocked the old man himself to the floor.

Uncle Arthur stood, a paper clutched in his hands, as though he was on his way out of the room to meet someone.

Oliver's mind went immediately blank. He stood in the doorway with his mouth open, foolish as he'd ever been. What was he planning to say to his uncle? Why had he barged into the room this way? What was he doing here?

Ah, well, he thought. *May as well go on as I have begun.*

"Uncle, we must come to an agreement as soon as possible. You know I've done the work to find the best outcomes for the house and property, and I hope you understand I've tried to find a solution that's best for you and Max as well."

It felt strange to refer to Maxwell by his diminutive name. Before this visit, he'd never even seen the boy, yet now he felt a gently protective swelling in his heart for his cousin. He'd hate to see the illness grow stronger while his uncle refused to see sense.

"I need your signature on the contract from the Campbell Company. The offer will not wait."

A voice in Oliver's head whispered that his uncle already knew his justification and the timeline. If the man hadn't been convinced before, a repetition of the same facts and figures wouldn't change his mind.

Oliver needed a new tactic, and it was a simple choice. It hadn't left his mind all night.

"I witnessed one of Maxwell's fits tonight, and I never want to see such a thing happen to the poor boy again. We need to get him out of this place. He needs the care and protection of a specialist, a doctor who has seen many patients with Max's symptoms. He needs to be near hospitals and institutions and medical schools. There are people in London who can help him, and I intend to find them."

Oliver realized his voice grew both louder and faster as he continued to speak. He felt strongly about helping Maxwell, but he didn't want to ruin any chance of his uncle listening to him by being too emotional.

"Please, sir, consider the boy."

Uncle Arthur seemed to grow several inches taller and wider before Oliver's eyes, like an animal puffing itself up to terrify its prey.

"How dare you suggest you know better than I how to take care of this house." He did not shout. Each word came across cold and measured. If any shaking remained in the old man's voice, it was the tremble of rage.

Before Oliver could point out the damaged exterior walls, the crumbling facade, the tumbledown outbuildings on the property, Arthur continued. "You have no idea what the house wants. You never did listen. You seem to consider Shadowbrook to be already your own, but this is *my* house, and as long as I live, I am the one who decides how I will dispose of my property."

He thrust a bony finger into Oliver's chest.

"So long as you choose to remain here, you will honor my wishes. You will cease your foolish errand of selling my property, and you will leave all discussion of Maxwell's care to those who know and understand."

Habit forced Oliver's head into a nod.

"You will leave my private wing now." Uncle Arthur's words came louder and louder. Surely, Jenkinson waited around some corner or other, and any moment the intimidating butler would come to drag Oliver away from the forbidden hallway.

After an evening so full of emotion, he would be happy to avoid that humiliation. Oliver turned and walked away, past the clock and its straining gears, and down the creaking stairs.

As softly as he moved, his footsteps weren't silent. Pearl opened her door and stepped out into the hall.

She looked at him like there was something she wanted to say, but when she saw his face, she stopped. "Are you ill?"

Oliver breathed a humorless laugh and shook his head. "Only a terrible nephew. Nothing I try will please my uncle."

She quirked that lovely eyebrow. "Maybe your efforts are misguided."

Oliver felt equally amused and frustrated by her dismissal of all his years of work. "Is it impossible to consider I might be right?"

She nodded. For a moment, he was pleased she saw things his way. Then he realized what he'd asked. Her nod of assent meant *yes*, it was impossible.

His words floated toward her on a sigh. "You are a surprising woman, Miss Ellicott."

"And you are incredibly frustrating, Mr. Waverley."

The snap and sparkle in her eye suggested she didn't mind a bit of frustration.

Oliver considered how to proceed. A list of possible next steps flowed through his mind and then were entirely erased as Pearl took a step forward, went up on her toes, and took Oliver's face in her hands. Before he fully realized what was happening, she pressed her lips to his in a kiss as warm and welcome as the first pleasant day of summer. Surprise did not prevent him responding, and he leaned into the kiss.

When she pulled away, she looked neither embarrassed nor disappointed. She held his gaze in silence. He knew he should say something, but she'd wiped all language from his mind.

"I—I thank you," he stammered.

Her bell-like laugh rang out quietly between them. "You're welcome. And you're still frustrating."

He felt his face heat with a blush.

"Good night, Mr. Waverley." She touched his shirt, just above his heart, with a gentle finger before stepping back into her room and closing the door behind her.

A mere second later, he was alone once again.

Had he imagined the whole encounter?

If he had, he'd happily reimagine it over and over as he took himself to his gloomy bedroom and fell asleep.

CHAPTER 14

When she awoke in the morning, Pearl listened to the sounds of Shadowbrook House. The wind seemed to whisper her secret into the room around her. She lay in her bed a few moments longer, reliving her stolen moment with Oliver.

It wasn't a dream—she'd really done it. She'd kissed Oliver Waverley. The thought made her blush at her own presumption. But not with any sense of repentance. Not a single regret. He may be the most infuriating man she'd ever met, but he was also the most handsome, and, despite his tendency to sometimes say thoughtless things, he acted with kindness and care. She liked him a great deal.

She'd been so bold. And he'd been so willing. She put a finger to her lower lip, remembering the feel of his mouth against hers, and traced the line of her smile.

She dressed quickly and went to Maxwell's door, pausing only a few seconds in the spot outside her room, just *there* where her feet had been planted so near his. The place she was sure she'd stop and remember every day from now on.

In his bed, Maxwell lay with his arm across a large pillow, his face still pale, but breathing gently. Water oozed from the damp spot in his ceiling, and she hoped a few days of warm fires and any stray sunlight she could coax inside might dry the leak. The sharp tang of mildew hung stronger in the room this morning. She would need to gather some pine boughs to repel the unpleasant scent.

She pulled aside his window curtains and greeted him with a smile, hoping her expression hid any lingering fear about his health. "Good morning, Master Ravenscroft."

"Hello, Pearl." His voice was quiet, but not as ragged as it often was the morning after a prolonged coughing fit.

She rested the back of her hand against his forehead, finding him warm but not overheated. "How were your dreams? Did you embark on any grand adventures through the night?"

It was their usual morning conversation, but Pearl wished for once he might ask her about her dreams. Or even about what might have preceded them. Not that she'd share many details with Maxwell. But the temptation to tell someone of her moment with Oliver was strong.

"There was a flood in my dream. The river rose higher and higher over the banks until the main floor of the house was entirely underwater. But we didn't mind. All the staff moved upstairs into the rooms beside ours. Oliver and I stood at the landing and cast fishing lines down the stairs."

Pearl laughed. "And did you have any luck?"

Maxwell shook his head. "Before we could catch anything, Oliver dove down the stairs and swam away. I tried to catch him with my pole, but I didn't want to hurt him. Only bring him back." Rubbing his fists against his eyes, he asked, "Will you go get him and bring him to me? I want to tell him about his terrific dive."

"I've got a better idea. Let's get you dressed and go out to the dock. Oliver can meet us there, and you can tell him."

Maxwell shook his head. "I want to stay inside."

Pearl knew Maxwell felt most safe and comfortable indoors, but she was sure a walk in the fresh air would help him breathe easier. She put a singsong lilt in her voice. "We can't stay inside all the time."

"Maybe you can't, but I can."

She didn't want to begin the day with arguments, but there was one angle she hadn't tried. "Should we ask Oliver if there's anything on the property he'd like to show you? A place he loves?"

"I don't think Oliver loves the house at all. I think he's afraid of it." The boy's voice softened to a whisper. "I think he's a bit afraid of me, also."

It might be true. Maybe Oliver's thoughtless comments last night were based in a worry he didn't even know he had.

Instead of answering, she lay her cheek against his hair and stayed silently beside him for a few moments.

"Would you like to look at your new book?" Pearl recalled she'd not even been able to show him the puzzles Nanette had chosen for him.

Maxwell slid down deeper into his covers. "I should sleep."

"You've had a lovely rest. Let's get up."

He shook his head against his pillow. "The house wishes me to sleep more."

Such talk wasn't a good sign. She did not like to hear him say these things. After a bout of illness, sometimes Maxwell wallowed in his bed for days. She knew rest was helpful, but only to a certain point. Afterward, too much time in bed seemed to make him weaker. And lately he'd taken to telling her it was what the house wanted. What the walls told him.

When he spoke this way, she shuddered. His conversations with voices she couldn't hear was a childish fancy, but she wished it would stop. When she asked, he told her the house had always spoken to him. Didn't it talk to her?

She refused to engage further about it. Not only because it frightened her, but because she was sure it couldn't be good for him. His reality was already so foreign to her; illness and confinement were not elements of her childhood.

He pulled the blanket near his chin.

Another hour's rest shouldn't hurt him. In any case, an argument certainly wouldn't help. But she'd offer him one more chance to change his mind.

"If you wish more rest, I'll leave you to it." She grinned at him, forcing aside lingering thoughts of what the house wished. "I'll go discover a new place for us to explore."

When he didn't toss aside his covers and leap from the bed, she saw he really was feeling low.

Maxwell's murmur sounded flat. "Don't find all the house's secrets while I sleep."

She bent close and touched his nose with her fingertip. "No more than one or two, I promise."

She could see he was attempting to smile for her, but the gesture was weak and sad. "You always know more about Shadowbrook than I do."

"Well, of course. I have to stay at least one step ahead of you. It's what your grandfather pays me for." Her teasing tone and wink might have masked the concern she felt, but his lethargy and sadness worried her. He appeared more ill the longer he stayed in his bed.

The boy's next words were so quiet she almost missed them. "Please don't leave me."

Swallowing the lump in her throat, she shook her head. "Of course not. I'm happy to stay. I'll pull the chair up to the bed and read with you."

Maxwell shook his head and half covered his face with his hands, as if he needed to hide from her before he could say the rest. "I don't mean while I sleep. I mean, please don't go away from here."

Pearl leaned across the side of the bed and took Maxwell's

hands in her own. "I promise you I will be here at Shadowbrook House for as long as you need me. I will grow old by your side if that is what you wish."

His eyelids fluttered, and his mouth opened wide in a yawn. "It's a dangerous world outside these walls. Stay here. Stay safe. Stay with us."

Before Pearl could ask any of the questions Maxwell's strange words brought to her mind, his eyes closed again.

She would never abandon the boy. Never. Not while staying near him was in her power.

Maxwell Ravenscroft looked nothing like Pearl's younger brother—Eddie had spiky, dark locks and the ruddy cheeks of children who played outside regularly—but when he slept, Maxwell reflected the sweet rest of her brother after he'd tired himself from a day of running and play. The slope of Max's soft cheek, eyelashes resting against it like tiny flower petals, always brought her brother to her mind.

She knew only too well how quickly a child could go from healthy and tumbling about, making far too much noise and laughing constantly, to silent and still. She had, after all, only been gone from home two nights. That terrible winter, two nights were enough to change everything.

The illness had attacked her family that quickly.

And Pearl had not been home to stop it, nor to comfort them, nor to ward away the sickness or succumb herself. The influenza carried off her family before she returned home.

She would not allow such a thing to happen again to someone else she had grown to love.

Looking out into the hall, she saw Oliver's bedroom door hung open. She walked past, glancing casually inside. He wasn't there. Maybe he was in the kitchen.

She'd only made it halfway to the stairs when she noticed Violet fluttering through the room across the hall from Oliver's.

Pearl had never seen that door open. It was one of the many rooms at Shadowbrook that had always been locked up tight.

She put her head inside.

The room's walls were hung with a warm, golden paper, as if regardless of the stormy winter day, the sun shone within. A huge four-poster bed dominated the floor, but even with such a massive piece of furniture inside it, the room was larger than Pearl's or Maxwell's by half again. Large enough for three windows, the far wall stretched wide, letting in more gray light than any of the other bedrooms Pearl had explored. Pearl was surprised to find such a lovely room in such good condition. Why was it always locked?

At the side of the bed, Violet shook out a long linen sheet, snapping the cloth midair and snatching the far end into her hand.

"Would you like help?" Pearl asked, though it was clear Violet had linen-folding skills Pearl couldn't match.

The girl glanced up and smiled, holding one side of the sheet toward her. "Thank you. I'd appreciate another pair of hands."

"I've never seen this room open before. What's happening here? Is Mr. Ravenscroft moving rooms?"

Violet's eyes widened, and she looked at the door. "Oh, no, Miss Ellicott. And if he were, I'd not be allowed to prepare his bed."

"What do you mean?"

The girl became very interested in smoothing the sheet against the bottom edge of the mattress. "I haven't yet proven myself. Only Mr. Jenkinson and Mrs. Randle are permitted inside the master's room."

"I doubt that has anything to do with your skills. I think he simply dislikes company. And as he rarely leaves the room, the straightening and cleaning would require someone to arrive at a moment's notice. You're kept too busy throughout the house for such complicated timing."

She watched Violet's face relax into her usual pleasant smile.

"Who are you preparing the room for, then?" Pearl directed the question to the linens so as not to appear to be interrogating the girl. "Seems unlikely we'll have another visitor so quickly after Mr. Waverley's arrival."

"It is soon. I didn't have much warning. She'll be here any moment."

She? Who was *she?* Pearl wanted to know everything. Immediately. But she did not wish to appear too eager for gossip.

"Don't worry. I'll help you finish in here." Pearl unwrapped a few down-filled pillows from their dustcovers and plumped them against the massive headboard.

Violet nodded in thanks and kept working.

Pearl's patience was getting her none of the answers she hoped for. She'd have to ask pointed questions. She played her hands across the leaf-patterned spread folded on a divan and asked, "Who is coming?"

Violet looked up, surprise in her widened eyes. "Why, Madame Genevieve. Surely Mr. Ravenscroft told you."

Pearl remembered the letter she brought from the post office, but she shook her head. "He didn't tell me there would be another visitor."

"But you must know her. She's in the papers."

"Oh?" Pearl didn't trust herself to ask further questions. She was at a complete loss.

Violet looked at Pearl and nodded sagely for an eleven-year-old. "She's in different papers than you read, I think."

Violet gestured to the rumpled blanket across the bed, as if pointing out the obvious.

Pearl moved to the other side and pulled the linen across the mattress. "But you know of the woman? What do you think I need to know?"

Violet pulled the linen tight. "I would think Mr. Ravenscroft would tell you about the plans to have her here. Especially since you're among the chosen."

Chosen? By whom?

Unbidden, the image of Oliver's smiling face came to Pearl's mind. Whatever Violet's comment meant, it couldn't be what Pearl was thinking of. She cleared her throat with a delicate cough.

"Chosen for what?"

Violet looked away. "I beg your pardon. I've spoken out of turn."

With a smile, Pearl moved to the chair in the corner and began to fold the holland cover draped over it. "No pardon is necessary. I assure you, if I were to take offense, it wouldn't be for being chosen."

Violet stammered. "It's what the maids say. Mr. Ravenscroft sees you. He talks to you—you and Mr. Jenkinson and Mrs. Randle. He doesn't talk to the rest of the staff. We're invisible. But you're part of the house. Part of the family."

Pearl's attempt to snap the covering into a fold in midair was nowhere as neat as Violet's had been. She folded the sheet awkwardly as she considered the girl's words.

"I'm not part of the family. I'm not part of any family."

"You eat with him." Violet didn't seem to be arguing, simply explaining.

"Very rarely."

"You have permission to go visiting. You sleep in an upstairs room with windows and a fireplace."

The girl's words struck Pearl. She enjoyed a different set of privileges from most of the staff, though she'd never thought how that might appear to the others.

Pearl placed the poorly folded sheet at the edge of the bed. "Violet, I apologize if I act as though there's any difference in my station and yours. I am an employee of this house exactly like you are. But you're definitely more skilled than I am in many areas."

The girl smiled at the compliment. "You're doing just fine."

The sound of jangling bells floated into the room through the open window.

Violet dropped the blanket and hurried to the window. "She's arrived."

Pearl followed her to the window. The strangest carriage she'd ever seen pulled to a stop in front of the house.

A covered landau that might have been in fashion fifty years earlier, the carriage was hung with an abundance of small silken flags fluttering from every edge and corner. Long poles obscured by dozens of metal bells reached up from the rear. Whorls of bright paint across the sides of the carriage gave an impression of smoke swirling through a room. Pearl thought the carriage's appearance might be quaint if the whole thing didn't seem so very loud.

Then the carriage door opened and an arm emerged.

Pearl and Violet looked at each other. When they looked back out the window, the arm shook as if to remove an insect from a sleeve, but instead of a flying creature, scarves unfurled. Dozens of brightly colored, gauzy scarves.

Violet leaned close to Pearl. "Is she waving at us?"

The extended hand snapped its fingers, and the driver leaped from his seat. It was a testament to the garishness of the carriage that Pearl had not noticed him. His top hat, at least twelve inches high, was bedecked with ribbons that matched the bright silken flags decorating the carriage. One sleeve of his tailcoat was bright orange, the other green. Thick blue-and-white stripes stretched across his back.

He scuttled to the open door and held out a hand toward the extended arm.

A flick of the wrist brought him to a halt. Over the sound of more jangling bells—the horses, Pearl had suddenly noticed, were as gaudily appointed as the driver and the carriage—she heard the man say, "Right. Of course." Then he dropped into a low bow.

Upon straightening his posture, he took the offered hand. The scarf-bedecked arm was followed by the rest of the woman, every newly visible inch of her more unbelievable than the last.

Dressed in layers of flowing fabrics, she looked as unlike the fashionable ladies of the new decade as Pearl could imagine. Where corsets tightened most bodices, this woman wore drapes of filmy cloth. As she stood and let each layer of fluttering silk settle around her, she patted the sides of her brassy orange hair. With the movement, dozens of metal bangles clanked together, joining the ringing bells on the horses' harnesses.

Tilting her head upward to take in the expanse of the jagged roofline, she sighed loudly enough for Pearl and Violet to hear through the open window. In a surprisingly deep and sonorous voice, she said, "Ah, Shadowbrook. At last we meet."

CHAPTER 15

Oliver sat at the edge of the Shadowbrook dock, his shoes beside him, trouser legs rolled up to his knees. His feet dangled into the gentle flow of the river. When he'd sat here as a boy, his feet had only reached the water when the river was close to overflowing its banks.

He stared into the water, remembering the way he'd watched boats slip along the current, squinting toward the wooden hulls, imagining how his life might be different. If he were a cabin boy, he could climb the mast of a huge vessel, scurrying up to the crow's nest to deliver a message or spy out an approaching ship. On a ship, he'd be useful. Needed. Seen.

A life at sea was never truly an option for Oliver. It was only a fantasy. His tutors made it clear his uncle expected him to excel in more gentle pursuits, so he studied his lessons, even if half-heartedly, and he drew his pictures. Sketches of things he saw and things he dreamed filled pages of notebooks. He covered each scrap of paper he found with his drawings. And then he hid them away, knowing such a frivolous hobby would displease his uncle.

Only when Oliver left Shadowbrook to attend school did he allow himself to consider sketching as a talent worthy of his effort. This led to rewarding work with builders, architects, and restorationists. He knew his circumstances as heir to Shadowbrook didn't require him to seek a profession, but the modern age allowed him to explore options that would not have been available decades before.

Options such as the sale of the house.

Here on the dock, Oliver could picture a busy workforce loading and unloading fabrics and clothing, a smart factory building rising behind him. It could employ so many of the local families, give a new opportunity to those who previously had few choices if they wished to remain in this part of Hampshire.

Oliver opened the prepared contract, rereading the words written by the Campbell Company's solicitors. He knew their offer was based on an agreement he'd made without Uncle Arthur's approval, and Oliver would need to convince the old man to see the sale of the property his way before he signed. But he also knew any further delay would put the entire operation in jeopardy. The Campbell's agent required a signed contract before the end of the month, and the days were passing faster than he could have imagined.

He needed to move the process forward to its inevitable and best end. After the sales arrangement was finalized, there would be no further need to discuss Shadowbrook. Money would be plentiful, and new opportunity would open itself to Oliver and his uncle.

He only needed to convince Arthur the sale was the best outcome for Maxwell.

Since Maxwell was Uncle Arthur's priority, it should be an easy task.

Oliver turned around and faced Shadowbrook. Which room was Uncle Arthur in right now? What was the old man doing? Why was he determined to deny Oliver this—the only thing he'd asked for in years? As he turned back to gaze over the water again, a gust of wind ripped the contract from his hand and sent it fluttering out to the water.

With an agility he hadn't made use of in years, Oliver ran after it. He saw the white paper spin in an eddy at the river's edge. Before he reached the water, the paper had sunk beneath the ripples and disappeared.

He considered going in after it, but only for a moment. It was only paper. He could request a new copy of the document.

But there was little time for such setbacks if the contract was to be completed this month.

Gentle, misty rain began to fall, the spreading branches of the nearest trees forming a frame for the gray drizzle.

Oliver wished Maxwell was well enough to come out and join him. There was no pleasure like feeling a soft mist while listening to the rushing sounds of the water from the Shadowbrook dock. And getting the boy away from the smells, the noises, and the permeating fears and worries of Shadowbrook House could only do him good.

Oliver leaned against a tree trunk and pulled another folded paper out of his pocket. The barest sketch of Maxwell's face, head thrown back in a joyful laugh, peeked out of the charcoal lines.

He took the pencil from behind his ear and began again, letting each line grow beneath his fingers. Instead of a realistic representation, the sketch gave the idea of Maxwell. The curve of his ear, the upturned wrinkle at the corner of his eyes when he smiled.

Without thinking about it, he moved his pencil to the space opposite and sketched another line, this one longer and more delicate. He added a few short strokes, a curve, and a shaded area, and Pearl's image emerged out of the marks. He was far more comfortable drawing buildings than people, but her face was firmly etched in his mind—the fine lines of her lashes and the curve of her lips.

The sounds of the river tumbling by accompanied the soft drift of his pencil across the paper, and before long, he had filled the page with sketches of Pearl's face, her hands, her mouth. In each drawing, she smiled out of the paper at him as she had last night, her face holding both invitation and challenge.

He hoped that expression would always be so easy to call to his mind.

None of the drawings showed Pearl's look of frustration she often wore when Oliver was nearby. She told him he was frustrating. Infuriating. But the smile he called to mind showed she also felt something different about him. Something more pleasant. Something that led to late-night kisses in hallways.

What would Oliver need to do to give Pearl a reason to see him in this more positive light? His words to Uncle Arthur had hurt her, and she forgave him when he apologized. He was sincere in his regret, even if he still firmly believed Maxwell needed more specialized care than he could get at Shadowbrook. The words were wrong, even if the ideas behind them were for the best. He'd take care never to speak with such thoughtlessness again, but how could he prove to her his suggestions were only in the interest of the household? Why did she resist the change so clearly best for Maxwell?

All his attempts to discuss it had resulted in her irritation and annoyance. He understood her experience at Shadowbrook was different from his, but it seemed impossible she couldn't see things from his point of view. Convincing her might take as much effort as talking Arthur into selling the house, but Oliver looked forward to giving Pearl an excuse to change her mind.

CHAPTER 16

By the time Pearl arrived downstairs, Jenkinson had already led Madame Genevieve into the entry hall. A break in the storm allowed the woman to enter without getting rained on, and Pearl thought Madame Genevieve's extraordinary appearance depended on remaining dry. If her scarves were damp, they'd not flow with every dramatic lift of her arms, not to mention what might become of her halo of frizzy orange hair.

Jenkinson led the woman past Pearl without a word or a glance, as though she were a decoration in the entryway. Pearl said nothing but watched as Madame Genevieve resettled her scarves and shawls and arm bangles. The woman gave what Pearl thought was a wave, but then she repeated the gesture, and Pearl saw she was simply testing how her flutters looked while she was on the move inside the house.

She waited outside the door of the nearest parlor, and less than a minute later, the butler returned. He walked past Pearl, and she turned and fell into step with him.

"Who is she?" Pearl used her practiced voice of friendly discussion as if they were in the middle of a comfortable conversation. Jenkinson had never responded in kind, but she was sure some day he might. This could be that day.

This was not that day. He walked silently, his steps a touch faster than she could comfortably match. She jogged along beside him. As long as she kept her breath, she could continue to ask questions. Maybe one of them would nudge the butler into answering.

"This is the woman who sent the letter. I understand she's some kind of public figure. Have you read about her in the papers? Why did she choose to visit Shadowbrook? How did she meet Mr. Ravenscroft? Does she have a connection with the house? Is she a friend of yours? Someone you knew before you went into service?"

At that last question, Jenkinson turned his head just enough to glare down his nose at her. He didn't speak a word, but Pearl thought he'd answered her all the same. She had no idea if the answer was yes or no. Jenkinson gave very little away, but he'd reacted, which he rarely bothered to do.

Jenkinson stopped outside the housekeeper's small office near the kitchen. Knocking twice, he opened the door enough for his head and shoulders to disappear inside. "Tea is required. Entry parlor."

Pearl heard the scrape of a chair and the rustle of skirts. Mrs. Randle scurried out of the room. Pearl planned to follow, interested in anything she might pick up from Mrs. Randle's orders to the kitchen staff, but a new sound distracted her.

High-pitched and insistent, the noise conveyed some level of distress. In a house like Shadowbrook, full of twisting halls and false doorways, determining location by sound was a fool's errand. Even so, Pearl thought the noise came from the entry hall.

She retraced her steps and arrived back at the front door to find a pile of luggage, a steamer trunk, and a leather bag. A fluffy white head with a golden star on its center poked out of the opening of the cracked and worn red leather.

Upon seeing Pearl, the small dog barked more demandingly, clamoring for attention.

Pearl looked around, and, seeing no one, lifted the dog from the carrying bag. "Hello, there," she said, and the dog responded by raising its furry head and licking her chin.

Laughing, she tucked the dog, which was not much larger than a folded bedsheet, into her arms. The barking, though unceasing, seemed to decrease in intensity, or at least in desperation. Was it possible for a dog to bark with happiness?

Another glance at the stack of luggage proved the animal belonged to Madame Genevieve. Each piece was a different color, and all handles and straps were wrapped in bright ribbons.

Pearl looked down at the dog in her arms, its fur brushed and shiny, its tiny snout quivering. "You are an excellent excuse to get some answers," she whispered.

The dog licked her chin again.

With only a second's hesitation, Pearl opened the door of the parlor where Jenkinson had left the visitor. She strode in as if it was her place to do so.

"Good day," she said. "I believe this is yours."

The dog struggled to jump from Pearl's arms, but Madame Genevieve didn't raise her hands to receive it.

A long, slow nod was followed by a long, slow sigh. "Ah, Misty." The woman smiled at the dog, her words drawn out into several notes and several extra beats. "There you are."

Those few words seemed to take far too long. The woman's low, husky voice seemed to stretch and carry every syllable into two or three. For the first time, Pearl knew what authors meant when they used the word *intoned*.

"Poor dear has had a long trip and must be quite exhausted by my company." Hums and sighs punctuated the woman's drawn-out statement.

She still made no move to take the squirming dog from Pearl's arms. Maybe she was the one who was tired of the dog.

"Do take a seat, Miss Ellicott."

Pearl wasn't certain which surprised her more, the comfortable way this stranger gave orders or the fact that she knew Pearl's name. Either way, Pearl followed the dramatic waving gesture and sat, holding the dog in her lap.

With eyelids half-lowered, Madame Genevieve lifted one arm in a fluid gesture that meant nothing at all but looked like part of a seated dance. Circling her hand in the space above her head, she stared at Pearl unblinking.

It did not take long before Pearl felt uncomfortable, and she stroked the little dog's head, grateful she had a reason to look away from the woman's gaze.

When Madame Genevieve spoke again, her words shed no light on what she might be thinking. "Do you have it?"

The woman couldn't be referring to the dog. With no idea what else she was supposed to have, Pearl shook her head.

Slowly, dramatically, the scarf-bedecked woman pulled words from wherever she stored them, stretching them like a knitted stocking. "That is a pity. The Sight would help you heal."

Pearl didn't know what to make of that sentence. The sight of what? And heal how? "Perhaps you misunderstand. I am not ill."

Another slow nod, and the woman gave a half smile that lowered the curtain of her eyelids a fraction more. "People who do not have the Sight never understand the full extent of their own pain." She seemed to recall the arm still raised above her head and lowered it gently, making full effect of both fluttering scarves and jangling bracelets.

There was information here if Pearl could understand it. Was this person a fortune teller? What did she mean by "the Sight"? What did she expect Pearl to see?

Madame Genevieve explained nothing, just continued to watch Pearl. In response, Pearl looked down at the dog in her lap. It was only her curiosity that kept her eyes returning to those half-lidded ones.

Many long minutes of heavy silence passed before Pearl

attempted one of her own questions. "Did you say your dog's name is Misty?"

Madame Genevieve brought her hand in front of her chest and waved it from side to side as if she were an orchestra conductor keeping her own words in somber time. "Ah, yes. Short for 'The Mists of the Veil Between Realms.'"

As long as it took Madame Genevieve to drag all those words forth and place them into the space between them, Pearl did not quite have time to school her features. She dropped her eyes again to the dog in her lap, whose name was a burden no animal should have to bear.

What silliness was this? And how long did it take Mrs. Randle to boil a kettle of water? As soon as tea arrived, Pearl would have an excuse to leave the room. She'd invited herself in, but she regretted doing so. No answers would come from this strange interview, only more questions.

"Even without being gifted with the Sight," Madame Genevieve said, "you must be able to see them occasionally. Of course you can hear them. Ghostly music rings from the walls. The chatter's deafening. So many voices. The house is full to bursting."

Them? Who did the woman mean?

The sound of Mrs. Randle's quick, light footsteps preceded the housekeeper into the room. Relieved, Pearl stood to excuse herself, but Mrs. Randle waited only for Pearl to put the dog on the floor before placing the tea tray in her hands.

Pearl gave a short shake of her head. "I need to check on Maxwell," she whispered.

The housekeeper pressed the tray more firmly in Pearl's direction. "Mr. Ravenscroft wishes you to stay with his guest."

With no choice except to obey, Pearl took the tray and settled it on the table next to her chair. Before she could sit, the little dog leaped up and claimed the seat, settling herself onto the cushion. She tucked her pointy little nose beneath a paw and closed her eyes. Pearl would have wagered the small dog wasn't sleeping at all, but she was hardly in a position to call the bluff of an animal named The Mists of the Veil Between Realms.

There were three cups on the tray, and Pearl poured tea into each. She handed a cup to Madame Genevieve and watched as the woman helped herself to most of the sugar in the dish. She spread her hand, with silver rings on almost every quivering finger, over the selection of cake and biscuits before placing several along the rim of her saucer as if Pearl might take them away before Madame Genevieve had a chance to sample each one.

With each sip of heavily sugared tea and each nibble of sweet treat, Madame Genevieve seemed to sink farther into her chair. Both hands full, she made no further gestures to set her scarves aflutter, nor did she continue their conversation. Pearl was relieved.

Until the woman began nodding and shaking her head in turns as if she was having a conversation Pearl couldn't hear. This hint of madness made Pearl distinctly uncomfortable.

After a few long and awkward moments, the woman hummed a long, sustained note. "Mmm. I see."

Pearl raised her eyes in question, but Madame Genevieve did not elaborate.

No clattering footsteps warned Pearl of the next arrival. Instead, the door opened and Mr. Ravenscroft entered, his soft leather shoes making barely a whisper along the floorboards.

He glanced at Pearl and then turned his attention to his visitor.

Pearl was eager for Mr. Ravenscroft's dismissal. She couldn't wait to leave the room. Although Madame Genevieve's appearance was entertaining, their interview had gone on long enough. Would Mr. Ravenscroft send her away before she even finished her refreshment? Not a problem. Since the dog had taken her chair, she was still standing, teacup in her hand. She'd like to pocket one of the almond biscuits for Maxwell before she left.

Mr. Ravenscroft made an awkward bow to Madame Genevieve. He cleared this throat and glanced around the room.

"How do you find the place?"

It was a strange way to begin a conversation with a guest, but Pearl knew conversing with guests was not something Mr. Ravenscroft did regularly. Or ever.

A breathy sigh seemed to draw Madame Genevieve to the edge of her chair. "Oh, Arthur," she murmured, her voice a deep, sonorous hum. Pearl hid her shock at hearing the woman refer to Mr. Ravenscroft by his given name. "We were correct. Your house is, indeed, a divining rod. Powerful spiritual energy resides here. We shall find great success in our efforts."

Mr. Ravenscroft pressed his hands together at his heart in a surprisingly warm and gentle gesture. He appeared to breathe in comfort at Madame Genevieve's words.

More talk of spirit and auras and resonance spun in the air between Madame Genevieve and Mr. Ravenscroft. Pearl felt she was intruding on a private moment and began to inch her way toward the door, keeping her steps light. The others seemed intent on their conversation. This was an excellent time to make her escape.

But such a plan was not to be. Mr. Ravenscroft straightened and turned to face Pearl. "A moment, Miss Ellicott."

Pearl stopped.

"You will sit with Madame Genevieve and answer her questions in preparation for her meeting with my grandson."

Pearl responded without thinking. "You want Maxwell to speak with this woman?" She managed to soften the disbelief in her voice before the final words escaped her.

He squinted at her. "She will do him a world of good. And you may find yourself benefiting from her services as well."

Mr. Ravenscroft spoke to Pearl infrequently. Unless he was giving a direct order, he rarely aimed his words to her. She nodded to show she'd heard him.

"Very well. I'll leave the two of you to your discussion."

Mr. Ravenscroft did not offer his hand to Madame Genevieve, but she reached for him, pulling on his forearm.

"You will not regret bringing me here. Many doors will unlock at my touch."

Pearl had no idea what that meant, but Mr. Ravenscroft nodded. "I'm counting on it."

He turned and left the room as silently as he'd entered.

"Funny old bloke, inn't he?"

The words came without a hint of the moaning, musical tones of Madame Genevieve's previous statements.

Pearl spun around. "I beg your pardon?"

It was as if Pearl watched the woman put on a new face. Her mournful expression returned, as did her flowing gestures. "The dear, sorrowful man. He puts a great deal of trust in us both, I think."

Why, you're nothing more than a fraud, Pearl thought.

Masking her disapproval, Pearl nodded as she lifted the dog from the chair again and sat with Madame Genevieve. "I believe he does."

CHAPTER 17

Oliver walked into the house through the kitchen's door, and at his arrival, he heard the hush fall over the room. Three maids and the cook stood in the sudden silence. It was clear whatever they'd been discussing was not for Oliver to hear.

The cook raised her hands to her hips and lifted her eyebrows. "What can we do for you, Mr. Waverley?"

This was not the elderly cook he'd known in his childhood. This woman was all angles, from her bent elbows to her peaked eyebrows. He'd not spoken to her before, but she knew who he was.

"I came to see how I can be of service to you. I'm sure my arrival caused a stir, and I'm not eager to make your work any more difficult than it already is. Is there something I can do for you?"

The cook's stern expression melted a degree or two. "You came in from outside to ask how you can help with meal service?"

Oliver couldn't tell if she was being playful, but he guessed she was. He grinned. "All my best ideas come when I'm near the river."

A quiet laugh came from behind him, and he was sure if he turned to look at the maids, he'd see them all smiling at him, but he knew his job was to win over the cook. He kept his eyes locked on the tall woman's face. She made no move and said nothing. Oliver redoubled his effort.

"I don't have your skill of cooking for a household, but I can arrange a vase of flowers."

The cook's pointy eyebrows rose up her forehead at his admission. Perhaps flowers on the dining table weren't a priority at Shadowbrook.

"Or I can carry a barrel from the cold storage. Or wash dishes. Whatever you need. I'm a quick study."

He saw the cook's arms loosen at her sides, and she pressed her lips together in a small smile. "It is good to have a new recruit for the kitchen staff. But don't worry yourself. Even with the latest arrival, I think we can manage the feeding of the household."

"Latest arrival?" Oliver repeated. "Does my uncle have another visitor?"

It was as if his question was a magnet. All the women in the room leaned closer and began to murmur, all speaking at the same time. Unused to conversations like this, Oliver attempted to isolate each voice. He heard the word "woman" several times and quite a few instances of the word "strange."

They all must have seen the confusion on Oliver's face, because the maids fell silent, but they didn't back away. The cook took pity on him and said, "There is a woman from the city who's only just arrived. From Mrs. Randle's instructions, we assume she's staying quite a while. She has very particular demands."

The arrow eyebrows pointed up toward her cap once again, but Oliver didn't understand her meaning. Demands? Oliver couldn't imagine what sort of person would enter Shadowbrook and begin making demands.

Was it gossiping to ask for details? Oliver didn't know, but he wanted more information. "What kind of demands?"

"East facing windows, so the morning light of the rising sun can align her heart for the day." The smirk on the maid's face was enough to tell Oliver what she thought of such alignment.

Another of the maids chimed in. "She requires a lady's maid

to assist her with her hair and her clothing. As if anyone in this house is trained as a lady's maid. We've all got work enough to do."

A young woman in an apron that matched the cook's placed both hands on the table and leaned closer. "Her dog needs two eggs and a plate of chopped chicken each morning and night. That's four eggs a day, and only for the dog."

Violet grinned. "The dog must sleep on a pillow wrapped in bedsheets which must be changed every day."

"And she doesn't like gas lighting, so we need to keep her room stocked with candles."

One of the maids cackled. "To be clear, we're not talking about the woman. It's the *dog* who has opinions about gaslight."

Oliver laughed along with the staff. He'd never been present for such a conversation, and he hoped his inclusion meant they would continue to talk to him about how daily life functioned at Shadowbrook. This was by far the least nervous he'd felt around the staff.

Just as he felt himself relaxing fully into the moment of harmless gossip, a hush fell over the room. Mrs. Randle hurried into the kitchen, her shoes clacking against the floor. "If you've got time to stand around here, I'll gladly assign more tasks to each of you." Then she turned to Oliver. "Mr. Waverley, I've been asked to speak to you about Mr. Ravenscroft's new guest."

"Wonderful. I'm looking forward to knowing more about her."

He heard Violet suppress a giggle.

Mrs. Randle shook her head and pointed to the door. As he followed her out of the kitchen, she spoke to the air in front of her. "You're not to seek out the visitor. You're not to ask her opinion about your plans. You're not to attempt to turn her mind to your takeover of the house."

Oliver stammered a reply. "Takeover? I don't know what you mean."

Mrs. Randle shook her head. "It isn't what I mean. It's what your uncle wishes. Stay away from Madame Genevieve."

The shock of the demand pushed the strange name straight out of Oliver's head. Whoever this new guest was, he was commanded to keep clear of her. After all the women in the kitchen had said, he didn't think it would be a chore to stay away.

But why would his uncle demand such a thing?

As soon as the question went through Oliver's mind, he was certain he knew the answer. His uncle was worried she'd side with Oliver. Whoever this guest was, she must be intelligent enough to know the house couldn't survive many more years before total collapse.

CHAPTER 18

Sipping her lukewarm tea with the dog curled on her lap, Pearl waited for Madame Genevieve to speak. Again, her voice rolled to Pearl in long, mournful tones. "I understand you must feel shy in my presence. Meeting a person one has only read about in newspaper articles or heard discussed in hushed, respectful voices can be intimidating."

Without lifting her head, Pearl raised her eyes to glance at the woman. "I assure you, I've never read about you."

Far from being offended by Pearl's uncharacteristically rude comment, Madame Genevieve smiled. One hand waved the air in front of her face, setting her bracelets clinking. "No matter. You know me now." The woman rolled her hands around each other as if using a towel to dry them. "Let us discuss the poor boy."

Pearl knew this was Mr. Ravenscroft's wish, but she did not feel she had to make it easy on the charlatan. "Are you here as a physician?"

Madame Genevieve gave a wide smile. "Of course not. I'm here to see to his spiritual being, not his physical."

Pearl nodded. "I see. You're a representative of the clergy, then?"

One hand drifted up and straightened the tail of a scarf wrapped around her crown. It looked more like a bandage than a turban. "I think you know I'm not."

"In that case, I'm not at all sure what you are doing here."

Pearl didn't intend her comment to invite an introduction, but Madame Genevieve smiled as if the cutting remark was exactly what she hoped to hear.

"I reside between the planes of the seen and the unseen."

Pearl hummed in assent as if such words made any sense at all. "Except for today, when you come to reside at Shadowbrook House."

Madame Genevieve chuckled, and a note quavered deep in her voice, reminding Pearl of the reverberations at an organ concert.

"Indeed, I do. As do many of the spirits of the departed."

Pearl did not feel herself equal to making an appropriate response to that, so she stayed silent.

"As you have certainly surmised, dear Arthur requires my help in communing with those he has lost."

"I surmised no such thing," Pearl answered. She wanted no part of this woman's charade, but being accused of understanding or expecting this person's employment at Shadowbrook appealed least of all. Yet Mr. Ravenscroft had instructed Pearl to help her. To give her information about the house? About Maxwell? The idea was repellent.

Pearl wished Oliver had not gone out today. She had a feeling he'd see through Madame Genevieve's pretense as easily as she did, and together they'd be able to convince Mr. Ravenscroft to send the fraud away. Surely the man would listen to his nephew, even if he rarely invited any counsel from Pearl.

Pearl decided she had better take in as much information from the woman as she could. Arguing with her did not appear to work in Pearl's favor.

She looked the woman fully in the face. "Madame Genevieve," she said, choking on the gravity the address required, "my only concern is to care for Maxwell. The state of the household directly affects the boy. If his grandfather thinks you can be of some assistance, I'm willing to extend whatever help you need. But please do not assume I understand what you're about. Your interests seem to be as foreign to me as any city on the other side of the earth."

In answer, Madame Genevieve performed another deep sigh. Her words came as slowly as before, causing Pearl to wish she could speed her up.

"I appreciate your honesty, but I'm curious why you are so resistant to my work. Work you claim not to understand. You're an educated girl. Tell me what you've gleaned. Surely, I'm not such a mystery."

Visibly relaxing, Madame Genevieve sat deeper into her chair. A nod of the head and a wave of her hand seemed to suggest Pearl was forgiven for not knowing the woman's reputation.

"You're a medium?"

"I prefer the word *spiritualist*, but it all comes down to the same thing."

"And you think you hear ghosts—understand them."

Madame Genevieve inclined her head. "In much the same way you think you understand the work of being a governess."

Trading insults was not Pearl's habit. She knew she'd begun whatever conflict she was engaged in now. She could revert to a more formal politeness. "I suppose we all have a limited knowledge of any situation or experience."

Madame Genevieve smiled. "Exactly. We think we know what we are about, and then we learn more. As we look back, we see how much we've grown in our capacity and our understanding."

Pearl shook her head. "Whether you choose to believe me or not, I must restate my claim not to understand anything about your business."

Madame Genevieve breathed out a deep, audible sigh and

launched into what Pearl assumed was another practiced presentation. "The realm of spirits is here among us. Those of us blessed with the Sight rub shoulders with the departed in every moment."

The same drawling, moaning tones underscored the woman's every word, but Pearl had no intention of interrupting Madame Genevieve. The more she refuted the woman's strange claims, the longer this conversation would last.

"There are, of course, peak locations: places where spiritual energy is more concentrated than others. I am attuned to these places and to those who reside in them, both the seen and the unseen. My work is to reach beyond the shroud of forgetfulness that obscures you people who suffer with a literal mind and connect you with those whom you have lost."

Pearl felt strongly the discomfort of the sudden use of "you" in Madame Genevieve's performance. This was not about Pearl. But she was determined to let the woman get through her monologue and ask her questions so Pearl could escape this parlor and get back to Maxwell.

"Most of the departed remain close to their places of death, but it's not unheard of for spirits to travel, especially when they're following someone they loved in life. Perhaps some of your dead have come here to share in your company."

Pearl couldn't help it—she scoffed. Then she gave a small shake of her head and lowered her eyes so the woman wouldn't find her confrontational.

"It's very rare for one not blessed with the Sight to trust easily, but I will extend my best efforts so your doubt and lack of confidence don't stand in the way of healing for dear Arthur and his grandson."

Madame Genevieve stared at Pearl with what might have been a serious expression of concern, but Pearl kept herself busy imagining rebuttals, so she barely spared a glance in return.

The woman paused long enough that Pearl's curiosity grew unbearable. She had to look at her.

When their eyes met, Madame Genevieve made a quiet humming sound. Not the moaning wail of her performance voice, but a suggestion of understanding.

"I hope there's some room for healing yourself here as well," she said in a soft, normal voice.

Pearl looked at the dog in her lap, unsure how to answer.

With a dramatic wave of her arms, Madame Genevieve brushed away the momentary distraction. "Maxwell Burton Ravenscroft is a lad living close to the edge of the worlds. He has lost his parents, tragically, in his earliest days. And he suffers from an illness that keeps him repressed in body and mind."

Repressed in his mind? Did Madame Genevieve insult Maxwell's intellect simply to get a response from Pearl? It was possible she was only continuing to perform nonsense, but her words touched a raw nerve.

Her answer emerged from her mouth, spiky and sharp. "There is nothing lacking in Maxwell's mind. He's as bright a child as I've ever known. If Mr. Ravenscroft suggested Maxwell's illness has in any way altered his mental capacity, he was mistaken."

Madame Genevieve's mouth twitched in a smile. Whatever she was hoping for, it appeared Pearl had provided it.

"Does the boy use his bright mind to speak to you of his deceased parents? Does he ask you about yours?"

That was a step too far. Mr. Ravenscroft could require her to converse with this woman, but no one could force her to discuss the loss of her family.

"Maxwell and I have many things to talk about every day without resorting to silly mysticism."

Madame Genevieve nodded. Her answer was spoken without any of the shuddering breaths or drawn-out moans. "Don't imagine it escaped my notice that you didn't answer my question."

She didn't wait for Pearl to reply, and with a flutter of sleeves, the spiritualist gave another deep, groaning sigh. "There is much to uncover here, and many secrets to bring to light. I look forward to learning more at your side."

Pearl knew a dismissal when she heard one, no matter how long the words dragged on. She stood, set the sleeping dog on the chair, tossed a nod in Madame Genevieve's direction, and walked out of the room.

Why in the world had Mr. Ravenscroft brought that silly woman here? What could she possibly think Pearl would tell her? And to what end? What did Madame Genevieve want?

By the time she'd climbed the stairs and reached Maxwell's door, Pearl had spun her mind into a tangle. What had she learned from the interview? Was the woman laughable? Certainly. Did she exert a certain hold over Mr. Ravenscroft? It seemed so. Was she asking far too many impertinent questions? Undoubtedly.

Pearl wished she could simply dismiss the presence of this stranger in the house, to ignore the uncomfortable feeling her questioning brought. But Madame Genevieve's first half hour at Shadowbrook had been anything but subtle. She'd not slip out of Pearl's thoughts as long as she stayed in the house.

Gently tapping against Maxwell's door, she waited for his invitation. It wasn't impossible to think he'd still be asleep, and she feared his mood was morose, as it so often was when he chose to stay in his bed for many hours.

"Come in." Maxwell's voice floated out into the hall.

The curtains were pulled over the windows again, so either Maxwell had climbed out of bed to close them or Mrs. Randle had been in to bring him breakfast.

Pearl peered into Maxwell's face, which looked healthier than it had yesterday. She needed to tread gently. If she pushed him too far too fast, he could fall into a far more serious bout of illness. Dr. Dunning made it clear Pearl needed to give him sufficient rest to strengthen, but not too much. Finding that balance was one of the most difficult aspects of her work.

"Shall we go for a wander?" she asked brightly.

Slowly, he sat up in his bed and shook his head. "Can we stay in here? I want to know about Oliver's plan for the house. Teach me about ready-made clothing and factories."

It was rare for the boy to ask for information concerning something Pearl knew nothing about, but this was one of those instances.

"I'd need to do a fair bit of learning before I could teach you anything about that. Ask Mr. Waverley your pressing questions. I believe he'll talk with you about it."

Maxwell shook his head. "I don't want to be a bother."

"You're never a bother." Pearl wished she could scrub such thoughts from the child's mind. There was no one in the household who found it troubling in the least dedicating themselves to his care and comfort.

Resettling himself against his pillow, he said, "I think I'll sleep some more."

Pearl saw the curtain of sadness begin to descend over Maxwell.

"Maybe some music?" she suggested.

"If you like."

Pearl hurried across the room to the shelf where they kept the instrument they'd found in one of their explorations. She lifted the old violin from its case, holding it carefully. Once she'd tightened the bow and run its hairs across the block of rosin, she went back to Maxwell. She'd often offered to teach him to play, but he wasn't interested in learning. He said he loved to listen to her play, that the sounds of the instrument felt familiar and comforting.

Standing at the end of his bed, she began playing one of his favorite chamber pieces and could see immediately how the music calmed him.

After a time, she moved from chamber pieces to country dances.

When she saw Maxwell's feet rocking from side to side beneath his sheets, she chose another joyful song, and then another. Soon he was grinning and pretending to direct her, his hand waving in perfect time.

Just to make him laugh, she skipped around the room for the last few counts of the song, finally dropping onto her back at the foot of his bed in a display of exhaustion she didn't feel. Making music filled her, fueled her. She always heard music in her head. It kept her company in the cold and silent halls of the house. She could play for Max all day, especially when she saw how it cheered him as well.

Max applauded. "Well played, Miss Ellicott," he said in an echo of the plummy expression she sometimes used when she read to him in character voices. "What will we do now?"

She sat up and schooled her face into a stern expression. "Lessons."

Sometimes such a look and statement would inspire a joke from Maxwell, a pretended disgust for study, but the boy didn't seem to have the energy to argue with her today, even in jest.

Their mathematics lesson lasted less than half an hour before Pearl noticed Max tiring. First a slump of his shoulders, then a casual rubbing at his eyes that went on too long, and finally a great yawn.

Pearl took the book from Maxwell's hand and asked the final question. "If you rest for twenty-seven minutes, how many seconds will pass?"

He reached for the paper and pencil, but she shook her head. "Try it inside your head only."

She didn't actually expect the boy to figure complicated numbers in his mind, but she thought it might keep his brain busy as he fell asleep. Dwelling on numbers was much better for him than wondering why his illness had struck him yet again.

Pearl took her usual chair by the fireplace, the one angled slightly toward the door. It was her habit to sit there with Maxwell and read to him, which she'd done since she first came to Shadowbrook. Of course the boy couldn't read for himself then, but even after he learned, he still loved for her to read aloud. She picked up the book they'd been reading, and she realized the last time they'd been inside the pages was before Oliver arrived.

He'd upset their household routines, but more than that, he'd altered Pearl's thoughts and feelings. Her heart was never quite settled anymore. For all the infuriating, frustrating bother Oliver brought, she couldn't deny her attraction to him. He was a contradiction, a push and a pull, and Pearl was incapable of deciding whether she was more charmed or repelled.

None of that made any difference in her work. She was here to care for Max, to teach him and to love him.

It was silly to think life at Shadowbrook was any different now. Her daily routine would be the same as it had always been. The heir to the property was present, and she couldn't pretend he wasn't fascinating, much in the way an unsolvable puzzle was fascinating. But nothing fundamental in the household had actually changed. Except for the addition of Madame Genevieve, of course. And the dog.

She realized she hadn't told Max about the dog. Glancing over at the bed, she saw him breathing steadily, his eyes closed.

There was some sense of relief in not mentioning Madame Genevieve to Maxwell. The woman was not Pearl's concern, nor did she need to be Max's. Now that Pearl had answered—or refused to answer—the woman's strange questions, maybe they could exist within the house in their own orbits; no need for them to collide again.

CHAPTER 19

Oliver wandered around the house for half an hour hoping to cross paths with Pearl and Maxwell. He moved carefully, not opening any closed doors. Accidentally coming face-to-face with his uncle's latest visitor wasn't an appealing idea.

When he didn't hear any sounds of laughter and playing, he moved upstairs toward the bedrooms. The room across the hall from his own had its door flung wide open, a stack of brightly colored cases on the floor. This must be where the guest was staying, and at such close quarters, it would be difficult for Oliver to avoid her. He'd done harder things. He could keep his distance.

He knocked at Pearl's bedroom door, but there was no answer. He moved to Maxwell's room, and at his knock, he heard Pearl's voice softly invite him inside. Upon opening the door, he noticed once again the sharp stink of the room, barely masked by the gently burning fire and the mound of pine boughs on the mantel.

Max slept in his bed, his hands tucked beneath his cheek. Pearl sat at the small table with a notebook open in front of her.

"Oh, there you are," she said. "Give me a moment to finish these notes."

Oliver warmed at the thought she'd been expecting him. He walked into the room and put his back to the fire. Its pleasant warmth was only part of the appeal of this situation. From here, he could stare at Pearl's long, slender neck as she worked.

After a few minutes, Oliver asked, "What are you writing?"

Without looking up from the paper, she answered him. "I always take notes about Maxwell's episodes to give to his doctor when he next comes to Shadowbrook. It helps him to know the details."

"Such as?"

"I suppose all the usual information. The duration of the attack, its specific symptoms and how long they remain in evidence, when comfortable breathing is restored, and what Maxwell was doing before the onset."

"I can help you with some of that, since I was there." An idea landed in Oliver's mind. "In fact, I could take you to the rooms we explored. It might do you good to get out of here."

He couldn't mention the strange smell to Pearl—what if the sharp odor was an effect of Maxwell's illness? But he could take her away from it.

He reached for her hand to help her from her chair, and the moment their fingers touched, he felt the same sparking thrill run through him as when they'd kissed. Now there was twice the reason to leave the sleeping boy's room.

He kept her fingers held in his, and she made no move to pull her hand away. They walked along the bedroom wing and toward the stairs. Pearl looked over her shoulder a few times, but when she didn't see anyone or anything to alarm her, she walked with Oliver up the stairs.

The squawking of the wooden steps beneath their feet didn't seem as loud as Oliver's footsteps felt when he climbed the stairs alone in the dark.

"Max and I decided to explore the left side of the upper floor's wing. He said the two of you haven't gone into many of those rooms."

Pearl hummed in assent. "Once we looked into a room that

had a broken window. The floor was covered with several beautiful old carpets, one on top of another, and so much water had come in through the broken window that the floor squished beneath our feet. It was unsettling."

Oliver chuckled. "That's one word for it. Another word is *disgusting.*"

"Exactly."

Oliver thought he might get away with a comment about finalizing a purchase contract and walking away from the mess, but he didn't want to risk souring Pearl's mood. It was probably best to keep the conversation away from disposal of the property or Maxwell's health. He didn't want to argue with her.

He wanted to kiss her.

Not that he'd make any assumptions about her willingness. Just because she'd kissed him once didn't mean she wanted to do it again. But he dearly hoped she wanted to do it again.

They reached the landing on the upper floor. Hallways led off in several directions. They bore to the left into one of the halls. He opened a door and led Pearl into a passageway with doors placed irregularly along both sides.

"Most of these were locked when we came here together, but Maxwell has a couple of old, ornate keys. He told me he's had them for years. He tried both keys in each door, but none of the locks budged for him. Then we got to this door."

Oliver turned the knob. The room was small, but its walls were covered with mirrors of all sizes, some framed in ornate gilt moldings, some circular, and some small squares of glass set side by side.

Pearl gasped.

Oliver, still holding her hand, pulled her to the center of the room. "It's lovely, isn't it?"

Pearl looked around the room, turning slowly and keeping Oliver at her side as she took it all in.

"Look." She pointed to a large mirror in a thick wooden frame. Its surface sent back not only the two of them but also their reflection from the mirror on the opposite wall. Their images doubled and tripled on and on, the slight curvature of the glass causing the reflection to bend toward the right edge of the mirror, giving the impression that the image was being reproduced in perpetuity.

"There's something magical about the illusion that anyone could go on forever." Her whisper sent a ripple across his skin.

Oliver guided Pearl closer to the huge, framed glass. She held his gaze in their reflection. He felt a pulsing of pleasure at the ease with which they stared at each other while standing side by side and both looking straight ahead.

She reached out a finger and touched the reflection of Oliver's shoulder. He imagined he could feel the pressure.

"Have you ever considered that the closest you've come to seeing what you look like is a flat reflection in an imperfect looking glass?"

"Never," he admitted. "But it seems you have, and I'd love to hear you speak about it."

What he didn't say is that he'd love to keep hold of her hand as he watched the reflection of her lips moving.

"If someone were to paint our likeness right now, we'd have a record of the moment, but it would be no more *us* than this reflection is. Just an image, and one that shows only a single expression. I've seen reflections of myself, but I don't suppose I really know what I look like."

"Allow me to tell you." Oliver's words slipped out before he thought about them. When she didn't stop him, more words fell from his lips as easily as the thoughts gathered in his mind.

"You know perfectly well the silky blackness of your hair, but did you know it shines almost blue in the candlelight? The way a raven's wing catches sunlight and sends it back as a hint of a deep ocean. And your eyes are so expressive, I can see what you're thinking about before you speak. When your lips speak words, each carefully formed syllable changes the shape of your mouth. It's a mesmerizing transformation I could watch for hours."

She put a finger to her mouth, her lips parted and perfect.

"I'm afraid if I begin to describe the curve of your throat you'll think I'm trying to write poetry, which I would never attempt. I know my limits. But the line from your chin to your collar is in perfect proportion. I speak as someone who has studied drawing. And, to be fair, as someone who has studied the line of your neck."

Oliver sensed he was speaking nonsense, but he couldn't seem to stop himself. "Your hands, at least, you can see as well as I can. Those elegant fingers, so capable of creating beauty or soothing a wound or stirring the blood inside me."

He didn't miss the catch in her breathing when she released his hand, and he felt his own gasp as she faced him, placing both her hands around his neck. "You do know how to say pretty things, Mr. Waverley."

"Only things I know to be true." He ducked his chin, bringing his face a sigh away from her own, his lips almost touching her cheek.

She shifted, and her hands settled on his shoulders, fingers digging into the fabric of his coat. "Only things you *think* are true. You're not always right, you know."

"Miss Ellicott, do you really want to argue with me right now?"

She tilted her head, and her nose drew near the space beneath his ear. He felt the whisper of her breath. "Did you have a better idea?"

"I'm so glad you asked. In fact, yes. Quite a few good ones."

"I've heard enough of your ideas to know you should let me evaluate them. See if they're sound." Her words were a soft murmur he felt as much as heard.

"Something tells me I ought to place my hands at your waist." His palms barely grazed the fabric of her dress.

"Scandalous." He immediately released her, but she put her hands over his and pressed them to her sides. She took a step closer, a thing he would have considered impossible only a moment before. She resettled herself so she could look at his face. He didn't mind the shift.

"Mmm," she hummed. "Any other ideas?"

"You should put your hand on my face the way you did before."

"Like this?" she asked, her fingers trailing lightly through the hair above his ears.

"You see? Another excellent idea, and perfectly executed."

She smiled at him while shaking her head. "You really can't take all the credit, you know. It's a combined effort."

"Speaking of combined efforts," he began, his smile growing with each word.

She blinked her eyes with exaggerated slowness. "Yes?"

"I believe I'd quite like to kiss you now."

She gestured to the mirror-covered walls. "Here? In front of all these people?"

He dragged his eyes from her face to glance into the reflections. "They all look fairly busy. I don't think they'd take any notice at all."

As it happened, he was right.

Oliver held Pearl close, and they began to sway. After a moment, he pulled back and cocked his head, listening. "Do you hear that?"

"Is it the sound of your better judgment telling you this isn't the moment for asking questions?"

He loved the way she leaned close to him and whispered the words, but beneath the sound of her voice, he heard the music again.

"Sounds like a violin."

She shook her head. "Sometimes I hear that. It's the wind."

"The wind doesn't play melodies."

"Of course it does," she argued, and she took a step away from him. "It sings everywhere: through creaking branches of trees and reeds on the riverbank and between the bricks of this house. When it sounds particularly tuneful, it's the memory of music you've heard before."

Oliver knew that wasn't true. He was sure he heard the strains of ghostly songs, the same way he'd heard them when he'd lived here as a child.

He didn't want to argue with Pearl, especially when he knew they could be spending their time together in much more pleasant ways. But would she continue to deny what her senses told her?

"Are we hearing the same thing?" He pointed to the wall to his left and hummed along, a fraction of a second behind each note. "You're telling me that music is the wind?"

"Of course it is. It's certainly not a ghost, which is what the staff would like to make me believe," she said.

"And those are the only two explanations we can consider?"

Her expression now void of all playfulness, she met his eye. "The sounds we're hearing are another way this house is crying out to stay, and for us to stay with it. You can't destroy a place with such miraculous abilities."

Oliver felt the surprise play over his face at the same moment he saw her reaction. She must have seen how her answer startled him.

She went on. "I don't mean actual miracles. I mean, this house is damaged and suffering, but it's also beautiful and full of marvels." She made a slow turn, taking in the mirrored walls. "Much like each of us. You can't destroy it."

Oliver tried not to sigh in frustration. "I don't want to destroy anything. I just want to put the past aside and move forward."

She started shaking her head before he finished speaking. "Some of us need the past."

"Better things are ahead for all of us."

"You can't know that is true, and you must stop saying it's so. Many of us in this house have already lived the best days we will ever see."

His breath of incredulity came out almost like a laugh. "I refuse to believe that."

"Which is why you'll never understand us."

Oliver stepped close to Pearl, reaching his hand to stroke her arm.

"I want to understand you."

Maybe she thought he meant everyone in the house, but in his heart, he cared most about her. About knowing her mind and her soul. About learning to read her mood, about seeing her feelings in her eyes.

"I think you mean it, and that's why you're so infuriating. I'm trying to explain, but you're simply not hearing. Your uncle needs this house. Max needs this house, and so I need it too. You want to take it away from us all."

Oliver shook his head. "That's not true. I simply know there's so much better out there."

Pearl sighed and turned away. "There is no promise of anything better. For any of us."

Oliver watched her walk out of the mirrored room, and the music floating through the walls turned melancholy.

CHAPTER 20

Pearl hurried down the stairs, eager for a moment alone with her thoughts. How could Oliver misunderstand her—and himself—so thoroughly? And why did she feel such a strong attraction at the same time as such serious frustration? He was maddening.

A voice rose up the stairs as she descended. "Miss Ellicott." Madame Genevieve's performative, moaning wail sounded like someone pretending to be a ghost.

Pearl closed her eyes and breathed deeply before putting on a polite expression.

Madame Genevieve stood at the landing, waiting for Pearl. "I wonder if you'd prefer to be present when I interview Master Maxwell."

Pearl thought she had better not specify precisely what she preferred.

"Of course I would. I'll let you know when he's feeling up for a visit."

She continued down the stairs, hoping if she didn't say more or make eye contact, the woman would go away, but Madame Genevieve's drawling, tremulous voice stopped her again.

"Oh, no, my dear." How did she make her voice sound like it carried its own echo? "I will see him now."

The nerve of the woman. Pearl shook her head. "This is not a good day for Maxwell. He is not well enough for a conversation with a stranger."

Madame Genevieve's eyes twinkled. "I'll only be a stranger until we get to know each other." She turned toward Maxwell's room.

Would she dare enter right that moment, even when Pearl had told her not to?

It appeared she would. Pearl muttered something impolite and jogged into the bedroom wing after Madame Genevieve. The woman moved fast; by the time Pearl caught up to her, she was stepping through Maxwell's doorway.

Had she even bothered to knock? Did she plan to show him any sign of respect at all? Pearl caught the handle of the door before it closed in her face.

Madame Genevieve strode into the room, one arm raised in front of her and the other trailing behind, as if she was performing a strange dance.

"Maxwell Ravenscroft, you are a boy whose mind whirls with questions." On the word *whirls*, she flung both arms in front of her as if to stop an oncoming charge with the strength of her hands. Pearl was certain the move was designed to give maximum dramatic effect to those ridiculous scarves.

"And I, Madame Genevieve, Seer of the Hidden Realms, Communicator with the Departed, Oracle of the Beyond, have come to help you uncover your answers."

She clasped her hands together at her chest, closed her eyes, and breathed heavily for a moment, as if the rush into the room and the performance of her introduction had winded her.

She didn't appear to be an old woman, but her costume made it difficult to guess her age. Pearl thought she could be thirty-five or sixty. The hennaed hair might have been covering some streaks of silver, but now Pearl saw a youthful exuberance in the woman's expression. She pulled her eyes away from Madame Genevieve and looked to Maxwell.

He sat up straight in his bed, a book fallen from his lap to the blanket beside him, his mouth open in wonder.

As Pearl made to move to his side, Madame Genevieve stepped in front of her, settling herself with every possible ceremony into Pearl's chair beside the bed.

Had the seat always appeared so regal? The thought surprised Pearl, especially because her general impression of Madame Genevieve was that of an overpainted, overdressed charlatan. But in this moment, seeing her at Maxwell's side, Pearl wondered if she'd misread the woman.

Maxwell's cheeks glowed. Pearl couldn't tell if it was excitement or fever, but his eyes shone with the joy he often displayed when learning something new, not the frightful sheen that accompanied a troubling illness.

"You can speak with ghosts?"

Max sounded breathless, more so than Madame Genevieve had only a moment before. Pearl saw his hands clenched around his bedcover, gripping it tightly.

Pearl wanted to put a stop to this immediately, but there was no time for her to interrupt before Madame Genevieve raised her arms to her sides, her hands framing her head. "I can hear the whispers of memory."

Pearl recognized, from her own work with children, a master at responding to a question without giving a specific answer. A bit of grudging respect unfurled in her.

"You have lost a great many loved ones." Madame Genevieve's words were not a question, but Maxwell nodded in agreement.

"My father was gone before I was born, and my mother never recovered from my birth."

Pearl had never heard the boy say such a thing; the self-blame in his voice pained her.

He kept speaking without any prompting. "My father must have had a family, but nobody will tell me anything about him.

Not even his last name. That's why I'm called Ravenscroft. And that's why my grandfather lets me stay here even though I'm a great deal of trouble to care for."

Each word felt like a physical blow. Pearl had spent every day for the past six years with Maxwell, yet she'd never heard him speak this way. The guilt he seemed to carry must press against his heart like a millstone.

She waited for Madame Genevieve to tell the boy his parents' deaths were not his fault, but instead, the medium closed her eyes and lifted her chin to the ceiling, as if smelling the air.

Maxwell watched silently. Pearl struggled between the desire to go to him, to comfort him, and wishing this woman's strange ways would cause Max to open up and say more about his heartache.

The woman scooped the air in front of her close to her face. "I hear the sounds of water lapping against wooden boards. I hear the creak of a mast and the flap of heavy canvas. We are surrounded by salt and fish and fresh air. Strong men pull ropes in sun and rain. Your father was, I believe, a sailor."

What was Madame Genevieve doing? How dare she invent a story about his deceased father? And to what purpose?

Maxwell clapped his hands together. "That's smashing! A sailor!"

Pearl hadn't heard Max so excited about a story in many weeks. She wished he understood it was as fictional as the pirate novel they'd been reading at the fireside.

"I wonder if he was strong enough to carry those huge barrels. You know the barrels I'm thinking of? The ones sailors store food and water inside?"

Madame Genevieve, her eyes still closed, nodded. Which part of what he said was she agreeing to? And how long would this falsehood continue?

When next he spoke, it was in a hushed tone. "Did my father

die at sea? In a shipwreck? I do hope he was surrounded by his friends. Sailors are so brave. They never fear death as long as they have their crewmates beside them."

Pearl gasped. This was the message Maxwell carried away from the adventure stories she read with him? The danger and the possibility of death at any moment? Not the daring, last-minute rescue. Not the reunion with loved ones at the docks as the sailor's feet once again touched solid ground.

"I believe you are right about sailors' bravery," Madame Genevieve drawled. "But in order to know more about your father, all we need to do is ask."

Maxwell looked at Pearl. She could practically see his mind whirring with all the questions he'd been asking for years. Questions she could not—and his grandfather would not—answer.

A log popped in the fireplace, and Maxwell returned his attention to Madame Genevieve. His voice was a whisper. "I'm not sure anyone knows the answers."

With another wave of both hands through the air in front of her, she sighed long and slow. "Your father knows."

Pearl hadn't seen Maxwell move as fast as he did then, shifting from reclining to kneeling. Hands clasped at his heart, he was the image of a supplicant. "I hear voices here all the time, but I never hear him. Can you speak to him? Ask him to talk to me?"

Pearl resented the way she tilted close to hear Madame Genevieve's answer. She wouldn't trust the woman's words, no matter how her body was currently betraying her.

"If you are willing, and if we all set aside our doubts, we shall try."

A shiver ran down Pearl's spine. She knew perfectly well the words about doubts were for her. Now if Maxwell couldn't— What? Commune with his dead father?—it would be Pearl's fault because she was not a believer.

Max, still on his knees, nodded vigorously. "I am willing. What do I need to do?"

Pearl couldn't sit by silently any longer. "Wait. Wait, please."

Both of them looked at her: Max with patient curiosity and Madame Genevieve with thinly veiled amusement.

"Yes, Miss Ellicott? What is it?"

Confound the woman, she knew Pearl couldn't stop her now, at least not without becoming the villain in this bizarre story. But Mr. Ravenscroft could—both stop her and be the villain. Simple.

"Wouldn't you rather discuss this with your grandfather?"

Maxwell nodded. "Oh, yes. Let's invite him."

Madame Genevieve nodded as if the idea was her own. "One must not rush these things. We are in the preparatory stages of our exploration. Today you have only one assignment, young Master Ravenscroft."

Maxwell wiggled on his bed until he was even closer to the chair where Madame Genevieve sat. He was the picture of compliance. What might this ridiculous woman do with a child so eager to please?

"You need to gather all your happiest memories."

Pearl looked from Max to Madame Genevieve. That was not what she expected.

The woman went on. "Of course, the most powerful memories would generally be those connected with the deceased. In a different situation, those recollections of your best times together would forge the strongest bonds. Since you didn't ever have the opportunity to make such memories with your father, you must work doubly hard. Consider your happiest times. Remember your best days. Ask the house to help you. Take time to write the stories down. Talk them over with your governess. She ought to do this exercise as well." Without missing a beat, Madame Genevieve turned to Pearl. "Did you know your father while he was alive, dear?"

"What? Yes, of course I did." Pearl felt herself spluttering in her surprise.

The smallest twitch appeared in the woman's eye. She had just tricked Pearl into formally acknowledging her father was dead.

Not that it was a secret, but Pearl had no intention of sharing her personal information with a pretended medium.

Maxwell was already asking for paper and pencil. Sensing the opportunity for a dramatic exit, Madame Genevieve swept from the boy's room. With her hand on the doorknob, she turned to Pearl.

"It's a worthwhile exercise. For both of you. You need to see his joy. And you need to find your own."

Did Pearl imagine the tone of the woman's voice settling into a more normal cadence, or was she simply growing used to the wailing and moaning that underscored all of Madame Genevieve's pronouncements?

In any case, Pearl didn't imagine the wink. Madame Genevieve was not a subtle woman, and Pearl couldn't have missed that wink unless she was turned around completely.

She wanted to ask Madame Genevieve what she meant by her suggestion to *ask the house*, but the woman slipped out the door.

Max drew her attention back to him with a sweet demand. "Pearl, hurry. I have loads of ideas to write down. I don't want to forget any of them."

CHAPTER 21

Oliver wasn't avoiding his uncle's invited guest. If he managed to move through the bedroom wing of Shadowbrook without ever crossing her path, that was his good luck. As well as some careful maneuvering. But not hiding. The secondhand instruction to keep his distance from the woman was easy for him to obey.

He made his way to Maxwell's room and knocked on the door. Pearl answered, her smile warm.

"Hello, Mr. Waverley." Her eyes sparkled, and Oliver wondered if she was remembering the best parts of their meeting in the mirrored room the day before. He hoped she could ignore the worst.

"Good afternoon. I came to invite you both to join me at the dock. We could spend an hour watching boats and ships." He wanted to get outside, and he was sure an outing would be good for Maxwell.

Pearl pointed to the boy's small table where Maxwell sat, his head tilted to the side.

"What is he doing?" Oliver whispered.

"Listening."

"To what?"

Pearl gave a quiet sigh. "His happy memories."

"I can't tell if you're pleased about that or not."

Pearl drew Oliver away from Maxwell. "I'm very happy he's

focusing on something pleasant. But the woman who suggested it—have you met her? Your uncle's friend?"

Oliver shook his head. "The kitchen staff find her odd, and Mrs. Randle suggested I keep my distance."

Pearl's one-sided grin landed directly in Oliver's heart. "Amazing you've kept her at bay this long. I don't know how long you'll be able to manage that. She took her evening meal alone in her room last night, and I stayed here with Max."

As if on cue, Maxwell's door creaked open, and a tiny dog wearing a fluttering gold ribbon around its neck pushed its way into the room.

"What is that?" Oliver knew the answer, of course, but he couldn't quite make the animal's existence fit into Shadowbrook House.

"That's Misty. She came with your uncle's houseguest."

The dog's bark was far too loud for such a small animal, and Maxwell leaped immediately from his chair. Clearly, the boy was smitten. He knelt and held his hands out for a sniff.

Pearl pulled Oliver farther away from Max and the dog. Could she be looking for reasons to tug on his arm? To speak to him in a low voice? "The dog's already figured out her way around the house. She's come to visit Max in his room several times. He doesn't want to stay in bed for long hours if there's a chance of playing with Misty."

"I would never have dared ask for a pet when I lived here. It wouldn't have crossed my mind. I can't believe Uncle Arthur allows it."

Pearl shook her head. "I don't think he expected his guest to travel with an animal."

They watched Maxwell tumble with the little dog for a few minutes.

Pearl crossed her arms over her stomach. "Is it ridiculous that I'm trying not to resent an animal? It seems easy for Misty to get

Max playing. I have to convince him, sometimes beg him, just to get out of bed."

A crack of thunder shook the windows in the room. Misty buried her head under Maxwell's arm and whimpered. Max whispered comforting words into her coat.

"Maybe now isn't a great time for a trip to the dock." He walked over to Maxwell and placed a hand on his head. "Have you shown your little friend the library yet?"

Maxwell looked up at Oliver. "No. Do you think she'll like it?"

Oliver grinned. "I like it. You like it. I think even Pearl likes it. Chances are good the dog will like it too."

Maxwell scrambled to his feet and lifted the dog into his arms. "Come on, Pearl. We're going to show Misty the library."

Oliver was glad it was so easy to get the boy to agree to leave his bedroom. He didn't think he'd ever get used to the sickly smell of the place, and he was grateful the air in his own room didn't carry such a sour, sharp scent.

Following Maxwell and Pearl across the landing to the east wing, Oliver listened to Max chatter at the little dog, telling her about the treasures they'd find in the library.

When they reached the library's door, Oliver pulled it open for Max and Pearl. Inside, he knelt at the hearth and started a fire, listening to Maxwell as the boy introduced the little dog to some of his favorite titles.

Once the flames were licking at the logs, Oliver turned and sat on the floor, his back to the fire, and watched Pearl and Maxwell as they wandered along a wall with floor-to-ceiling shelves stuffed with books. He watched the way Pearl's hand trailed along the shelves, fluttering across spines. He could practically feel her fingers tracing his shoulder with the same feathery touch.

After a few minutes, Oliver heard Maxwell call his name. "Was this library here when you were a boy?"

"Probably for several hundred years before I was born."

"Did you have a favorite story?"

Oliver got to his feet. "I kept my favorites on a low shelf out of the way—just here—but I'd be surprised if they were still here. They weren't great or valuable or even pretty to look at." He pointed to a section of the shelves where he'd stored ragged copies of the adventure books he shared with his friends, each boy taking the stories home in turn. His collection of illustrated books, none written specifically for children, had been his most treasured, providing pictures that he tried to replicate in his notebook. Of course, none of the books belonged to him. But his uncle hadn't seemed to mind Oliver's takeover of a few books. The old man may have never even noticed.

He knelt in front of what he'd always thought of as *his shelf* and was surprised to find the same selection, relatively untouched. The exciting stories, pages ruffled from water damage and childish treatment, stood like sentinels of his boyhood memories. He pulled one of the illustrated books from the shelf and held it out to Maxwell.

"These helped me learn to draw."

Max flipped through the pages, giving several of the illustrations a long look as the dog ran circles around his feet. Over his shoulder he asked Pearl, "Do you remember my picture books?" He turned to Oliver. "We used to read them a very long time ago."

Oliver caught Pearl's knowing smile. "A very long time ago" meant something different to an eight-year-old than it did to an adult.

"I do remember. Would you like me to find one for you?" Her voice made the question sound like the effort would be a pleasure.

Maxwell's smile widened and his eyes sparkled. "Oh, yes, please."

Pearl seemed to know exactly the books Max meant. She pulled two from a shelf and handed them to the boy, who took a seat in the middle of a velvet couch, tucking the dog into his lap. He patted the cushion beside him, and Oliver obediently sat. Pearl came to Maxwell's other side and watched Maxwell show Oliver the playfully colored pictures as the small boy expertly guided the dog's nose away from the pages.

Pearl's arm rested on Maxwell's shoulders as he eagerly explained the story. Oliver leaned in to look closely at the pictures, casually resting his own arm across the back of the couch. When their sleeves made contact, Pearl glanced up at Oliver. Instead of moving away, he drew his arm an inch closer.

The smile she gave him was not as playful as her expression occasionally was; she looked at him with serious eyes. He held her gaze many long moments as he answered Maxwell's unending questions.

When Max closed one book and reached for another, Oliver shifted. He ought to pay better attention to what Maxwell was showing him. But he kept his arm close enough to Pearl's that he could rest a finger on the fold of her shirtsleeve's fabric. Could he feel her heart beating there near the crook of her elbow? Or was that his own blood pulsing into his fingers?

"I always get a new book by Mr. Caldecott for Christmas, even though I'm too old for them now." Maxwell turned the first few pages of a well-read book, its papers soft at the edges, to find a favorite illustration. Oliver smiled at the thought anyone would ever fully outgrow a beloved book.

They spent more than an hour there, Maxwell eager to share the books he'd loved. Oliver thought he could be perfectly happy to join Pearl and Maxwell in the library every day and stay for hours. At least as long as the house stood and they remained in it. What, he wondered, would he do with the books upon the sale of Shadowbrook? Surely the Campbell Company would have no use for them.

His thought was interrupted by Maxwell's laugh as Misty turned around and lifted herself onto her back legs, her front paws on Maxwell's shoulders. The boy wrapped his arms around the furry, white body and laughed harder, both leaning into the dog's obvious affection and tilting his head away from some of the more intense friendliness.

"Her tongue tickles," he said with a giggle.

His laugh turned to a cough, and Pearl leaped up from the couch. She picked up the dog and set her on the floor, then reached for Maxwell's hands. Instead of taking Pearl's hand, the boy wrapped both his arms around his chest and curled into himself.

Oliver stood, his own breath hitching, wondering if this would turn into a dangerous fit.

With one hand rubbing slow circles on Maxwell's back, Pearl spoke softly. Feeling helpless, Oliver stepped close and put his own hand on Pearl's back, echoing her gentle circles. She never stopped speaking words of comfort to Max, but she turned and sent a small, grateful smile in Oliver's direction.

How was it possible she eased his worry when he set out to offer her comfort?

Maxwell's cough subsided, and his breath—a thin wheeze—slowed. After only a few minutes, he sat up and lowered his arms to his sides.

"I'm all right now."

Oliver might have believed Max if he hadn't needed to breathe in the middle of the short sentence.

Pearl's responding smile was brief, and it didn't reach her eyes, but Oliver was impressed she was able to manufacture even the echo of happiness in the frightening moment. There were elements to her strength that fascinated him.

Maxwell must have noticed the falseness of her expression, because he reached for Pearl's hand and held it in both his own. "I really am fine. See? This was a good adventure. No one got hurt. The library is a good room. It's so quiet here. No angry whispers. We should come here again. All of us."

As if in agreement, the dog barked and jumped onto the couch, turning two full circles before settling on the seat next to Maxwell.

Oliver felt Pearl's laugh in the hand he still held to her back. Maybe this effort wasn't a disaster. He would keep trying to convince her he was worth the occasional frustration.

CHAPTER 22

Pearl found it was easier to avoid Madame Genevieve in the following days. Each evening after Maxwell said good night, the woman would join Mr. Ravenscroft in whatever parlor or drawing room he chose. Pearl made sure to move Max quickly from his grandfather's side to the library where they'd sit with Oliver and read a story. Pearl loved the evenings when it was Oliver's turn to read aloud.

Pearl asked Violet about the evening visits one morning as the maid prepared the fire in Pearl's room. "What do they do when they meet after we've left?"

"It seems like they sit and talk. Nothing more."

Pearl wondered what "more" Violet expected.

"Have you heard them? What do they speak about?"

Without looking up, Violet shook her head. "We hear nothing."

Pearl laughed. "I know better than that. We who work for Mr. Ravenscroft hear far more than he knows."

Violet turned and grinned. "Very well. They speak of those Mr. Ravenscroft has lost. His parents. His wife. His sister. His daughter."

Pearl knew what she wished to ask, but the proper wording eluded her. She didn't want to frighten Violet with her suggestion, but there was a strong chance the girl heard much more than Pearl would. That didn't give Pearl the right to press the girl about it.

Her next question came out halting and fractured, heavy with self-doubt.

"Does she . . . attempt . . . to reach them?"

The subject didn't seem to bother Violet at all. "A séance, you mean? Oh, no, nothing like that yet. We're all waiting for it, though. Might help clear out some of the ghosts hanging around this house and muttering all the time."

Pearl inspected the fingers on her left hand, trying hard to seem casual. "Do you think there are truly ghosts at Shadowbrook?"

Violet answered in the same matter-of-fact voice as she scooped the last of the cold ash from Pearl's grate. "You must hear them. All old places have them. Nothing to be afraid of, though. Like the marks left on a wall when a picture gets taken down. Just like footprints in a dirt path. People leave traces."

Pearl had never heard the phenomenon described so simply, so clearly. Violet's words gave Pearl the strangest feeling she was missing something.

She no longer pretended at disinterest. She moved closer to the fireplace and handed Violet the small brush from the stand.

"Do you see them?"

Violet turned and sat back on her heels. "I don't have the Sight. My gran did, and when her mind went, she'd sit in a room smiling at the corners of the walls, nodding and whispering. Maybe you have to be a little crazy to see. But sometimes I feel like I'm not all by myself in an empty room. I hear the music, of course. We all do."

Pearl's stomach clenched. She knew what Violet would answer, but she asked her question anyway. "What music?"

"The violin. I hear it best from the stairs, because it comes from somewhere in the middle of the house. Or from Maxwell's room, but that's when you're the one playing."

The girl heard violin music playing in the house. Madame Genevieve heard it. Oliver and Maxwell heard it. Pearl also heard it, but she had been certain it was only inside her head. At least, she had been certain until a few days ago. She shuddered.

Violet shook her head. "It's not frightening. The music is lovely, even when it's sad. And feeling like someone's nearby is good. If anything, it's better than being alone. Someone was here before me, and someone will be here when I'm gone. It's nice."

Pearl recognized the strangeness of having this discussion with someone less than half her age, but she wanted to understand. "Aren't ghosts supposed to be angry and destructive?"

Turning back to pick up her cleaning tools, Violet shrugged. "I sometimes hear a sort of muttering, but evil ghosts are mostly in stories. If anyone trapped forever in this house was of the hostile kind, there'd be no secret about it. We'd all know it. Sad, though? Yes, I'd say there's a sad feeling here. In almost every room, but not all the time."

Of course. The mildly oppressive air within Shadowbrook might be explained away by such superstitions and old wives' tales. Pearl knew better, though: The feeling came not from haunting, deceased souls but from the haunted ones who lived here now.

Violet picked up her work bucket and smiled at Pearl. "Sometimes the voices seem cheerful, don't you think?"

Pearl wondered how she'd given the girl the idea she heard the voices Violet spoke of.

"But when Maxwell is sick, everything's gloomy. I bet his illness draws the sadness close. It only makes sense."

Pearl found herself nodding, but she wasn't sure if it was agreement or farewell. Violet seemed so certain, but Pearl didn't find any of this clear or even possible.

A few evenings later, Pearl walked Maxwell from the music room Misty had chosen as her domain down to the south parlor to say good night to his grandfather. She planned to go with him as far as the room's entrance, as usual, and then step away to give the two of them some privacy.

She knew this habit of walking Maxwell to the door was one she likely couldn't justify for much longer. Max was hardly a small child who might get lost or frightened in the house, but she enjoyed their explorations together, and she relished the moments he'd reach for her hand. It reminded her of walking with her brother all those years ago.

As Pearl led Maxwell to the door, Jenkinson put out a hand to stop her. "Mr. Ravenscroft wishes you to stay."

Pearl tugged the skirts of her dress into place and stepped inside. Madame Genevieve was already in the room. Pearl gave her a nod and turned to Mr. Ravenscroft.

"What can I do for you this evening, sir?"

"We hear you play the violin."

She nodded. Was she supposed to say more? Would Mr. Ravenscroft reprimand her in front of his company?

"I'd like you to provide some entertainment for our guest this evening." He gestured to Madame Genevieve, who smiled and gave a convincing display of modesty.

Her drawling voice spread her words across the seconds like jam over toast. "I'm sure we'd all love to hear you play, but please, don't trouble yourself on my account."

Pearl knew how she was supposed to respond. "It's no trouble at all. I'll go upstairs for the instrument."

When she arrived back in the room, Maxwell was speaking animatedly to his grandfather. "And then I wrote the whole thing down again so Oliver will have a copy to keep with him when he has to leave. I think it will make him laugh."

Pearl knew the boy referred to a story he'd told her that morning, one of the happy memories he'd been collecting according to Madame Genevieve's counsel. As much as Pearl resented the woman for tricking Mr. Ravenscroft with her fraud, she couldn't deny the value of Maxwell's new habit. It truly did seem to be increasing his joy to consider the things that delighted him.

Hovering at the door, she waited for Maxwell to finish telling his grandfather the story. After a few minutes, she felt Madame Genevieve's eyes on her. The woman winked at her, and Pearl's back stiffened. What were the winks supposed to mean? Did the spiritualist think they shared something? That there was a friendship or understanding between them? Because there wasn't.

As Pearl stepped into the parlor, Maxwell turned and saw her. "What will you play, Pearl? A chamber piece? One of the country dances? One you've made up yourself?" He turned to Mr. Ravenscroft. "What is your favorite song, Grandfather? I'm sure Pearl can play it."

She gave Maxwell a smile of gratitude for his belief in her while at the same moment hoping his grandfather didn't take the boy's words literally. She was proficient, but she could not simply play anything she'd ever heard.

Instead of making a request, Mr. Ravenscroft turned to Madame Genevieve. "What kind of music do you enjoy?"

The woman clasped her hands together in a move that set her scarves fluttering. "I like what I hear in the night here in this house. The long, slow notes."

Pearl stared at her. Would Madame Genevieve claim the songs were played by ghosts when it was simply the wind blowing through the house?

Mr. Ravenscroft bowed his head and closed his eyes, as if her words were a prayer he wanted to join.

Max nodded. "Sometimes I hear that music, too. I used to think it was Pearl, but I hear it when we're reading or playing sometimes."

Madame Genevieve nodded. "There's a memory in this house of someone who loved music." She shifted in her seat and hummed a melody that sounded like a song Pearl often heard in her mind. "I do enjoy a soaring romantic piece."

In what was by now a reflexive response, Pearl lowered her chin to hide the rolling of her eyes, but to her surprise, she felt a sincerely amused smile flicker over her face.

Of course that sort of music appealed to Madame Genevieve.

Pearl raised the instrument and played the most romantic, most soaring piece she could recall.

She followed that piece with another, and then another. As she swayed in time to the notes, she heard in her mind an echo of harmony, as if her memory supplied a second musician to round out her songs.

When Maxwell stood from the couch and asked her to play a lively dance, Pearl nodded and shifted the tone of her playing. The boy stepped in front of Madame Genevieve, offered her his hand, and raised her from her seat to dance with him.

Pearl watched him as carefully as her playing allowed, keeping time with his steps. If he was unable to leap, he skipped across the room, one hand on Madame Genevieve's arm and the other wrapped in her ring-bedecked hand. They spun in gentle circles, and Pearl's heart soared to see Max tilt back his head and laugh.

If a portion of Pearl's heart held back from fully enjoying the moment for fear Max would suddenly burst into a lung-wracking cough, it was a smaller portion than usual.

She glanced at Mr. Ravenscroft and saw he was as still and stiff as usual, but the fingers of his left hand tapped on his leg as if along imaginary strings, playing along in his mind. Pearl knew those taps. She did the same when she listened to someone play.

At the end of a country dance, Maxwell dropped onto the couch, his head resting on Mr. Ravenscroft's shoulder. "Maybe it's your turn now. I'm worn-out."

Mr. Ravenscroft caught Pearl's eye. He glanced from the top of Maxwell's head toward the door.

Pearl nodded in understanding. "I believe it's time for bed, Max. You've worked hard this evening, and we still have many stairs to climb."

"Do you know what this house needs?" Maxwell asked, his voice weary after his exertion. He stifled a yawn. "A dumbwaiter. All the best houses in stories have dumbwaiters to carry sweets and secrets and tired adventurers up and down the house's levels."

Pearl was ready with a response, but Mr. Ravenscroft surprised her by leaning over and whispering in Maxwell's ear. If the boy's brightening expression was any indication, there might be an unexplored shaft he'd be very interested in discovering.

What was happening? Who was this man snuggling Max and whispering secrets into his ear? She'd never seen Mr. Ravenscroft so tender and playful. She'd never even imagined it possible.

She was rarely invited to join the Ravenscrofts for their nightly visit, and she'd never witnessed anything like what she was part of tonight. She wondered if Mr. Ravenscroft had ever behaved this way with his nephew. From Oliver's words about the lonely childhood spent in his uncle's house, she doubted it.

What was different? What had changed?

Before Pearl could follow her thoughts any further, Madame Genevieve held out her hands to raise Maxwell from the couch. As he stood before her, she brought her face close to his. "More happy memories for your book. And this time, consider any stories you've heard about your parents. See what the house will tell you about your mother's childhood here. We don't need to have been present for memories to hold power."

Maxwell practically disappeared as Madame Genevieve wrapped both her scarf-fringed arms around him. Pearl's throat thickened at the sight. Was she jealous that Max was being affectionate with someone who wasn't her? Or did she wish someone would enfold her in an embrace like that?

Either way, in a moment, Maxwell was at her side, his small hand in hers.

She tucked the violin under her arm and nodded her good night to Mr. Ravenscroft. His face wore his familiar look of lowered brows and downturned mouth, and he did not offer thanks for her playing, nor did he smile at her the way he did at Maxwell and Madame Genevieve.

"That was very well done, my dear," Madame Genevieve said as she followed Pearl to the door. "I hope you'll repeat that performance regularly. Music has a way of drawing the spirits close. And the spiritual accompaniment was as perfect as if the two of you had practiced together."

Pearl did not dignify that silliness with a response.

The woman smiled as though she knew exactly what Pearl was thinking. "Any time you're ready to speak with me about your own lost ones, I'm available to you."

Pearl shook her head. "That's very kind, but unnecessary."

"There is healing in bringing the spirits of the departed into your daily life."

She wished Maxwell was not standing right beside her. She chose her words carefully. "I am not ill, Madame. I don't require healing. But I appreciate how you've begun to help here."

Madame Genevieve reached out an arm covered with jangling bracelets and traced a gentle line across Maxwell's cheek. "It's my delight to share the gift."

The mantel clock struck the hour, and Pearl heard the reverberations of the large clock upstairs. Leaning closer to the woman's ear, she lowered her voice. "I still feel it's only right for me to be in the room any time you speak with Maxwell."

Madame Genevieve winked. In the deep, drawn-out, quavering tones of her performance voice, she said, "I'm sure you do."

CHAPTER 23

Oliver continued to offer to meet with his uncle about details of the sale, to suggest he write a letter inviting a representative of the Campbell Company to come speak with them. Uncle Arthur refused to discuss anything to do with the inheritance.

Disappointed and frustrated, Oliver walked away from his latest attempted conversation with nothing more than the image of Jenkinson standing in front of a closed door. He felt his sigh, long and loud, as he made his way down the last few stairs.

He turned toward the bedroom wing and saw Pearl.

"Goodness, Mr. Waverley. You look done in."

He gave a rueful chuckle and shook his head. "I appreciate your careful observation, and I believe you're right. I can't pretend to be delighted by my continued failures."

"Walk with me, then. We can reminisce about the ways you've brightened up this house since your arrival."

A small, framed painting slipped from the wall and fell to the floor with a thud.

"Can the house hear you? Even the walls disapprove of my presence." As soon as he said the words, he wished he could take them back. He didn't want to sound petulant, especially in conversation with Pearl.

"I am quite pleased with your presence, but perhaps we ought to walk outside. To protect the artwork."

He saw her cheeky grin and felt an echo of it grow across his own mouth. Pearl may have felt frustrated with him and his plans, but she wouldn't allow him to sulk.

She led him through the music room, stopping to attach a lead to Misty's jangling collar.

"Is caring for this animal part of your work now?" he asked.

Pearl shook her head. "I'm happy to take her out now and then if it saves effort for the rest of the staff. Max drifted off to sleep after our lessons today, and I find myself at my leisure."

"And you choose to spend your free time with the neglected pet of my uncle's strange houseguest?"

She opened a door at the end of a hallway and led the dog out into a small courtyard. Instead of answering his question, Pearl asked her own. "You've met Madame Genevieve, then?"

Oliver shook his head. "I know the woman only by reputation, and that is enough for me. I've devised a contest for myself: I win if I never actually come across her face-to-face."

Pearl chuckled. "I imagine she's saving your meeting for a dramatic moment. Conjuring dramatic moments seems to be her specialty. I'm surprised you've avoided her so well."

Oliver swallowed his response. He didn't need to admit to Pearl how easy it had always been to disappear into the halls of Shadowbrook and not be seen for hours, days, and even weeks. Not that he'd made such an attempt to avoid his uncle when he was a child. It seemed Arthur avoided him as much then as he did now.

The little dog led them into a walled garden. Pearl let her off her lead to run, but before too many minutes, the dog contented herself with circling Oliver's feet, forcing him to watch her every move so he didn't accidentally step on her.

"This isn't precisely what I had envisioned for our walk together," Pearl said, an apology in her tone.

Oliver picked up the dog, and she immediately began to bathe him with her tongue.

Pearl laughed. "She adores you."

"The feeling is entirely one-sided, I assure you."

Pearl tucked her hand into Oliver's arm. "She'll have to share you with me, but I promise not to be so affectionate."

"I wouldn't mind if you were." Oliver nearly blushed at the thought of Pearl kissing the space between his jaw and his ear. He hoped if such a thing happened, he'd be able to forget the dog.

As if she could see the thought in his face, Pearl shook her head and grinned. "Misty and I have different ways of displaying our regard."

"Right. She licks my chin, and you tell me I'm a fool to give up all of this." He kicked at a rock in the path, sending it skittering into a crumbling section of stone wall, causing a shower of pebbles to rain down.

He hoped she would laugh and their conversation could continue to be playful, but Pearl sighed.

"We're not going to agree on this, not ever. And if you can't consider waiting a few years . . ." Pearl's voice trailed off, and Oliver knew she was thinking about how long she could expect Maxwell to survive. He wanted to assure her the boy could grow strong. He wished she believed in the London doctors' abilities. And she didn't seem to realize what a boon the Campbell Company's offer was, nor how critical their timeline. As certain as he was she had committed to the wrong belief, he couldn't argue his point any further without causing offense. He'd much rather go back to teasing about how her affection was different from a dog's.

He watched Pearl look up toward the cloudy sky. He hoped it wasn't a trick for holding in tears. Had he made her cry? He put the dog back on the ground and turned to face her, both his hands resting lightly on her shoulders.

"We don't have to talk about it. I'm sorry I've upset you."

She returned her eyes to his. There was an obvious shine, but she lifted the corners of her mouth. He thought this particular expression, her smile pushing past impending tears, made her more beautiful than he'd ever seen her.

"If we never speak of the things you do that upset me, ours will be a nearly silent relationship."

He followed her lead and grinned back at her. With an attempt at a careless shrug, he said, "I can think of interesting things to do without saying a word."

She shook her head. "You see, you're still talking."

He took her hint and made much better use of his mouth. And she, hers. He felt his hand was made to fit the curve of her neck.

After too brief a moment, a gust of wind brought icy rain. Pearl laughed and tried to cover her hair as Oliver scooped the dog into his arm and held the side of his coat out for Pearl. She tucked herself tight against his side as they scrambled toward the house. The sounds of their laughter and the dog's increasingly insistent barks almost drowned out the patter of rain against branch and stone.

Their arrival through the kitchen door was met with a flurry of excitement from the serving staff.

"Hundreds, she wants. Hundreds! I don't keep that many candles on hand for an entire year, much less for a single night."

Mrs. Randle stood with her hands on the sides of her head, quick steps taking her in a tight circle around the middle of the kitchen.

Oliver set the dog down on the floor and watched her run from the room. She must have been chased out of this kitchen more than once.

Violet skidded into the room and stopped in the corner, about a dozen partially consumed tapers in her hands. "Here's what I found in the maids' rooms, Mrs. Randle. I didn't dare go into the footmen's rooms without permission."

The housekeeper's brow, already stormy, lowered even farther.

"Well, of course you shouldn't go there. No one asked you to, you silly girl."

Oliver saw Violet flinch. He imagined the harried housekeeper had said something Violet interpreted as exactly such a direction.

"How can I be of help, Mrs. Randle?" Pearl gave the housekeeper her full attention.

"That woman wants several hundred candles for heaven only knows what reason. And she wants them tomorrow night. As if I am capable of making wax appear, dipping it, and allowing it to harden in thirty-two hours."

The timid housekeeper must be experiencing an unusual strain to speak so forcefully. He glanced at Pearl.

"Are you referring to Madame Genevieve?" Pearl spoke carefully.

The slightest hint of a scoff came from Mrs. Randle before she answered. "Madame Genevieve." She spoke the name as if it were made from bitter lemons. "She's putting together some sort of witchery. A *gathering*, she calls it. And it requires hundreds of candles. Not lamps or lanterns. Candles. And not dozens. Not even scores. One hundred won't do for Her Highness. She requires several hundred. I've no idea where I'm to find such things."

Pearl glanced at Oliver. "We might be able to help you. Please excuse us for a moment."

Without another word, Pearl grabbed Oliver's hand and hurried from the kitchen. He knew he'd follow her anywhere, and after their moment in the dormant garden, he knew staying silent had its benefits. She led him into a passage opposite their bedroom wing and walked to the end of the hallway. Standing in front of a blank stretch of wall, Pearl tapped a knot in the floorboard with her toe. The entire panel of wall swung into the hallway, opening on a hinge. Within, a narrower passageway led to a staircase. They followed the steps until the stairs stopped at another wall. The next door required a key, already in the lock. Clearly, she'd been here before.

The room was full of boxes, neatly organized by size and clearly labeled, unlike the random scattering of boxes in so many of the house's unused rooms. Oliver was astonished by the orderliness of the storage system, which allowed Pearl to select exactly what she was searching for. Running her hand down the boxes, she stopped when she reached one that read *Candles*.

Oliver expected to find damage to the tapers inside. Mice loved to nibble on wax, and if there were candles inside the box, they might not be usable. The layer of dust covering the entire room suggested Pearl was the only person who'd been inside in many years.

Opening the crate, she uncovered a large ceramic vessel with a tight-fitting cork lid. She levered the cork out, and Oliver saw dozens of candles inside, standing at attention as if they anticipated being needed on a day much like today.

Pearl pointed to two more boxes with similar labels, which held more candles than they could carry. Even if the crocks were empty, they were large enough to be prohibitively heavy. As Oliver hefted the first of the crates into his arms, an eerie sound stopped him cold. All the hair on the back of his neck stood on end, and the flesh on his arms puckered.

The unmistakable tones of violin music floated in the air. A keening, heartbreaking tune.

Oliver set the crate back on the floor. He pointed to the wall. "Do you hear that?"

A hesitant moment passed before Pearl nodded.

Oliver whispered, "Have you heard it before?"

She looked from one corner of the room to another before she answered, her voice thready with emotion. "Never so loudly. I've always been able to convince myself it was my imagination, or the wind. I often hear songs in my mind, probably the way you see pictures in yours."

"Do you think it's a . . ."

At Oliver's hesitation, she placed her hand over his mouth. Her eyebrows drew down her forehead. "Do not say ghost."

He moved her hand so he could whisper again, this time closer to her ear. "What else could it be? You think Jenkinson is an accomplished musician?"

"Whoever it is, it's a masterful touch." She continued to look around the room. Oliver watched her study the space as it filled with sound, as the music circled around the stacks of boxes and filled every inch of empty air with a sound Oliver could only describe as grief.

They stood together and bore witness to the agonized tune.

When the music stopped, they looked at each other for a moment, then lifted their boxes and carried them silently back to the kitchen. Oliver didn't know how to explain what that devastating music had made him feel, and Pearl remained quiet as well. After they set the crates of candles in the kitchen, they wordlessly turned and walked back to the hidden door and the winding staircase passageway.

Silence met them at the door. Whoever, whatever played the song had stopped. There was nothing more to hear.

No. Not nothing.

A creak, then another. A slow, repetitive shushing sound connecting the creaks. Rustling silk? Unfurling wings? Whispers of hidden voices? Or was it something without form at all?

Oliver shuddered. He gestured with his head toward the passageway they'd followed. Pearl nodded in silent agreement and followed him back out of the room. The farther they went from the hidden room, the more foolish Oliver felt. Surely all this talk of ghosts and spirits had addled his mind. Oliver didn't believe in things he couldn't see. Not since he was a boy.

His imagination had overpowered his mind while in the gloomy, secret space awash with such a mysterious, painful tune. Anyone would have been affected. It didn't follow that the explanation must be supernatural.

Though consider as he might, he couldn't think of another answer.

CHAPTER 24

Lives were lived and then ended. History was the past. What was gone was gone. Only a fool would believe someone like Madame Genevieve had the power to speak with spirits.

A fool—or someone whose heart broke at every thought of those who had passed.

Pearl was not such a person, but she dearly loved a little boy who was. This love propelled her to the door of Madame Genevieve's room. She gave a quick, quiet knock.

"All right. Come in."

Pearl opened the door and stepped inside. Scarves were draped on every surface, including each bedpost and all the framed paintings on the walls.

Madame Genevieve sprawled on the bed, one arm slung over her face as though protecting her eyes from a too-bright light.

"Did you find it?" she asked, her accent as sharp and spiky as someone hawking fish in the marketplace.

"I beg your pardon," Pearl said. "I don't know what you mean. Were you expecting someone else?"

With a gasp, Madame Genevieve sat up. "Lands, girl. You gave me a fright." She looked around Pearl at the door. "Just us, then?"

The harsh accent was stronger than when Madame Genevieve had slipped into it before, and as unfamiliar to Pearl as the strange moaning had been before she'd grown used to it. Was this the real voice of Madame Genevieve? Perhaps nothing was real with this woman.

"I've come alone. But I won't interrupt you if you've made plans."

Madame Genevieve moved until she was sitting upright, her back against the bed's headboard. She shifted something in her lap, and Pearl saw the little dog curled up, asleep.

"Nothing as solid as all that. Just sent a maid to find some cheese for Misty. Come in. Sit, if you like." She gestured to a chair near the window. On it lay a black gown with flowing sleeves. Tiny white dog hairs clung to the fabric. Pearl folded the skirt to one side and perched at the edge of the seat.

"What brings you to my diggings tonight? Need a reading, do you? I'm not quite prepared for that just now, what with the gathering we're planning, but we can see about a private session in a free moment while I'm here."

Pearl gave a quick shake of her head. "Not a reading. Not a session. I have questions."

Madame Genevieve's laugh emerged from her throat as a bark much like her dog's. There was nothing of the floaty sound of her performance voice. "Don't we all, dearie? Well, I don't guarantee I'll give you any answers you haven't thought of yourself, but go on."

It was as if the performer was a different woman than this. As if none of Madame Genevieve's pretense was needed now that the two of them were alone together.

Pearl unlaced her fingers and ran her hands across her skirt. "How long has Mr. Ravenscroft been communicating with you?"

"Not going to beat about the bush, are you? Diving right in?"

Even across the dimly lit room, Pearl caught the woman's eye and held it. "In order to keep the household peace, I believe we can be direct with each other."

Madame Genevieve gave a single nod before she answered. "I hide only what I need to hide. I reckon you do the same."

Pearl felt herself stiffen defensively. "Doesn't everyone?"

Madame Genevieve chuckled and sank back into her pillows. "Aye. We're all hiding and seeking. It's the universal game."

"How long have you been working with Mr. Ravenscroft?" Pearl asked again.

"It's been right near three years now. One of my longest-standing clients, he is."

Three years seemed a terribly long time for Mr. Ravenscroft to buy Madame Genevieve's particular brand of comfort. "And how did he originally become connected with you?"

"Like any business, I do my advertising. I'm *le-git-i-mate*." She enunciated the word carefully, as if to prove her claim.

"He discovered you in a newspaper?"

Madame Genevieve lifted her hands in a gesture that either meant she didn't know or she wasn't holding anything. "Many of my clients have read about me in a gazette or a journal or a herald. I appear in stories often enough."

"And what is it you offer?"

Madame Genevieve sat silently for a few long seconds, staring at Pearl as if to read the thoughts behind her expression. After a moment, she shifted to the foot of the bed, her knees close to Pearl's.

"Most folks choose a group meeting, where we sit around the table and commune. It's the most economical option. We gather together, join hands, and attempt contact, you know."

Pearl did not know, but she could imagine.

"There's a bit of showmanship involved. Tables rattle, candles blow out. The whole package. Everyone likes a show. But mostly, they come for the words. Quite often, the messages I report back to them serve to comfort more than one of the gathered clients. It's a skill I continue to sharpen as I grow my business. Make an answer seem personal, but not too personal. Vague enough to satisfy many of the hopes the patrons have come with. Simple messages for simple minds. But that won't do for our Mr. Ravenscroft. He prefers a private session by letters."

Pearl nodded, hoping the woman would continue.

She did. "We write to each other of those he's lost. He tells me stories. Shares his memories. Flogs himself over his past mistakes. They all do that, of course. Everyone speaks his own guilt when talking about the past. He asks me questions. I try to give him helpful answers."

"Helpful?" Pearl didn't hide the skepticism in her voice.

"He gets what he pays for. And he keeps writing back. He's brought me here, and that's the mark of a satisfied customer. Now I can see and hear what's happening in this house for myself."

"And you consider it *helpful* to trick him into believing you're communicating with the dead?"

Madame Genevieve chuckled again and scratched the sleeping dog behind the ears. "You wouldn't last a day in my line of work. You've got no sense of the mystical. And it's no trick. This house is noisy with the murmurs of the dead."

"Then why don't I hear them?"

Pearl was surprised by her question though Madame Genevieve clearly was not.

The spiritualist smiled at her. "Are you ready to know the answer?"

She couldn't honestly say whether she was or not.

Madame Genevieve took Pearl's hand in her own surprisingly soft one. "Many whispers clamor for our attention, from the living and the dead. When you press your hands to your ears to block the ones that might hurt you, you may also cut yourself off from those who could bring joy. You can learn which voices to listen to and which to ignore."

"And you can teach me that?"

The woman nodded, and her fluffy orange halo bounced back and forth. "I count on you learning well enough to help Maxwell do the same. It might save his life."

She was unwilling to show the woman how uncomfortable that sentence made her feel. Not knowing how to reply, Pearl stood. "I believe you have answered my questions. Thank you. And I apologize for the interruption."

Walking with Pearl toward the door, Madame Genevieve said, "No apology needed. Come see me any time. But the next time, I'll have to charge you." The woman grinned and winked as if they'd shared a great joke. "If my other clients find out we had a session for free, I'll be flooded with demands for trial runs. Keep that dry, will you? Won't do my pocketbook any good if such news gets about."

Pearl wanted to deny they'd had a *session* almost as much as she wanted to "keep it dry." Nobody would hear about this from her.

As she walked into the hall, Pearl felt Madame Genevieve's hand on her arm. "Small comforts can't hurt anyone. I reckon you've got one or two of your own. Don't deprive others of theirs."

Pearl looked into the woman's eyes and saw genuine kindness, although shrouded by the layers of costume and face paint. It didn't surprise Pearl she'd been slow to see past the showiness of Madame Genevieve's theatrics.

The woman took Pearl's hand and squeezed it gently. "We're not so different, you and me. We're both in the business of comfort and teaching."

Pearl couldn't help herself. She laughed. "We go about it in quite a different way."

Madame Genevieve gave a nod of assent. "Aye. And why not? Each to her own, I say."

CHAPTER 25

Pearl might have argued with Madame Genevieve's claims. Lies could hurt. Being tricked, as well. But she let the woman's other words settle in her mind as she walked back to Maxwell's room. Madame Genevieve had a point, after all. Some days, small comforts were all Pearl had.

She knew there was a chance Maxwell had fallen asleep, but she wanted to look in on him. Offer him some "small comfort" in her own way—one that did not include flowing scarves or rattling tables.

He was not asleep. He sat up in bed against his pillows. As soon as she closed the door, he said, "Did you speak to her?"

Was there nothing this child couldn't see in her face?

"To whom?" she asked, buying herself a second or two to form a better answer.

"The lady. Genevieve. You met with her, didn't you? Did you ask her to see me again?"

She wouldn't lie to him, but she could select which of the questions to answer. "No. She's busy planning her meeting for tomorrow. And I don't think a visit with her is in your best interest."

Maxwell shook his head. "You're wrong. I need her. To help me understand."

"Understand what?"

He looked to the side of the room where the spot of damp darkened the corner of the ceiling. "What the house needs from me."

Pearl couldn't decide how to respond to that. She wanted to take the boy in her arms and hug away all such thoughts. He was not suffering from his lung disease because Shadowbrook House demanded a sacrifice. The idea was foolish and frightening.

But if he believed it, even in a tiny part, she would do everything in her power to assist him.

"We'll see what she can tell us at her gathering."

He looked at her, his eyes shining. "You'll come? You'll listen to her?"

Pearl realized she was no longer dreading the woman's performance. A small but growing part of her looked forward to it.

The next afternoon, Pearl helped Maxwell into a fine suit of clothing he kept in a wardrobe but had never worn. Every year or two, Mrs. Randle brought him a wrapped packet of what she called "visiting clothes," but as he never went visiting, he had no occasion to put them on. Whenever he grew a few inches, the old suit would disappear from his bedroom and a new one would arrive.

He tugged the jacket's sleeves, and Pearl saw how his discomfort of the restrictive fabrics matched the excitement of wearing a costume. She remembered the feeling.

"You look very handsome. I wish I had a beautiful dress so I could match your finery."

Maxwell carefully wet his hands, pressed them to his head, and combed his hair over to the side in the same style as his grandfather. He didn't need to know that it stood up in the back like the little-boy version of peacock feathers.

He stood before his looking glass and inspected each angle of his reflection. Pearl hid her smile as he twisted his shoulders to try to see how his back appeared in the structured jacket. It was not vanity but simple curiosity. She could practically hear him wondering how he'd look in a suit when he was a man. The thought was both delightful and tragic, as they both knew hope was a luxury, and Maxwell would not likely see adulthood.

When he finished his self-inspection, he turned to look at Pearl. "You don't have a fancy dress? Then what are you going to wear? You can't go to the gathering in that."

There was no stifling her laugh this time. "Do I look so awful, then?"

He quickly apologized, shaking his head hard enough to dislodge a few strands of his thin hair from their carefully combed state. "No, only this is a special occasion, and you should wear your prettiest dress."

"Which one is that?" Did the boy even notice the clothes she wore? Did anyone?

His answer was decisive. "Something red."

She could not imagine what he might be thinking of. "Max, I don't own a red skirt or a red blouse. I'm not convinced I could even dig up a red ribbon for my hair."

"In stories, ladies are always dressing in scarlet silks."

"I don't have either scarlet or silk. But the words do sound lovely together."

Max leaned against the edge of his bed and let out a soft sigh. He repeated his argument. "This is an important occasion. We should both be dressed accordingly."

She collected all her restraint and didn't laugh. "Of course. How about I put on something blue?"

"Blue is nice."

"Very well. I'll go change, and when I return, you will tell me I look nice in my blue dress in three different languages of your choice."

Max grinned, and the twinkle returned to his eye. "Then you need to fix your hair, because I haven't learned to lie in French or German."

Pearl pretended to scowl but laughed herself out of the boy's room. Whatever happened at Madame Geneviève's gathering, it was worth seeing Maxwell so animated and happy.

She fastened the blue skirt at her waist, choosing to put on both her underskirts. It was not often she dressed herself as though for company. Madame Geneviève's gathering was reason enough, she supposed, to enhance the silhouette of her dress.

As she brushed through her long, dark hair, she wished someone would come stand behind her and pin it up for her. She was proficient in setting her own hair, but there was a luxury in someone else's hands performing such a personal action. Not a lady's maid or a servant, but someone who loved her. A mother. Maybe, in another kind of life, a sister.

The moment Oliver's face came to her mind, she tried to brush the thought away. But the idea of his hands caressing her hair was too lovely to ignore, so she allowed herself to sink into the waking dream as she looked into the glass. She saw her expression and knew all her secret feelings were laid bare.

She spent a few extra moments performing a more complicated twist than she would normally do, and in a fit of silly pride, she pulled some curling strands loose to frame her face. According to the papers, it wasn't a fashionable look this year, but she knew it suited her. And she hoped Oliver would notice.

Satisfied that Maxwell would not need to lie about her appearance in any language, she hurried across the hall to his room, performing her knock as she pushed open the door.

One step into the room and she stopped. Oliver stood in front of Maxwell's looking glass, pressing a damp hand to his own hair and combing it over to the side to match the boy's.

"Much better," Maxwell said with a smile. "You look ready for company now." Turning to Pearl, the boy said the most unnecessary words: "See how nice Oliver looks."

As if she could take her eyes from him.

Pearl wondered how she'd breathed easily only a moment before. Now, with Oliver standing so close and his hand on hers, her heart pounded in her throat, and she had to think carefully about how her legs supported her.

How long did she stand there blinking up at Oliver? She thought it would be a wonderful idea to continue for hours. Days, perhaps. She'd never felt so sympathetic to the fainting heroines in the novels she and Nanette enjoyed. There were situations to which fainting was the perfect response.

Maxwell interrupted her reverie. "You look lovely in your blue dress." Then he repeated the sentiment in French and in German. His pronunciation was decent, and his expression seemed sincere.

Oliver leaned close and whispered, "He's right. You look truly lovely."

Pearl forced her eyes from Oliver's smiling face. She gave Max a curtsy. "Thank you. Merci. Danke."

Without waiting for more language tutoring, Maxwell went on. "Oliver hasn't met Madame Genevieve yet. It's only good luck he's already met Misty."

Beside her, Oliver murmured, "Very good luck indeed."

She turned and almost convinced herself it was only to be polite as she asked him a question. Not to stare into his deep brown eyes.

"Does your uncle know you're coming to the gathering?"

Oliver laughed. "I didn't receive a formal invitation, but I imagine he knows I've dressed for the evening. Nothing goes unnoticed by Jenkinson. I only hope Uncle Arthur doesn't toss me out into the rain when he finds me in the parlor."

Max shook his head. "Of course he won't."

The look that passed between Oliver and Pearl suggested neither of them was quite as certain as the boy.

Pearl thought she knew how to secure Mr. Ravenscroft's

permission for Oliver's attendance tonight. She excused herself from the room for a moment, promising a quick return.

Her knock at Madame Genevieve's door was answered quite differently from the day before. The voice Pearl now thought of as Madame Genevieve's performance tone wafted into the hall, slow and deep and mournful. "Do come in, my dear."

The spiritualist sat at her dressing table, several candles surrounding her, staring at her reflection. She caught Pearl's eye in the glass and waved her inside. With a gesture from a heavily braceleted arm, she pointed to an empty chair. In the same slow murmur, she said, "Make yourself comfortable."

Pearl wasn't in the mood for polite small talk. Any remaining awe she felt for Madame Genevieve was simply respect for the drawn-out game the woman was playing. "I don't want to bother you while you're getting ready for a show. I need a favor."

The woman raised one eyebrow as if in question but didn't break character.

"Mr. Waverley and his uncle are not on good terms. If you could speak for Oliver's welcome at your performance this evening, I think Mr. Ravenscroft would accept his presence more readily."

A hum rumbled low in Madame Genevieve's chest. "It is not my place to manipulate dear Arthur's feelings and opinions."

Pearl crossed one hand over the other on her lap and smiled softly. "We both know that's not true. Manipulating his feelings is precisely what you've come for."

Madame Genevieve avoided responding to Pearl's comment by facing the mirror and picking up a cosmetic pencil to darken her eyebrow. With a hint of a smile, Madame Genevieve perfected the curve of her brow and tilted her chin in the barest of nods.

Pearl took the gesture as assent. "We understand each other, I believe."

Madame Genevieve answered Pearl through the mirror. "Half

of that statement is true. We do, in fact, understand each other. And when you finally believe, my efforts here will have been met with success."

Pearl smiled as she stood. "You've certainly got your work cut out for you if that's what you're waiting for. Focus your attentions on Mr. Ravenscroft, receive your payments, and enjoy performing your routine. That is more than enough to keep anyone busy. And thank you in advance for encouraging Mr. Ravenscroft to welcome Oliver."

Madame Genevieve's voice drifted through the room and followed Pearl to the door. "Keep your mind open to all possibilities."

Pearl closed the door softly behind her. When she returned to Maxwell's room, she stopped at the threshold. Max sat in his chair by the fire reading aloud from the adventure story he and Pearl were enjoying. Oliver sprawled on the floor at his feet, his own long legs stretching almost into the fireplace. He leaned back on his elbows, his face turned toward Max with a look of absolute delight spread across his features.

To see these two together, relaxed and happy and well, swelled Pearl's heart beyond measure.

She watched quietly as Max read a difficult passage flawlessly. Oliver hung on his every word.

Only the tolling of the clock in the upper hall stole Pearl's attention away from the sight. She would have been happy for time to stop completely, but the evening was only beginning.

Pearl coughed softly. The other two turned to the door. Oliver leaped from the floor with enviable energy, and Pearl smiled to think she was the reason for his eagerness.

"We ought to go down and take our places," she said, reaching for Maxwell.

The boy took her by one hand and Oliver by the other and tugged them out of his room.

As they walked to the stairs, Oliver glanced at Pearl over

Maxwell's head. She felt glad about the extra care she'd taken to make herself presentable.

"What are we calling this event we're taking places for?"

Max looked up and answered him. "The gathering."

Oliver's answering chuckle sounded nervous. "Gathering of what?"

"Ghosts. Restless spirits." Max spoke as if such things were obvious. Commonplace.

Pearl was not so caught up in the delight of Oliver's presence that she couldn't respond to a teaching moment.

"Maxwell, we don't know what Madame Genevieve has planned. Whatever it is, we will enjoy the performance and treat your grandfather's guest politely. And when it is finished, she'll return to the city."

A day ago, Pearl might have been relieved to see the end of Madame Genevieve's stay, but she realized she'd grown fond of the woman. If anyone asked, she would admit she liked Madame Genevieve quite a lot, fraud or not.

Oliver grinned over Maxwell's head at Pearl. "I'll finally meet my uncle's guest."

"Even when you see her, you might not believe her."

CHAPTER 26

Oliver clutched the handrail as he walked with Pearl and Max down to the main floor. He knew at any moment he might become so absorbed in staring at Pearl that he'd tumble down the steps. Not that he was in the habit of losing his equilibrium, but Oliver was in definite danger of falling for this woman.

Danger? No. He could admit it to himself. He'd already fallen.

None of them spoke as they made their way through the entryway and down a hall that seemed to curve and twist rather than turn at a normal angle.

Gaslight sconces burned so low that their glow centered near the middle of the walls, leaving the floor and ceiling in darkness. The yellow light flickered, seeming to beckon to Oliver.

Max tugged on his hand and pulled him through a wide doorway. Inside, the room was golden with candlelight. A shimmering, flickering glow hovered over every surface, covering tables and spreading over the fireplace mantel, even pooling on the floor. The effect was magical. Oliver was sure he'd never been in this room before, but in any other state the space would be unrecognizable.

Whatever was happening at Shadowbrook tonight was unlike anything he was prepared for.

He looked at Pearl, and the shining candlelight reflected in her eyes. He wanted nothing more than to take her in his arms and stare into those eyes for hours. Forever.

Maxwell pulled Oliver deeper into the room and out of his daydream.

"This is Madame Genevieve."

Oliver turned and stared. The woman's hair hovered around her head like an orange cloud, and she was dressed as a stage performer. She took Oliver's hand and pressed it between her own, and he felt the imprint of her thick rings on each of his fingers.

"At last we meet." Each word came slowly, with a deep warble. "Mr. Oliver Waverley, heir to the blessings and challenges of Shadowbrook House."

What was he supposed to say to that? "Erm, hello."

She smiled from behind a shocking layer of facial cosmetics, and Oliver realized he had no idea how old Madame Genevieve might be, or how likely he'd be to recognize her out of her current costume. Whatever her age or natural aspect, she certainly had strong hands. He wanted to squirm out of her grip.

"Your mind is consumed with trivial matters. Open yourself to the portals of the infinite. If you allow it, you'll see wonders tonight."

She spoke so slowly Oliver had time for a hundred thoughts during the performance of each of her sentences. The most obvious of his thoughts was a wish to get free of this woman's clutch and leave this room.

Maybe she read his mind—or his face—because she released his hand. Oliver took a large step away from her and hoped no one was watching him. He didn't want to be rude, but he had no wish to let her look that closely into his eyes as if there was a message inside she could discover.

His long step away wasn't long enough. Madame Genevieve reached out and caught him by the sleeve, deftly steering him to the couch where his uncle sat, stiff and glowering, staring toward a wall.

"Dear Arthur, as I've told you, the forces of the universe have continued to work together to bring healing to this house and all who dwell within. How else would you explain the presence of both your dearest nephew and myself at this auspicious moment?"

Oliver wasn't sure what was auspicious about this moment, but he could explain his presence quite easily. He'd be wherever Pearl was as long as he could manage it.

His uncle didn't answer, so maybe Oliver didn't need to say anything either. He glanced over to see Pearl watching him. He sent her a look he hoped telegraphed his embarrassment and his wish to be standing nearer to her. At that instant, a clap of thunder shook the walls, and rain began to pound on the windows. As far as dramatic effect was concerned, it couldn't have been better timed if they'd been standing on a stage.

Oliver watched Maxwell step close to Pearl's side and throw his arms around her waist.

He reminded himself he was not envious of a little boy. He was not.

Turning back to Uncle Arthur, Oliver saw the old man watching him. Had he seen Oliver's expression of yearning? He must have noticed the look that passed between him and Pearl.

And why should he not see? There was no reason Oliver couldn't find happiness with a lovely and intelligent woman who happened to be an employee of his uncle's household. He had nothing to feel ashamed of. He simply hoped he wouldn't have to discuss his feelings with his uncle without hours of mental rehearsal first.

But this moment required someone to speak.

"Uncle, I thank you for welcoming me to the party."

Uncle Arthur looked unblinking into Oliver's face. He did not smile. He did not offer his hand.

Oliver attempted not to fidget under his stare.

Moments that felt like years passed before the medium laid a hand on Uncle Arthur's shoulder. Her tremulous voice flowed through the room. "What a joy to have you with us for this special evening."

Joy, was it? Nobody looked particularly joyful to him.

The scarf-draped woman lifted her arms as though she hoped a bird would perch there. "We shall now all take our seats. Pearl, this is your place." She pointed to a small sofa, and when Pearl sat in the center, the woman gestured to the side until Pearl moved over. "Maxwell, dear, you are here beside your grandfather."

Max settled himself much closer to Arthur than Oliver would have ever dared. The boy was comfortable with the old man in a way Oliver had never been. He wished he might have been so brave in his childhood. He knew it was too late now.

"Mr. Waverley," Madame Genevieve drawled. His name sounded far different in her voice than it did in Pearl's. "You will take the seat beside Miss Ellicott." She held his eye long enough to send him a tiny smile. What was the smile for? Did she think she knew something about Oliver's heart? About his hopes? He'd prefer it if the strange woman would ignore him.

As he walked to his designated seat, the little dog emerged from beneath the divan and leaped into the spot Madame Genevieve had pointed him toward. Pearl scooped the dog into her arms.

Oliver sat next to Pearl, and Misty leaped onto his lap, standing on hind legs with front paws on his shoulders and licking his chin. So much for sending a signal of sophistication. Pearl shifted, and Oliver was unsure whether he was more embarrassed or more pleased that the small couch allowed him no extra room. Even as one of his legs pressed against the side of the sofa, the other touched Pearl's skirts. Though they were not as full as those the fashionable women in London wore, the cloth still took up much of the space on the couch. Oliver felt a flush rise into his cheeks as Pearl shifted again and the blue fabric of her skirt covered part of his leg. The dog walked a circle over his thighs and then curled into a ball.

Oliver looked up at the rest of the people in the room,

surprised to see Jenkinson and Mrs. Randle sitting in chairs placed between the couches to form a circle. The young maid Violet was perched on the edge of her seat, looking excited. The cook sat with her arms folded across her chest. Another maid and two young footmen seemed to be feeling a range of emotions from willingness to dread.

Madame Genevieve began to speak, moving around the circle of seated guests. She fluttered and jangled and spoke some nonsense about opening hearts and minds to the mysteries of the beyond. She widened her circuit and stepped to the gaslight knob on the wall. With what had to be a practiced touch, she turned the gas down as far as it would go, leaving the sparkling candles as the only light source in the room. The rainfall outside sounded louder in the sudden quiet.

Without actively paying attention, Oliver heard the next words the woman spoke. "Only in this way will you be prepared for what is asked of you."

He leaned closer to Pearl and whispered, "What is being asked of me? I wasn't listening."

In answer, she placed a finger to her lips. Oliver knew the gesture was telling him to be silent, but instead it reminded him how soft those lips felt when she brought them to his own.

The smile he gave her likely hid none of his thoughts. She looked away, but not before he saw her answering smile.

"As everyone knows," Madame Genevieve intoned, standing in the center of the gathered seats, "the souls of our departed beloved remain in our realm for as long as they are needed, or for as long as they feel the desire."

Oliver leaned close to Pearl again, just for the pleasure of whispering in her ear. "Does everyone know this? It's the first I've heard of it."

Pearl gave him another smile, but quicker this time, before she turned her attention back to Madame Genevieve. Was Pearl simply being polite to a guest, or did this woman's patter mean something to her?

He might as well listen so he could discuss the charade with Pearl once it was over. He couldn't stop his smile, though, so he decided it best to keep his eyes off the performance, just in case Madame Genevieve could read his doubt and amusement.

Oliver's eyes traveled the circle, taking in each expression. One footman still appeared wary, and the older of the maids looked frightened. She sat straight against her chairback and twisted a handkerchief between her hands as if she needed to wring precious drops of water from it.

Maxwell was attentive, his hands pressed into the tops of his thighs and his eyes focused on Madame Genevieve's face.

Madame Genevieve was still in full flow, arms waving and voice warbling.

He shifted in his seat and looked at his uncle. Arthur Ravenscroft's brow was furrowed, his mouth pulled down. There was no better description of that face than *stormy*. Was the old man regretting his decision to bring this stranger into the house, to let her direct the activity of the evening?

Oliver watched his uncle for a long moment, noticing the stiffness with which he held himself. Whatever the purpose of this evening's event, it didn't make Arthur Ravenscroft comfortable.

Madame Genevieve crossed in front of Uncle Arthur and seated herself on his other side. "Now, as we focus our energy on our most treasured memories, we must join hands in a circle of connection."

She raised her hands in front of her, looking for all the world as though she was ready to be handed a tray. When nothing happened, she glanced to the footman at her left. He slowly reached out and took the woman by the tips of her beringed fingers. Oliver felt a wave of relief that he was seated opposite the strange woman. Not to mention beside Pearl.

He held his hand out to her, and Pearl slid her fingers into his as if the action wasn't an absolute miracle. Her hand felt perfect within his, small but strong, soft and sure.

He looked to his other side. Mrs. Randle stared straight ahead, making no move to link herself to him. On the other side of the housekeeper, Violet held her hand out like an offering. Oliver wondered if Madame Genevieve recognized what a bold request it was to require this group of people to make physical contact.

He slid his right arm across the space between himself and Mrs. Randle so she only had to clasp the hand in front of her. She made the move quickly, placing her hands atop the two reaching toward her. The housekeeper was still visibly uncomfortable, but at least she'd completed the assignment, and Oliver knew how much Mrs. Randle valued completing assignments.

"And now, as we are all physically connected, let us close our eyes and take a moment to consider our spiritual bonds."

Oliver didn't know what that was supposed to mean, but Madame Genevieve didn't elaborate. She simply bowed her head and breathed audibly and slowly. The others stayed silent.

The rain continued to fall, and a low whisper of wind encircled the house.

Glancing once more around the room, Oliver thought how little attachment he felt to most of these people. But when his eyes landed on Maxwell, his mind settled. The boy's charming demeanor and sweetness, his intelligence and humor had captured Oliver from the moment they first met. Even though they'd only known each other for a few days, Oliver felt sure Maxwell was his one relation for whom he felt immediate, easy love.

He purposely did not look at his uncle. There was nothing easy about his feelings where the old man was concerned, and he'd rather consider someone else.

What exactly did Madame Genevieve mean by spiritual bonds? A connection between one mind and another? A bridge formed across the space between two people? Oliver hoped such a connection was forming between him and Pearl.

He had never worked so hard in his life to stay still. No one else was moving, and he knew he must do the same. He found himself breathing in the same rhythm as Madame Genevieve. He wondered if she intended all the guests' breath to align. Maybe that was why her inhales and exhales were so loud. Or perhaps she was simply lost in the experience of sitting silently in a room full of silent people.

In the quiet, it seemed as if even the rain softened into near silence.

Oliver snuck another look at the people sitting across from him. Madame Genevieve, head bowed, rocked back and forth slowly. Uncle Arthur sat still and stiff, his eyes closed but his lids fluttering as if straining under the effort of spiritual connection.

Maxwell's eyes were squeezed closed, his nose scrunched up and wrinkled in exertion. Whatever it was he thought Madame Genevieve wanted, Max was giving it his full effort. Oliver risked turning his head to see the others; everyone sat with heads bowed and eyes closed. Had Madame Genevieve given some instruction he'd missed? Did everyone else in the room understand what was supposed to be happening? Finally, Oliver turned his head enough to take in Pearl. As she sat beside him, her long lashes resting on her porcelain cheek, a single tear made its way down her face. With one hand in Oliver's and the other holding onto the young footman sitting on her other side, she had no easy way to wipe the tear away or to hide it.

Oliver loosened his grip on her fingers, but Pearl made no move to release his hand. She simply breathed in and out and let the tear fall.

CHAPTER 27

Pearl felt Oliver's hand loosen around hers and hoped it meant he was relaxing. As much as she understood Madame Genevieve's display was full of bluster, there was a deep peacefulness in the moment of focus and stillness.

As the spiritualist asked them all to consider a moment of joy they experienced with someone who had passed on, Pearl worried. Would thinking about a happy memory with Edgar somehow dishonor the sadness she felt now that her brother was gone? Would her focus on a joyful time they'd shared cause her to release some of her grief? Would such an act mean she missed him less? She understood grief and mourning came about because of love. If she was not grieving, did she no longer love Eddie?

A single glance at Maxwell's face, eyes closed with an intensity that wrinkled his forehead, showed how firmly he was determined to follow Madame Genevieve's instructions. He would do anything in his power if it meant he'd be able to remember the parents he'd never known.

If he was willing to give such mental exertion to the evening's entertainment, Pearl could at least match his effort.

It had been years since she'd allowed herself to sit still and sink into a memory of her brother, that sweet, playful little boy who won her heart the first moment she saw his tiny, tight fists and those astounding baby toes.

The pain of losing him, the agony of being absent when he died, clawed Pearl's heart and threatened to steal her breath. It had been this way all the years since the passing of her family. It was why she rarely let a memory of any of them linger in her mind. But somehow, Eddie's memory felt most tender—both most accessible and most dangerous to her peace.

Each thought of Eddie only made her more conscious of the need of careful observance of Maxwell. She could not allow Death to slink into Shadowbrook and steal Max away the way it had stolen Eddie.

Such comparisons hurt too badly to consider, so she simply never considered them. But now, watching Max work hard to remember people he'd never met, she knew she could spend a moment remembering someone she'd known as well as she knew herself.

She pictured Eddie's face—not as she'd seen it last, but as it had appeared to her for so many days and years before. The way his cheek dimpled when he laughed. How his left eye squeezed almost closed in a wink when his crooked smile stretched across his face. The dark locks that always tumbled over his forehead, no matter how often he slicked them back with water. How his face changed when he lost a baby tooth, and then again when a large one grew in its place. She felt his arms around her neck and could almost recapture the scent of his hair, warm from playing in the garden.

She welcomed these sensations, wishing she could hear him call her name. Wishing she'd been more encouraging as he tried to learn to play a simple song on the piano. Wishing she'd never left him alone.

An unexpected sense of calm flowed around Pearl and rested on her shoulders, a whisper of peace she'd never felt before. Idea more than words, the whisper told her she had done well her work of loving her family. She'd been a good sister, a good daughter. The tragedy of illness was not her fault, and she need not feel guilty for her own survival. She had permission to feel grateful and be glad for the life she was living and the strength she'd cultivated.

Only in a moment so still could she have received such a feeling. On an ordinary day in her usual routine, Pearl would have neither the time nor the inclination to seek out such stillness. In the constant chatter of teaching and playing, she would not have heard the sweet whisper to her heart. If this was what Madame Genevieve meant by reaching beyond the earthly plane, Pearl was grateful for it. She felt a tear roll down her cheek and knew it for a sign of growth and healing.

A few more quiet moments passed before Madame Genevieve called the members of the circle back to attention. She looked directly at Pearl when she said, "I do hope your sincere efforts were rewarded."

Pearl couldn't credit Madame Genevieve for any of the feelings she had, but the woman had arranged the setting in which she was able to feel them. She gave the spiritualist a small, heartfelt smile.

Their moment of unspoken communication was interrupted by the younger of the footmen, Steven.

"Well? When do you raise the ghosts?"

It may have been what many of them were thinking, but his question served to snap them all out of the reverie. Everyone shifted in their seats, dropping the hands they'd been holding. Even Oliver loosened his fingers from Pearl's.

Pearl took in the expressions of the people in the circle. Most of them appeared serene in the aftermath of the quiet exercise, but Steven looked impatient. "I thought we'd see something flickering, or tiles would fall from the fireplace. Maybe some of that moaning to shake the walls. That's what you're known for."

Madame Genevieve shook her head. "This is not an entertainment provided for your amusement. We are making a *connection*." She gave the word weight.

Steven muttered something Pearl couldn't hear, but Madame Genevieve continued to speak as if following a script.

"We are not alone here. The room is full not only of voices but also of memories, and what is more eternal than that? Perhaps you received a message this evening. Perhaps you struggled to link yourself with the spirit of one who has passed. I will be available during visiting hours tomorrow and every day I stay here at Shadowbrook to discuss your experience. And now I will share mine."

The woman shifted and resettled herself on the couch, her plumage and her bluster making Mr. Ravenscroft seem to fade into the furniture. "The clear message I received tonight is that Shadowbrook House requests a party. Not just any party, but a formal Christmas dinner."

Pearl looked around the circle. If Madame Genevieve was expecting her suggestion to be met with excitement, she would be disappointed. All the adults in the room looked some shade of dismayed, and none more so than Mr. Ravenscroft.

The response to her announcement didn't deter Madame Genevieve. "The house communicated to me how long it's been without such a celebration. We shall commence preparations immediately."

Pearl, no longer shocked by Madame Genevieve at this point, was still surprised at the command the woman took in a situation that was not hers to lead.

All eyes turned to Mr. Ravenscroft, and the old man lowered his chin to his chest. Was it a nod of assent? Was he slumped in defeat? It was impossible to tell.

The silence carried into another uncomfortable minute.

When the tension grew to an almost unbearable degree, Maxwell burrowed himself into his grandfather's side. "I've never been to a Christmas party."

The boy's simple words sealed the arrangement. All else was detail.

Madame Genevieve stood, sweeping her arms in one of her characteristic dramatic gestures. "Young Maxwell, I am confident everyone present will work together to give you the most enchanting Christmas party that has ever been."

Those words seemed as much a dismissal as they were likely to get, so everyone stood. The maids and footmen hurried from the room, and Jenkinson took his place at the door.

Oliver leaned close to Pearl. "Would you excuse me? I believe I might need a moment for myself on the porch."

Pearl looked into his eyes, surprised at the churning feeling she saw in their depths. Had he experienced something as peaceful and as profound as she had? If so, she could not begrudge him a moment alone to process it.

"Of course," she said, smiling at him. "Take all the time you need." She glanced at the rain pattering against the windows. "Don't stray too far from the porch, though."

He followed her gaze, then returned her smile with one of his own.

She watched him slip from the room even as Maxwell slipped his hot little hand into hers.

"A Christmas party, Pearl," he breathed in awe. "Just like in a story. Won't it be wonderful?"

They left the parlor and made their way through the maze of hallways until they arrived at the main staircase, Maxwell chattering the whole time. "Did you hear voices as we sat in the quiet? I did. Someone spoke to me about making a new set of memories in the house. Someone else told me to keep to my bed until I've grown stronger. A voice told me there was enough to sustain us in the house for as long as we wish to stay here." He sounded rather breathless with excitement, and Pearl was sure it would take some time for him to calm enough to fall asleep. She was more than happy to listen to his sweet prattle with one ear. Her mind was full of thoughts of her own.

At the bottom of the stairs, Maxwell tugged her hand. She tugged back in the game they often played, the back and forth of swinging arms and shared jokes. But then, instead of telling her what he'd thought of Madame Genevieve's gathering or mentioning an interesting thing he'd thought of, Max pulled on her arm hard.

His sudden wheeze was a wounded sound, the gasp of a frightened animal. In a matter of seconds, Maxwell had folded his arms over his chest and curled around himself, lowering into a crouch and tucking his head. He coughed with a frail, weak sound. Barely a puff of air for all the force he was fighting. He looked as though he was being crumpled by a giant hand, and his gasp for air sounded fruitless and terrifying.

Maxwell rolled to his side, fighting for air.

Time seemed to slow, allowing every horrible thought to enter Pearl's mind and take root there. She somehow knew both what was happening to Maxwell and what would happen in the coming hours. She knew she'd spend days, weeks, maybe longer reliving this moment in sleep and while awake.

Far later than she would have wished, Pearl forced herself into action. She dropped to her knees beside him, clasping her hands together behind his back. She felt his muscles spasm as his chest continued to constrict, Maxwell growing smaller within the circle of her arms.

Would no one come help them? Could the others not hear the wretched struggle for every breath that overtook the boy? Could they not feel the change in the air around them?

No one passed by them. None of the household staff came near the staircase. Pearl and Maxwell might have been the only living souls in the house.

No one noticed Maxwell's suffering except for her. There was no one else to bear witness to his wracking pain. No one who knew as well as she how much his illness cost him. She lifted his body, strangely heavy with the clenching of his muscles, into her arms.

She forced her feet to carry them up the stairs, each step a struggle. It was several long, frightening moments before she realized she was speaking aloud, chanting.

"I'm so sorry, Max. I didn't mean to let it happen. This is all my fault. I took my mind off you and became distracted. I didn't mean to let you become ill. Please forgive me. I will never, never allow it to happen again."

She knew her words were desperate and foolish; she couldn't prevent an attack any more than she could have kept Eddie and her parents from dying of influenza.

She spoke the words anyway, and prayed she could make them true.

CHAPTER 28

Oliver found a relatively dry patch on the porch under the dripping eaves and watched the rain fall.

For all that he had been a skeptic when Madame Genevieve had begun the evening's entertainment, he was not sure he could say the same now that it was over. Watching the tear fall from Pearl's cheek had touched him in a way he had not expected. It had seemed to encourage him to follow Madame Genevieve's instructions and think of someone close to him who had passed.

Unbidden, the memory of his mother's portrait had risen up in his mind, and a stillness had settled over his heart. A wealth of feelings and memories had flooded through him, and while he knew he wanted to share them with Pearl, he also knew he wanted to keep them close to himself for just a moment longer.

He looked around at the crumbling edges of Shadowbrook, at the uneven steps leading to the porch and the tilting, sagging walls. Somehow the effect made him think of his uncle—a man who once had such hard and straight edges, now sinking into himself under the weight of loss and loneliness.

When he owned Shadowbrook, would he hire someone to fix the steps, the porch, the walls? Would he need someone to look after this section of the grounds, or would he do it himself?

When he realized what he was thinking, the idea shocked

him. He wouldn't own Shadowbrook. The Campbell Company would.

But even as the thought entered his mind, he looked around the dark, rainy night and knew this place would always hold a piece of his heart.

Drawing in a deep breath of air cleansed by the rain, he turned back to the house and opened the door.

Instead of sleepy quiet, he found Shadowbrook in an uproar. The maids and footmen ran up and down the stairs, and everyone was shouting. The little dog streaked underfoot. Even Jenkinson, who rarely spoke, was hollering directions toward the back of the house.

Mrs. Randle flitted from kitchen wing to entry twice in the space of only a few seconds. She didn't stop when Oliver called her name.

He turned around looking for an explanation for the chaos and nearly crashed into Violet. He caught the pile of blankets before they slipped from her arms.

"What's going on?"

"It's Maxwell," she said, her breath coming fast. "He's taken ill, and we're all trying to help."

"Ill? Another coughing fit?" Oliver remembered the utter helplessness that had overtaken him when Max had struggled to breathe.

The girl nodded. "A bad one. He's tucked up in his room, and everyone's frightened."

If Maxwell had fallen ill, Pearl would be with him.

"I'll take these up to his room, shall I? And you can help Mrs. Randle down here."

"Thank you, Mr. Waverley." She spun on her heel and ran toward the kitchen wing.

Hugging one side of the staircase, he jogged up toward

Maxwell's room. A footman ran the other way, an empty jug in his hands.

Madame Genevieve stood half in her bedroom and half in the hallway. With her shoulders slumped and her face slack, her gauzy black gown and bright scarves looked garish and out of place.

Oliver didn't stop to ask her any questions. He wouldn't trust her answers.

He walked quickly to Maxwell's open door and put his head inside.

The boy lay tiny in his bed, face pale and drawn, a sheet pulled up to his chin. Pearl stood on the other side of the bed, one hand on Maxwell's head as he wheezed and struggled to pull a breath from the air around him.

Uncle Arthur wasn't there. Oliver wasn't sure if he wanted the old man in the room or not, but something about his absence felt sad and heavy. His presence may have given Oliver some discomfort, but surely it would have helped Maxwell.

Assuming the boy could pay attention to anything but his attempts to fill his lungs.

A footman pushed past Oliver, shoving him into the room. He hurried out of the way as the others mobilized in formation. Pearl set a board across Maxwell's knees, and the footman set a large steaming cauldron on it. One of the maids pulled a fabric sheet over Maxwell's head, tenting him inside with the vessel of hot water.

The raspy cough was muffled from within the makeshift tent, but in a moment, Maxwell seemed to take in a breath with less effort.

Pearl looked toward the door and locked eyes with Oliver. He set the blankets down on a nearby chair, feeling useless and unhelpful. She walked across the room and took his hand, leading him into the hall.

"What happened?" He knew he sounded desperate, but the upheaval frightened him. "Is Max all right?"

"Not yet. It was terrible. The poor boy. He enjoyed the evening so completely, but the excitement must have been too much for him. We were almost to the stairs. He dropped to the floor, Oliver. His chest collapsed, and he hit the ground like a wet woolen blanket. The sound of his wheezing—it's the worst it's been. I'll never forget the sound . . ."

Oliver knew nothing he said would be helpful, so he stood there quietly, one arm wrapped around her waist, the other hand sliding up and down the length of her neck. She continued to speak, allowing Oliver to form a picture of Maxwell's attack and the frenzy of the house.

She didn't ask any questions, and didn't appear to require any verbal response from him.

If what Pearl needed was a support, he'd be that for her.

But he would do whatever it took to remove Maxwell from this house before Shadowbrook killed the boy.

CHAPTER 29

With Oliver next to her, the work of the night felt easier: keeping her vigil at Maxwell's bedside, watching his small, weak chest rise and fall in almost immeasurable increments, listening for the slightest change in his breathing. Each wheeze, each weak bark of coughing fell on her ears like an alarm. Maxwell slept fitfully, moans and gasps startling him into frightened wakefulness before exhaustion covered him again.

Pearl had no idea what she said to Oliver as he'd held her against his chest, but the release of the words helped her breathe easier.

The tolling of the magnificent clock on the landing above reminded her once again to rinse the cloth she used to wipe the boy's brow. How many hours had passed in that darkness?

Oliver stood from his chair two or three times through the night to place another small log on the fire, keeping the room warm but not too hot. He hadn't spoken, and as much as Pearl loved the sound of his voice, she was grateful for the quiet. She needed to keep all her attention focused on Maxwell.

Hour after hour, she heard only the snap of logs in the fire, the tolling of the clock, and the quiet echoes of the keening violin music she'd heard when she searched the storage room for candles.

As if the house saw her pain and wept for her. As if it knew she could not allow herself the indulgence of tears.

By an almost imperceptible increment, the room began to lighten. The painting of a ship in harbor came into focus first, then the darkest damp patch of wallpaper against the west wall. If the weak light was any indication, they were in for a stormy day. She heard the maids' gentle noises as they moved along the hallway.

"Good morning," Oliver whispered.

She turned to him and smiled, not sure she could command her voice to make a sound.

"I can imagine you've long been wanting me gone, but I can't bring myself to leave. I hope it's all right I stay a bit longer."

Pearl nodded and stretched her hands toward the fire. "He might not wake for a long time yet."

"But when he does, you'll be here."

Pearl looked at Oliver. "I will always be here."

He nodded. "Here by his side. But not always here in this place." His glance around the room suggested he found it less than ideal.

She couldn't exactly argue with that, but she'd made the room as comfortable as possible for the boy. "We can't move him, so this is where he'll stay. By extension, I'll stay as well."

"You say we can't move him, but the journey to the city isn't bad at all. I've recently taken it myself, remember? As has Madame Genevieve. And of course, Max won't travel the same way I did. If a train is too much noise and rush, a few days of slow travel on decent roads and we'll have him in the hands of the finest doctors anywhere."

Oliver was a very good man, but he couldn't possibly understand Max's situation. He didn't live here. He was only a visitor. "Maxwell already has a doctor. And he'll be here later today."

She knew he thought Dr. Dunning's lifelong service in the surrounding small villages made him appear something of a rustic, and maybe he was, but Pearl had grown to trust the man almost as much as Mr. Ravenscroft did.

"I know Dr. Dunning is a friend of my uncle's, and there's comfort in that. But he can't know everything the specialists have learned, even if he's in contact with doctors who have treated people like Max."

"There are no people like Max." Her words rushed out of her with heat and passion despite her exhaustion. She took a breath, knowing she would have to make an effort to restrain herself from snapping at Oliver. Her temper would only stretch thinner as the days of Maxwell's illness continued.

Oliver touched her arm. "I know. He's unique. And he's special to me too. But there are others who suffer with similar symptoms, and there are doctors who have treated many, many patients with similar illnesses. Doctors who have worked for years to discover which treatments are most successful under which sets of circumstances."

Pearl looked at the boy in the bed, motionless and pale. "I can't risk moving him, even if Mr. Ravenscroft would allow it. And he won't, Oliver. He refuses to take Max away. Maybe it's only a matter of time before Dr. Dunning's experience catches up with those city doctors."

"It doesn't seem we have time for a hope like that. Maxwell's situation feels too urgent to wait on the local village doctor to suddenly become a highly qualified specialist."

His words filled her with a desperate wish to both speed up time and slow it down. She fisted her hands at her sides. "Why is it so impossible for things to turn around? Fate can be kind. It has been in the past." Not very often, and not lately. But she could remember times when it was true.

Oliver's expression softened. "I hear what you're saying about removing Max from the house. But we really ought to get him out of this room. He's so vibrant and happy when he's exploring. Let's get him into new corners of the old place."

She shook her head. "Not when he's this low. He might stay in his bed for weeks or longer."

"Not a couch in a warm parlor? Not at a window with a river view?"

"All I can tell you is he demands to stay here. He says this is where he must be. It was his mother's room. It's held generations of Ravenscrofts. He says the room needs him, and I don't wish to argue with him about it."

Oliver gave Pearl a troubled look, but she was too tired to attempt to interpret it.

He took her by the hand. "I don't want to argue. It doesn't help Maxwell. Let's agree to see how the visit with Dr. Dunning goes, and if he feels confident his treatments will help, we'll hold off on seeking another opinion for a few weeks. Meanwhile, we can take him to other spaces in the house as he rests. Does that sound fair?"

Frustrated that he felt he had a right to an opinion on Maxwell's medical care, Pearl wavered between wanting to tell him to mind his own concerns and wanting to fall into his arms. He was so sure he was right, but what could he know? His confidence in these unknown city specialists must come from somewhere.

But he wanted to bargain with her, to negotiate, which suggested he was willing to give her ideas some credit.

The thought made her smile.

His answering smile made hers grow larger.

He lifted one hand and, with the lightest touch, drew a finger along the side of her mouth. "Ah, this is very good to see. Everything will turn out all right in the end. You'll see. Just relax."

His hands ran up and down the length of her sleeves, and she wished she could release her tension simply because he asked her to.

"I'm not sure I can do that. I need to stay attentive. I need to be responsive. Just in case." She couldn't say aloud *just in case what.* "I really believe things will get better. But they're not better yet. I'm not saying I expect anything to suddenly become perfect. I just want one good thing to happen today, and if I look away, I might miss it, Oliver."

Before she had finished saying his name, he brought his lips to hers. First, a feathery light touch, a memory of a dream. Then, when she lifted herself up on her toes to get closer to him, he wrapped his arms around her, kissing her fully and deeply.

When he pulled gently away to look at her face, he was smiling. "How's that for one good thing?"

Pearl heard a giggle from the doorway and pulled herself away from Oliver's embrace. Violet held a covered tray in both hands, so there was no way for the girl to hide her huge grin.

"I've brought breakfast for you all."

Pearl looked to the window. A shaggy tree whipped against the speckled glass.

"It hardly seems morning," Oliver said.

Violet, still grinning, set the tray on a table holding a puzzle box and several books.

"Mrs. Randle hoped Maxwell would be able to eat something this morning, so she's included all his favorites."

The softest white scones, still steaming from the oven, were surrounded by jars of bright fruit preserves. The cream pot was as full as Pearl had ever seen it. An apple, sliced into circles the way Maxwell liked best since he first grew enough teeth to eat them, lay piled in the center of the tray, and a cup of hot chocolate, full to the brim, awaited the boy's waking.

Pearl patted Violet's shoulder. "You've all been very busy this morning. Thank you."

"Anything for little Maxwell," she said, smiling.

Pearl knew the difference in age between Max and Violet was smaller than the girl thought, but Violet's body was strong and robust. Maxwell's thin arms and sloped shoulders made him look small enough that he must have appeared very young to Violet's eyes.

"Did Mrs. Randle mention when she expects the doctor to arrive?" Pearl asked, avoiding Oliver's eye.

Violet shook her head. "I heard her say no news had come from the doctor in the night. Maybe there's word now that it's daylight."

The day had still not lightened much, but Pearl nodded in shared hope. "Will you let me know what you learn about the doctor's plan?"

After Violet agreed and left the room, Oliver came to stand close to Pearl's side again. He spoke in a hushed tone. "He's sleeping so peacefully. Do you think Max would mind if we shared some of his breakfast?" He gestured to the tray brimming with more food than the three of them could comfortably finish.

"I didn't think I'd feel hungry, but I'll admit, the smell of those scones has my stomach singing."

"Why don't you sit here?" Oliver pulled the chair she'd spent the night in close to the fire. "I'll prepare you a plate."

Pearl was so surprised at the offer she didn't even think to argue. She should be the one to serve him, but he moved quickly to the table and pulled open a scone. "Jam first or cream first? Think before you answer. This is a very important question."

"Indeed it is, because if you did it wrong, I'd need to close my scone, turn it upside down, and eat it bottom to top."

"Ah, Miss Ellicott, you haven't answered my question, but you've taught me some things about yourself."

"Have I? And what might those things be?"

Oliver wagged a finger toward her. "Answer first, then I'll tell you."

"Cream first, obviously." Her smile grew wider by the word.

With a sigh and a shake of his head, Oliver prepared her

scone. "And here I thought you were the perfect woman. A shame you eat backward." He spread a generous measure of clotted cream over the scone and topped each half with a dollop of bright, sweet preserves. Handing her the plate, he smiled his forgiveness for her silly preference.

Pearl laughed softly. "I suppose you consider your way the proper way."

"Only because it is," he replied, spreading his jam and then spooning on a dollop of cream.

It took some mighty self-restraint for her to wait for him to finish preparing his own breakfast treat before she picked hers up and took a bite. It was as delicious as it appeared, and Oliver had overdone the toppings in the most generous way.

Between bites, she asked him what it was he thought he'd learned about her.

"First and most important, that you are the kind of woman who will allow me to be of service to you." He settled himself so his food was in easy reach and he could look directly at Pearl. "The trouble with a person of your competence is that you are perfectly capable of doing all things yourself. I imagine you're used to it. But you allowed me to prepare your food."

She was eager to know more of what he thought he'd discovered, but he took another bite of his jam-first scone, so she had a moment to ponder his comment. He wasn't wrong about her abilities. Nor about her habits.

It was her practice as well as her duty to perform service. It was what she was paid for. This morning, she was simply too tired to argue with him about the details. But her simple assent meant something larger to Oliver, and she was glad she'd agreed to his offer.

He raised the remaining bit of his scone toward her in a salute. "Second, Miss Ellicott, by your suggestion of closing the scone back up, I learned you prefer to eat each half separately, which suggests you are a person who does not object to more preserves and cream. I am in favor of more preserves and cream as well."

She nodded. "Bread in all its forms is merely a vehicle for whatever goes atop it. And this is a perfect, delicious vehicle."

His answering smile warmed her.

Without a word of warning, he reached across the short distance between them and touched his finger to the corner of her mouth, wiping a spot of sweet, sticky jam from her lip. A jolt of pleasure ran along her spine at the unexpected intimacy of his touch.

She couldn't take her eyes from Oliver's face. The moment required her to say something, so she asked if there was anything else he'd learned about her.

One of his dark eyebrows quirked in an arc that mirrored his smile. "At least one more thing."

"Oh, dear. Your expression worries me. Will I hate what I hear next?"

He made a show of lowering his brow and softening his smile. "I certainly hope not."

She smoothed the fabric of her skirt over her legs. "All right then. No fear. I shall bear your revelation, whatever it is."

Oliver leaned close and took both Pearl's hands in his own. "Just this: It's clear to me you're comfortable with us getting to know each other's secrets, at least a few of them. I see this as a good sign of things to come."

After so much practice disagreeing with Oliver, one corner of Pearl's brain wanted to argue that Oliver had discovered a few of Pearl's habits, but that didn't mean he'd unearthed anything secret. And she'd learned little or nothing about him. But the better part of her mind was full of Oliver's gaze, the warmth of his strong hands wrapped around hers, and the way his smile tugged the left corner of his mouth higher than the right. Not to mention his deep brown eyes, which were currently staring straight into her soul.

She had no practice speaking of such things to a man. When she talked of moments like this with Nanette, the subjects of their discussion were always fictional. But Oliver had opened himself to her. He had made, if not a declaration, at least a suggestion of a future for the two of them.

Pearl needed to say something. More, she wanted to. She tried to think of a clever response, but all cleverness was drowned in a flood of exhaustion. The best she could do was nod. "A good sign indeed."

Oliver still held both her hands in his. His expression turned solemn. "There's something I want to discuss with you, and I hope you'll keep an open mind."

Was he going to say what she thought he might say? If this were a story, this would be a perfect moment for him to make some sort of avowal.

It's not a story, she reminded herself.

"My mind is open," she said. As soon as the words were out of her mouth, she asked herself if her words were true. She was certainly open to discussion about some things.

Before Oliver could say anything, a gasp and a wheeze from Maxwell pulled Pearl's attention to the other side of the room.

Immediately, she was on her feet and at the boy's side. His eyes, still closed, seemed to dart from side to side beneath his lids.

A change in Maxwell's condition—but was the change positive or negative? Only time would tell. And she would stand beside him at every moment. She would not allow herself to become distracted, not even by someone as lovely as Oliver. No alteration in Maxwell's situation would happen without her notice from here on.

CHAPTER 30

Oliver stood at Pearl's shoulder, watching and waiting. He kept thinking she'd turn back to him at any moment. As soon as Maxwell's ragged gasps for breath became smooth. When his arms stopped twitching and rested easily at his sides. When the skin of his face regained some color.

But nothing improved, and Pearl's attention remained riveted on Max.

Logs snapped in the fireplace. Rain rushed down the window glass. Pearl kept her silent vigil, and Oliver was sure he was once more in the way.

Pearl didn't ask him to leave, but did she even realize he was still in the room? After the conversation they'd shared, he knew they'd made progress. He'd practically told her he adored her. That he had considered—hoped—the two of them would have a future together.

Of course, he didn't say the words, not yet. They still needed to get to know each other. This wasn't a hundred years ago when people met at a ball and became engaged the following day.

Oliver was a modern man, exploring the many facets life had to offer him, but the problem with modern life was that nobody had ever experienced it before. All was mystery.

Thirty years ago, his uncle would never have sought employment as Oliver had, and therefore Arthur missed out on some of the physical and intellectual opportunities Oliver now enjoyed. Without his work, Oliver would not have been able to see firsthand the skeletal structure of some of England's most miraculous contemporary buildings. He'd never have climbed a scaffolding and looked down over the city from new heights.

Oliver's grandfather wouldn't have considered selling the family house and creating something useful out of it. Fifty years ago, what was more useful than one's own property, after all? The age of industry changed lives in the best of ways, and Oliver enjoyed stepping into the future.

When he'd searched his heart as carefully as he searched his mind, he'd become more and more aware how much he'd like to take those steps with Pearl at his side. But did she—could she—feel the same?

There was so much Oliver wished to say to Pearl, but the time for talk had passed, at least for now. She seemed to need to stand as close to Maxwell as possible. Now wasn't the time to speak of his own feelings, but he could demonstrate them.

Oliver considered himself a man of action, and it was time to act, even if acting was only being a literal support. He placed both hands on Pearl's shoulders and ran them gently down her arms. With a sigh, Pearl leaned her back against his chest, then took his hands in hers and folded them across her waist.

They stood that way, his heart beating into her back, as they watched the boy in the bed.

No words passed between them, but Oliver hoped they were thinking the same things. Maxwell whimpered and stirred, proving whatever unconscious sleep he was experiencing was less than restful.

Finally, Pearl spoke. "It's been a long time since Max had a fit this exhausting."

Oliver knew he must not interrupt, even though his mind filled with questions. He would let her speak for as long as she wished to.

"There are regular coughing fits like the first one you saw, but those are somewhat controlled. At least he can make eye contact with me as his lungs press his air away." Pearl took a deep breath, and Oliver felt her posture change. He wondered if she was subconsciously breathing deeply on Maxwell's behalf, as if her breathing could fill his weak lungs.

"I help him try to calm himself, and he sees me standing by. I don't think my presence actually makes his stiff airways any looser, but he knows I'm close to him. That I haven't left him."

She moved one of her hands to wipe at her cheek, then returned it across his once again, sealing both their arms around her.

"The lung attacks frighten us both, but I know the end result will be easier breathing. Sometimes a steam tent helps. Sometimes sitting beside an open window. When he manages to catch his breath, he begins to improve." She clutched at his fingers. "But, Oliver, last night was nothing less than terrifying."

Oliver thought of the coughing fit he'd witnessed during one of his early nights at Shadowbrook. Horrible wheezing sounds. Maxwell's staggering steps as he clutched at his chest. The helpless fear Oliver felt on behalf of his little cousin. It startled him to think whatever happened the night before had been so much worse.

"Every stolen breath takes him to a place I cannot follow. His eyes roll back in his head. Each muscle in his body tightens and shakes. When it's over, every part of him is left aching for days."

She reached out and stroked Maxwell's hand, his fingers spasming. Oliver understood now the boy's muscles were still reacting to their ordeal.

He whispered in her ear. "There must be a doctor who understands how these illnesses affect a little body. Surely we can get him safely to the city and into proper care."

Pearl let her arms fall to her sides and stepped out of Oliver's embrace. Without turning to look at him, she said, "I appreciate that you think you've seen enough to allow you to understand what Max needs. But you don't. You can't. There is more to Maxwell's situation than a bit of coughing and some muscle twitches. Your city doctors and surgeons would not have time in their busy schedules and with their dozens and hundreds of patients to come to know the boy. They'd study his symptoms and learn about his illness, but no visit to an infirmary's bedside would allow a medical team to understand what makes him Max."

With her back still turned to him, she wiped at her face again.

Lower, softer, Pearl spoke again. "Not that any of this detail matters. Mr. Ravenscroft will never allow Maxwell to be taken away from Shadowbrook."

Oliver placed a hand lightly on Pearl's arm. She did not turn, but neither did she shake off his touch. "My uncle didn't allow me to come back here, either. I wanted to come, so I came. Some things are too important to wait for permission."

"You're wrong about this. Your uncle knows Maxwell's situation better." She didn't look at him. Every bit of her attention was focused on the boy in the bed. Oliver understood she wished to be alone with Max.

"I'm going to leave you two together for a while. I'll come back."

Oliver quietly stepped out of the room and into the hallway. Looking up, he saw Madame Genevieve standing at her bedroom door, as if she'd spent the night's hours waiting for Oliver to leave Maxwell's room.

"Young man, you look a fright."

The woman's frank assessment of Oliver's appearance might have offended a certain kind of person, but the blunt analysis amused him.

He ran a hand over his disheveled hair. He could use a shave as well. His waistcoat and jacket were rumpled, as he'd been wearing the same clothes since Madame Genevieve's performance. His collar wilted beneath his chin.

"Perhaps I will be more appealing after some rest."

Madame Genevieve pointed toward Maxwell's room. "Stayed in there all night, did you? How's the boy faring today?"

Not a hint of her warbling, wailing tones floated around this conversation. Neither was there any false depth or breathy whisper. This more genuine speech gave Oliver the impression that her question was sincere as well.

Oliver rubbed his forehead, hoping he could push away an ache forming above his eyes. "I wish I could tell you he's improving, but I don't know anything about his illness or his recovery. Pearl is on alert, so there must be something to watch for."

"She didn't rest, did she? Poor girl. It was an emotional night for her." Madame Genevieve glanced over Oliver's shoulder toward the closed door of Maxwell's room as if she could see Pearl through the wood. "She works as hard as anyone I've ever met not to feel her difficult feelings."

The words surprised Oliver. How would this stranger know something like that? Was it true? Was Pearl's calm demeanor merely a way to avoid thinking about what was too painful for discussion?

Nothing in the woman's tone suggested she found fault with Pearl for attempting to mask her hidden pain, but he felt the need to defend her.

"She takes excellent care of Maxwell."

The woman nodded, and her cloud of orange-brown hair floated around her face. "No doubt about it. She's very good at her work. The girl was made to love people. Protection and affection are woven in the very fibers of her character."

Oliver thought that might be a version of a line Madame Genevieve used in her performances, but he wouldn't disagree with the sentiment. How had this stranger come to understand Pearl so well?

"Have you spent a great deal of time observing Miss Ellicott, then?"

Madame Genevieve's eyes crinkled as she smiled. "Not as much time as you have."

He felt the skin of his cheeks heat. "She is a fine, intelligent, and genteel woman."

"And rather beautiful. I should think you'd have noticed."

"Of course I have." Oliver was unsure how the conversation had taken such a rapid shift.

"Your uncle was lucky to find Miss Ellicott to care for the boy."

"He was indeed. Having Pearl here allows him to disappear and still have someone look after Max." If Oliver was trying to hide his resentment, he wasn't doing a very good job of it.

Madame Genevieve tugged at the end of one of the scarves around her neck. "It's true young Maxwell needs the kind of care Pearl can provide. Not like you when you were small. You managed on your own."

Shocked, he said, "Did you speak to my uncle about my time here? Did he tell you I *managed*?" It wasn't a word he would have used. Struggled, maybe. Endured.

"One picks things up in a house like Shadowbrook."

"One does indeed. Gossip and a forced familiarity with solitude."

She made a humming sound of agreement. "Not to mention an occasional cold from the drafts."

Oliver laughed. The sleepless night was beginning to take its toll. He felt himself growing silly with exhaustion.

Madame Genevieve didn't seem tired, though. "You found connection beyond the house. Friends. Other children. You're still close with them."

He couldn't deny it, but her knowledge of his past made him uncomfortable. "Why do you think so?"

"Not hard to see there's something tying you to this place. It's not the house itself. You can't wait to see the building gone. You've got very few happy memories inside these walls. So, whatever it was you loved, you found it outside."

Oliver shook his head, hoping to clear away the cobwebs of sleepiness. "How in the world would you know that?"

Madame Genevieve shrugged. "It's a bit of a talent. Connecting the things I can see with what I know about how human hearts and minds work. How do you think I'm such a success in my work? I can read you. Well, to be honest, not *you* so much as people who are willing to be read. Imagine how much I could know if you weren't so determined to hide from me."

"I'm not hiding."

"You're not terribly honest, either, though, are you? Not that you'd lie. I can see that. But you're keeping much of your heart wrapped up tight. Very much like your Pearl."

Oliver was beginning to realize the woman was much cleverer than he'd imagined, and she had seen more about him than he was entirely comfortable with. He needed to change the subject.

"And are you here to read my uncle? Does he know that's what he's paying you for?" Oliver's questions came out sharper than he'd intended, edged with defensiveness.

"He's been working with me for many years through letters and has shared with me his heart's wishes and regrets. Of course, there is much he will not speak of. I don't believe he is ready to open every door of his memory. But he does not dismiss my gifts. I don't think he'd be shocked to learn I know a great deal about things he never speaks of. Subtext is my specialty."

"That, and scarves."

Madame Genevieve smiled but did not dignify his impertinent

remark with an answer. She kept talking, so Oliver assumed she was unoffended.

"Dear Arthur seeks answers. Connections. Resolution. He's lost so much."

"And you've come here pretending to help him find it? The lost connection?"

Madame Genevieve folded her arms across her chest, a shielding gesture. "Nobody's pretending, Mr. Waverley."

He sighed. "I don't mean to offend you. Clearly something is changing in my uncle. He speaks to Maxwell, spends time with him, and that's more than he ever did with me." The self-pity tasted like vinegar in Oliver's mouth, but he finished saying the words he wanted to speak to her. "I'm confident some of their relationship is due to your influence."

"Very kind of you to say so, but I believe it's all the boy. He's a special child."

The next words Oliver spoke seemed to shoot out of him without passing through his brain first. "Will Max be all right?"

For the first time, Madame Genevieve looked genuinely surprised. "How would I know?"

Oliver stammered and shook his head. "No, of course not. You're not a magician or a prophet. I don't think you're able to see into the future. I didn't mean . . ."

Madame Genevieve put her hand on Oliver's arm and stopped his speech with another serious look. "I do the work of bringing comfort. People wish to see that in different ways. Some like to gather in groups around a table in a dimly lit room and summon the spirits of their beloved dead. Others wish to speak to me alone, cataloging their life's mistakes. Your uncle wishes he could go back in time and heal the gashes in the history of his family, but years of grief have sapped his reserves. He thinks he's got nothing left to offer but protection behind these crumbling walls."

How was it possible this woman knew his uncle so much better than he did?

Oliver sighed in frustration. "Maxwell isn't being kept safe here. The house isn't protecting him from his sickness."

Madame Genevieve nodded. "I understand how you see the situation. But can you see it through your uncle's eyes? You know there's no guarantee the boy would survive a journey to London, and no promise of healing there either."

"Then he should bring a specialist from the city here to the house, someone who can actually help Maxwell heal."

"Arthur isn't eager to welcome strangers to Shadowbrook."

"He invited you."

Madame Genevieve made a gesture with one hand suggesting Oliver was only partially correct. "I'm hardly a stranger. And it wasn't as easy as you make it sound. We've been corresponding for years, and even so, I had my work cut out for me."

"I imagine it wasn't long before you regretted convincing him to bring you to this tumbledown wreck."

"Oh, no. Exactly the opposite. This house is astounding. There are so many memories locked up in the hidden rooms and hallways that I can feel them pressing against my skin. Shadowbrook House is a treasure trove of spiritual energy."

With a shake of his head, Oliver gave a grudging smile. He was beginning to like Madame Genevieve, to understand better how she operated, but this kind of talk frustrated and—if he was honest—frightened him.

"You resist my language, but all it means is the house is steeped in love."

A short laugh escaped him. "If you were to ask anyone who lives or works here what the house is full of, none of them would say love."

"Is that what you think? Maybe you don't know the people who live here as well as you think you do."

The clock in the upstairs hall tolled, and Madame Genevieve smoothed the sleeves of her dress. "I have to meet with your uncle now, if you'll excuse me."

Oliver held out his arm. "I'll join you. I have a few things I'd like to say to him this morning."

The woman shook her head. "This is not the time for your discussion. I suggest you get some rest, then you ought to reach out to those childhood friends we spoke of. Perhaps they'd like to see Shadowbrook again before anyone makes decisions that will change this house forever."

"Are you suggesting I invite people to come and stay? When I myself wasn't even invited?"

Madame Genevieve winked. "It is my intention to make sure you're invited now. If anyone asks, I'll say the house wishes to be filled with young people enjoying the Christmas celebration."

CHAPTER 31

Pearl had often known tiredness, but this was something new. She occasionally stepped away from Maxwell's side, but she'd not rested deeply since he fell ill. Her mind felt aswirl with colors and patterns she'd never seen anywhere but the backs of her eyelids. Flashes of light seemed to stab outward from behind her eyes. Floors tilted. Walls leaned. Edges melted into each other. And all the time, Pearl avoided shutting her eyes for longer than a blink.

She had to.

Someone needed to watch Maxwell.

She saw what happened when she lost focus. His breathing became shallower, his coughs weaker. There was no fight left within him.

She'd witnessed the boy's slow recoveries before, but this one was the most frightening. All signs forced her to consider the very real possibility of no recovery at all. She stood watch at his bedside, trying to ignore his lethargy, his rasping breath, his unwillingness to engage in conversation.

If Maxwell's momentary returns to full consciousness increased, would he wake unchanged?

She tugged at his blanket, patted his shoulder, and ran her hands across his matted hair. Was he truly not waking, or was he pretending to still be asleep?

"Max, sit up. Do eat something. Cook has outdone herself."

A small frown crossed the boy's face, but she could not tell if he was reacting to her words or some internal pain.

Another tolling of the clock, and she spoke to him again, pressing him to get up if only for a few moments.

This time, he cracked his eyelids and looked at her. "Hurts too much."

"Sitting up? I can help you."

He rolled his head side to side. "Not sitting. Being awake." He closed his eyes again. A thin cough turned his body in on itself, and she rubbed circles on his back until his breathing eased somewhat.

Standing beside the bed, his unresponsive hand clutched in hers, Pearl looked to the west wall. Rain cascaded in sheets down Maxwell's bedroom window, the drops silent as they flowed in a constant stream. Nothing outside was visible beyond a vague smudge of greenish gray, a hint of the wintering forest behind waterfalls of rain.

The damp slipped along the inside of the walls as well, rivulets making small bulges in the horrible wallpaper Max wouldn't let her change. He said the house needed the old paper.

A tap at the door spun Pearl around, Maxwell's hand still hanging limp in her fingers. Mrs. Randle stood at the threshold, her hands clutching a piece of paper, her eyes darting from Maxwell's still form to Pearl's bedraggled state and back.

"A letter has arrived." Although she spoke with her usual clipped diction, her voice was a deeper, heavier version of itself than Pearl was used to.

Pearl nodded, wondering why Mrs. Randle would want to distract her from her vigil for such a trifle. Then, through her exhaustion, a thought swam to the surface: The household awaited news.

"Has the doctor sent word? When can we expect him?"

Mrs. Randle made a motion with her head that appeared to be both a nod and a shake, and somehow gave the impression of neither. Pearl must be very tired indeed.

The housekeeper held out the paper. "Mr. Ravenscroft asked me to bring you this."

Pearl lay Maxwell's hand gently on his counterpane and walked to the housekeeper. The floor lurched traitorously beneath her feet, but she made it to the doorway and took the offered letter. Mrs. Randle turned and left.

It was addressed to Mr. Ravenscroft, and before she'd passed the second sentence, Pearl understood the most important things: The message was from Dr. Dunning, but he was not coming to look in on Max.

A wave of dizziness rolled over her, and Pearl clutched the letter and forced herself back across the room and into a chair.

Once seated at Maxwell's side, she waited for the spirals in her eyes to clear before she focused once more on the letter.

My Dear Arthur,

I know my delay in reporting to Maxwell's bedside has you concerned, but it's for the best I've kept my distance. Both my little ones have, for several days, shown signs of an infectious fever, and those awful indications proved true this morning. Elijah and Emma are both suffering greatly, and I fear I would only carry contagion into your house should I come.

In another case, I would recommend immediate removal to the city for you to seek the assistance of any of the specialists I've previously named who would be able to look after Maxwell in a dedicated facility, but I cannot in good conscience suggest travel with the child at this point. All roads will be dangerous in this weather, but none more so than the connecting paths between your home and Southampton.

This profusion of rain will have laid bare many of the river's banks, and even the heartiest horses might slip in the deep mud.

Please, Arthur, send word to one or all of the physicians I've recommended to you. Perhaps one of them will attempt the trip to see your boy.

And, naturally, as my children pull through their bouts of this insidious illness, I'll be at your side the moment further infection is not a danger.

Do take care of yourself, as well, Arthur. Your heart cannot bear many nights of worry like the one you described to me.

My prayers are with you and your household.

Dr. Denton Dunning

Pearl had to read the letter several times before she understood much beyond the doctor's failure to arrive.

Specialists.

Dr. Dunning had recommended—more than once, and possibly many times—the very assistance Oliver suggested, the path to healing Pearl so vehemently rejected. And why did she refuse such help? Because Mr. Ravenscroft assured her no one was better suited to care for Maxwell than Dr. Dunning?

He surely believed it to be true, but the doctor himself seemed firmly set on assistance from the more specialized physicians in the city.

Was it already too late? She looked at the boy lying in bed, pallid and still. She could not be sure he would ever recover his strength.

Pearl set the letter in her lap and took both Maxwell's hands. She began to speak to him in a whisper, slow and gentle words flowing from her as the rain flowed over the window glass.

"Max, my dearest Max. I know your body is tired. I know

this sleep you're in must feel renewing to you. You work so hard every day to stay well, and now you have a chance for rest."

The chair touched the side of the bed, but Pearl was not near enough to the boy. She stood and let the letter fall to the floor. Climbing up into the huge bed, she sat at Maxwell's side. Although she was fearful of disturbing him, she needed to hold him closer. She shifted herself and the boy so his head rested on her leg, and she placed both her hands lightly over his thin chest so she could feel every hint of his shallow breathing.

"Do you still feel such pain? Is there any relief in this sleep?"

She didn't expect an answer, but even so, the lack of any response was disheartening.

"Perhaps you've rested long enough. If it is time to wake, I will be at your side. I will stay with you, as I've always promised, as long as you might have need of me."

She stared at the beloved face, his wide forehead covered with a tumble of wispy curls. His eyebrows, just darker than his hair, in two perfect arches over the wise eyes now closed in what she could only hope was restful sleep. His cheeks, now sunken and sallow, would soon bloom in rosy health. They must. She had to believe it.

Another soft knock at the door pulled her attention away, and for a moment, she felt resentment that anyone would bother her and Maxwell, but then she heard Oliver's voice.

"Pearl? May I come inside?"

She looked toward the door, the walls sliding sideways even as she remained sitting.

Oliver appeared hesitant, keeping himself half in the hallway. "Will it disturb either of you to have me here?"

Pearl managed a shake of her head, which made the room spin again. She raised her hand from Maxwell's chest and placed it to her temple, as if her fingers could steady whatever was slipping inside her.

"Please, do come in. I'm glad to have you here. Take this chair." She knew she should stand to welcome him, but she hadn't the strength to move.

He looked from Max to Pearl with a question in his eyes. "Are you truly glad?"

Pearl sighed in her exhaustion. She attempted a weak smile. "How can you doubt it?"

"I won't doubt any longer, but I need to hear you say the words. I've disappointed you in so many ways, I can't help but worry you'd rather be finished with me."

She swallowed down the urge to cry. "Oh, dear. No. I'm not finished with you at all." She knew the words must sound foolish, but she hoped she could communicate both what she needed to say and what Oliver wished to hear. "I do hope you'll stay with us. With me."

Oliver stepped fully into the room, walking as close to her as he could. He'd changed his suit and possibly bathed. His hair was still damp, and he smelled of something that evoked clean, woody branches in the forest.

Pearl chose not to mention the lovely scent. In her exhausted state, any comment might sound very strange indeed.

Standing at the side of the bed, Oliver reached a hesitating hand to Maxwell's head. The man's large fingers grazed the boy's hair in the gentlest touch. Pearl's throat thickened at the sight of such a tender caress.

Before he took his seat, Oliver moved his hand from Maxwell's head to Pearl's face. With the lightest movement of his fingers, he slipped a dangling lock of her hair behind her ear then leaned close and placed his lips softly, tenderly on her forehead. It was the barest whisper of a kiss, and Pearl knew it would live in her memory as the most loving gesture she'd ever received.

Oliver lingered there, leaning toward her, for almost long

enough. When he straightened and sat in the chair, the air around Pearl grew colder.

He shifted the seat, making it easy for Pearl to look at him without either of them needing to turn awkwardly. His shoe grazed something on the floor.

"What's this?" He lifted the paper at his feet.

"A letter from the doctor. There is illness in his house, and he cannot come to call on Maxwell." Pearl was surprised how much the explanation cost her, both in effort and in spirit. Dr. Dunning was her great hope, and now he could not come to save Max.

Scanning the letter, Oliver was once again on his feet. "I'll go."

"No, please." The pleading in her voice surprised Pearl. She didn't want him to leave them again.

He reached for her hands. "I can ride to Southampton and take a train to London. I'll send messages to these doctors and bring one back with me. Surely someone will come."

Pearl shook her head, but she was no longer saying no. She simply didn't know how to communicate her gratitude to Oliver. His leaving to fetch a doctor was exactly what was needed. Why, then, did she wish it didn't have to be him?

"We could send a footman." Her voice shook, exposing her fatigue.

Oliver placed a finger beneath her chin. "I think you know the boys working here have never been farther than Riverwood. I am familiar with the roads. I have friends and connections in the city. I can discover a willing doctor more quickly than anyone else from the household would be able to do."

Pearl knew the truth of his words, but her chin trembled as she answered. "I don't want you to leave us."

Before she knew he was moving, his arms were around her. At his embrace, strength flowed into her. He whispered into her hair. "I don't want to leave you, not ever. Nothing but Max's well-being could take me from your side. I'll return as soon as I can, and when I'm back, we will see him well. Then we must discuss the future."

He pulled away, and she saw his smile. Whatever picture of the future appeared in his mind, it pleased him.

Oliver bent close to Maxwell's still form. He placed his hand against the boy's cheek. "Hold on, little man. I'll be back soon with someone who will help you. You look after Pearl for me while I'm gone."

As Oliver turned to step away, Pearl clutched at his hand. She drew his fingers to her lips and placed a kiss on his knuckle. "Thank you, Oliver. As much as I wish it didn't need to be this way, I know it's best. Please, be safe. Come back to us."

"I will always return to you."

As Oliver swept from the room and pulled the door closed behind him, the house seemed to sigh as in a release.

CHAPTER 32

Oliver rode hard to Southampton, and, at the station, he quickly sent a telegram to George, pleading with him for his help. He knew George was training as a surgeon, and he hoped his old friend could recommend someone to care for Max. Then he boarded the train soaking wet and covered in mud splatters. He managed a few fitful bouts of sleep, grateful for the hum of constant noise that drowned out too much thought of what and whom he'd left behind at Shadowbrook. Each time he jolted awake, he stared out the window for a familiar landmark.

As the train eventually slowed to a noisy, squealing stop at the London station, Oliver saw George and another man standing on the crowded platform. Case in hand, he stepped out the door before the train had fully halted. He barely heard the grumbling words from the station official as he leaped onto the platform and into the embrace of one of his oldest, dearest friends.

"It is good to see you," George said in his gentle voice. He stepped back from the embrace and gestured to the man beside him. "Matthew Nichols, this is Oliver Waverley. Oliver, this is your cousin's new doctor."

The man looked to be about the same age as Oliver, with an intelligent, confident expression and a quiet demeanor. His dark hair swept over his forehead in a fashionable way, and his coat was cut to perfection.

"He is a good friend of mine," George said, "and he comes highly recommended by two of the specialists you named in your telegram. He is training at a children's hospital specializing in lung disease. It's our good fortune he's available to travel with no notice."

The men clasped hands. "Thank you for attending us, Mr. Nichols. I can't tell you how grateful I am."

"I hope I can help your cousin recover." Nichols smiled, and Oliver could see a serious gentleness in him.

The train journey back to Southampton passed quickly, and Nichols asked intelligent questions about Maxwell's symptoms, and although Oliver didn't know how to answer many of them, he filled in the young doctor as much as possible.

"I'll give your cousin the best care I can manage with my full attention," Nichols said.

George slapped a strong hand against Oliver's leg. "And my humble assistance is always on offer."

Oliver knew George's years at St. Bartholomew's hospital had included intensive training in several specialties. He'd been drawn to surgery, but George had excelled in all his studies, and Oliver was sure his friend would be a tremendous help with Maxwell.

The men arrived at Southampton station without incident, and Oliver dashed off through the pouring rain to order a carriage as the others gathered their cases.

Approaching Shadowbrook's front entrance, Oliver wished he could offer the men a better impression. The old house was falling down brick by brick. He knew George wouldn't think less of him for inheriting such a wreck, but he wished he could help him feel the gentleness growing inside the crumbling walls.

Would his friend be able to see the changes sprouting within? There was sweetness taking root despite his uncle's frosty demeanor.

If Uncle Arthur even agreed to see Oliver's guests, there was no guarantee he'd be passingly polite to them.

The warmth spreading through the house had little to do with his uncle. Oliver was beginning to understand Arthur Ravenscroft's limitations, but the tendrils of affection growing inside Shadowbrook were because he loved Pearl.

Love. It was true; he knew as soon as he thought it.

As the carriage brought them all to the house, Oliver glanced at the facade, still as crooked and tilting as ever. But the house grew ever so slightly more appealing to him as each day passed.

Oliver thanked the driver and helped gather the cases before leading his friends to the vast front door of Shadowbrook House. He'd only just placed his hand on the knob when the door swung open and Jenkinson filled the doorway.

Oliver ushered George and Nichols past the stoic butler and into the house, and as they were removing their coats, he saw young Violet peeking around a corner. He waved to her. "Could you help get my friends settled into rooms? I'm sorry there was no warning."

Violet curtsied and nodded. "Madame Genevieve told me we'd have more company. There are rooms prepared." She added in a whisper, "The woman knows things."

He managed not to laugh and nodded his agreement. "She certainly seems to."

Mrs. Randle stepped forward and gestured to her right. "Gentlemen, if you'd care for some refreshment, please follow me to the east parlor."

Oliver glanced at Mr. Nichols hesitantly. He would not begrudge the man something to eat after such a taxing journey, but he also wanted the doctor to see Maxwell immediately.

Mr. Nichols shook his head and spoke to Mrs. Randle. "I'll be happy to take something cold to eat after I've seen the patient, if that's agreeable to you, ma'am."

Oliver didn't wait to hear Mrs. Randle's reply. He took the

stairs two at a time and heard Nichols's feet keeping pace with his own. He also heard strains of violin music, but whether it was the phantom tones of the wind through the halls or the stronger music he'd heard with Pearl, he could not say.

Approaching Maxwell's room, Oliver opened the door slowly, hoping to see Maxwell sitting up against his pillows.

Instead, he found Pearl standing at the foot of Maxwell's huge bed, the old violin tucked beneath her chin, her eyes closed, and tears streaming down her face. Maxwell lay twitching, his eyes closed, his face as pale as when Oliver had left the house.

So lost in her thoughts and her music, Pearl didn't hear Oliver and Nichols enter the room. He placed a hand gently on her elbow.

Her eyes flew open, and she drew the bow away from the strings. "Oh, Oliver. You're back. I'm so glad." She gave him a tired smile, then looked to the bed. "I thought maybe he'd like to hear some music. I know it's silly."

Oliver placed his arm gently across her shoulders. "Not silly at all. I'm sure he loves it." He turned her toward the door. "Pearl, this is Mr. Nichols, a doctor from London. Matthew, this is Pearl Ellicott."

The doctor bowed. "Miss Ellicott, do I have your consent to examine the patient?"

Pearl looked surprised. "Of course. You don't need my permission."

"You are the one who is caring for him. Of all of us, you know him best. I'll not proceed on any treatment plan without your agreement."

Pearl's "thank you" came out as a breath, a sigh. Oliver assumed Dr. Dunning did not defer to this extent to Pearl's understanding of Maxwell's condition.

"If you please, I would like to hear all your observations since the time of the latest episode."

Pearl picked up a small book and handed it to the doctor. "Here are the notes I've taken. I thought they'd be more coherent than my words. I'm a bit tired."

Nichols gave a nod of understanding and took the offered book. He flipped through the pages quickly, then went back and read each entry slowly.

Oliver watched Pearl as she straightened and tucked the bedcovers around the boy. He stepped close to the bed and took a careful look at Maxwell. "Has he wakened?"

Pearl nodded. "Occasionally." She drew close to him and whispered, "He may be awake now. He seems easier when he's silent."

"He looks strong, doesn't he?" It was untrue, but Oliver needed something to say, and if Max was awake, he wanted the words to be positive.

She stepped close to his side, and her sleeve brushed his. "He's been calmer. He's breathing easier."

Oliver wondered if her words were as much hopeful invention as his.

Still absorbing Pearl's notes, Matthew Nichols spoke. "He appears to be making progress."

Oliver wished the doctor's words were more clearly positive, but the meaning of his message was better than it might have been. At least he didn't say Max was lying so still because he'd worn himself out.

Finally, the doctor put the notebook on the side table. "Is there somewhere I can wash my hands before I examine the boy?"

Pearl pointed to Max's washstand, and with the doctor's back turned, Oliver took advantage of a moment's privacy. He leaned close and whispered, "Are you all right? How can I help?"

Pearl's eyes were still shiny from her earlier tears, but she smiled at him. "You've done more than I could have expected. More than anyone. I can't believe you've found a new physician to help him while also allowing him to remain here."

"I will always do what I can for Max, but I hope you know I meant to offer help to *you*. What do *you* need?"

Pearl reached out and took Oliver's hand, lacing her fingers through his. She pressed his hand with hers and looked deeply into his eyes. "For now, only this. And when we see him well, I'll have all I need."

CHAPTER 33

Pearl would have stayed by Maxwell's side, but Oliver seemed concerned they'd be in the way during the doctor's examination.

Holding Oliver's hand, she leaned across the bed and kissed Maxwell's cheek. "Oliver has been very busy on your behalf. And he's eager for you to meet his friend. May I invite them to come see you after your visit with the doctor?"

There was no hint of a reply. If Maxwell was awake, he was better at pretending than he'd ever been before.

Oliver tugged her hand gently. They stepped out of the room before he spoke. "Has my uncle been to see Max?"

Pearl shook her head.

Frustrated, Oliver huffed out a breath. "Why does he not look in on him? He acts at one moment as if he cares for the boy, then keeps his distance when Maxwell needs him most."

Pulling Oliver's hand close, she wrapped both of hers around his. "Max hasn't been alone."

He shook his head. "I didn't mean to suggest you'd left his side. I know you haven't."

"Perhaps Mr. Ravenscroft needs some time by himself to consider all that's happened. After all, in his solitude he feels most comfortable."

Oliver gave a dry chuckle. "True enough. When he's alone he's happiest."

Pearl shook her head. She knew Oliver's assumption was unfair. "I don't believe he's happy. But isolation does seem to be his most easy state."

"How does a person grow satisfied with solitude?" Oliver's question seemed to hold many more questions inside it, and Pearl had been searching her heart for just such answers.

"I suspect it's years of habit and practice."

He shook his head, not necessarily in defiance of what she said, but possibly in sadness. "I hope I never grow so comfortable with it."

Pearl reached a hand to stroke the side of Oliver's face. "You won't. You will always have people around you who love you."

He looked surprised, his eyes widening. "Do you think so? I don't feel that way. I live alone. When I was a child here, I spent all my hours on my own."

Pearl nodded. "More than you wished to, of course. And your family situation has certainly been solitary. But the gentleman you brought from the city has been a friend since your childhood. You will always have his love and support. And you have Maxwell. And Oliver, you have me."

She watched his face soften with each sentence. And her declaration, which should have cost her some measure of courage, flowed freely and naturally from her like currents moving in the river.

His reply came back to her with similar ease. His words landed on her ears, her skin, and her heart, covering her with warmth. "And you have me, Pearl. For as long as you might wish it, I am yours."

If their story were in one of Nanette's novels, the declaration would be accompanied by grand gestures, flowers, birdsong. Pearl thought their quiet reality was preferable. She would have a lovely time convincing her friend that a simple love story was best. She smiled at the thought.

Oliver pressed her hand to his heart. "I can't tell you how much I appreciate hearing you say those words. But you should realize my life in the city is different than it is when I'm here. Many more of my hours are solitary than otherwise. By no choice of my own, I have grown accustomed to being on my own. It's my most common state. The difference between me and my uncle is that I don't like it. I don't want it. And I certainly don't seek it."

"I wonder if he enjoys it as much as you think he does."

She watched Oliver take in her words. It was a step forward for him, she thought, that he didn't dismiss the thought outright. He was giving his uncle some new consideration.

"I've spent time in this house since I was a boy almost as young as Maxwell. I have seen my uncle more in this visit to Shadowbrook than I did in all the previous years. My childhood was spent searching for him, glancing around corners, holding my breath and walking silently so I didn't accidentally come upon him and startle us both."

He rubbed his thumb gently along the tips of her fingernails. "On my latest arrival, I recognized the change in him almost immediately, but I didn't understand how it came about. Now, I think I do. I know it's not a contest, but he clearly responds better to Max than he ever did to me. Having Maxwell here, having *you* here has changed everything. You both know my uncle so much better than I do."

Pearl would have listened to Oliver meditate on his feelings for hours, but she knew there was a piece of his uncle's story he was missing. "Mr. Ravenscroft has suffered greatly, for all his adult life. The catalog of those he's lost is long and tragic. Such losses affect a person, as we both know. In the face of your own tragedy, you sought for an uncle to share your pain. He didn't respond, so you widened your search and found your friends. Their affection over the years repaired much of the wound in your heart. But who was there for Mr. Ravenscroft? He lived here in this lonely house without his parents, without his wife and daughter, without his beloved sister, and then, after you left for school, without you."

Oliver rubbed his hand across the back of his neck. "He practically drove me away."

"He wouldn't have done so if he thought he could provide you what you needed to be happy and successful." Pearl was surprised to hear herself speaking the words. She tried to picture Maxwell's mother, a young woman living in such a situation. "Perhaps it was the same for him with his daughter. This could not have been a house where an affectionate young woman could flourish."

Oliver nodded. "She was gone by the time I arrived, and I never saw her here after."

She wondered at the pain Maxwell's mother must have felt as she cut herself off from her father's home. "He might have pushed her out as well, whether he meant to or not. Likely he struggled to hold her too tightly."

With a sigh, Oliver said, "I suppose there are many ways to turn love against itself, to allow fear and coldness to curdle what ought to be courageous and warm."

Pearl looked deeply into Oliver's eyes, pleased he was beginning to consider his uncle's pain as thoughtfully as he contemplated his own. "You have a good heart, Oliver. I believe such a thing is a family trait, no matter how deeply its tenderness might be buried."

Oliver kissed her fingertips once again. "I need to go speak to my uncle, don't I?"

Pearl pressed his palm flat against her cheek, soaking in the warmth of his touch. "I wouldn't dream of telling you what to do, but Madame Genevieve would certainly agree you ought to go seek him out."

They both smiled at the thought. For all Pearl knew, the

spiritualist was standing at her bedroom door, ear pressed to the wood, listening to them this very moment, nodding her fluffy head and waving her scarves in agreement.

"I don't want to leave you here alone."

Pearl turned her face to press a kiss against Oliver's palm. She loved the feeling of his skin on hers. "I'm not alone. I've got Maxwell. I'll attend the doctor as he examines Max, and when you come back, you can give us both a report on your visit."

Oliver rubbed the back of his neck again, a motion Pearl had seen him repeat in times of worry. "Assuming Jenkinson will let me into the room where my uncle is hiding."

Pearl pulled the letter from Dr. Dunning out of her pocket. "Take this with you. Tell your uncle what you've done. Show him the lengths you were willing to go to and that you love Maxwell as much as he does."

As Oliver took the paper from Pearl's hand, he clasped her fingers again. "Maybe I'll speak to him about something else."

She smiled at him but shook her head. "This is Maxwell's time. There will be hours and days and years to speak to him of other things. The rest of it can stay between the two of us a bit longer."

Oliver leaned down and kissed her mouth sweetly. He pressed his lips to her cheek and slid them close to her ear. "Between us and the service staff, you mean. I think we both know Violet couldn't keep what she saw to herself. We haven't exactly been discreet."

She wrapped her arms around his neck and pulled him closer. "I have nothing to hide, Mr. Waverley. Let them talk. This house could use some happy news."

CHAPTER 34

Climbing the stairs to the upper floor, Oliver's legs felt heavy, as if the staircase had grown steeper. He knew such an impression was all in his mind, but his mind was moving powerfully after all the emotion of the past few days.

Before he felt entirely ready, he found himself knocking at the door of the room he had discovered his uncle in during his last visit to this once-forbidden wing.

His uncle did not call for him to enter, nor did he tell him to go away. Oliver knocked again, and when there was still no response, he turned the knob and opened the door.

The room was vast. A huge bed rose from the center of the room with posts that seemed as tall as ship's masts. Dark-blue damask hangings draped the walls, windows, and bedposts. Large mirrors in gilt frames hung from two walls, making the enormous room seem even bigger.

The effect of the decorations must once have been elegant and luxurious, but to Oliver's eye, it looked dark and spooky.

"Uncle Arthur?"

There was no answer. Oliver stepped farther into the room. This was one of the many rooms in Shadowbrook House where builders had given no heed to squares and rectangles. The walls opened and formed as if they grew independent of any consideration for a room's standard proportions.

"Uncle?" Oliver called again. He moved deeper toward the room's corners and found an open passageway leading directly from the room itself, a path which seemed to connect the bedroom to another space. Oliver had never seen this section of the house, but he was beyond being surprised by Shadowbrook's twists.

He followed the passage, turning as the walls directed him.

Moving deep into the interior of the house, Oliver called out once again.

In reply he heard a whisper. A murmur. Was it a warning or a welcome, or was it only the wind and rain on the roof and walls?

The passageway seemed to rise beneath his feet. He felt himself climbing, even though there were no stairs. Oliver looked behind him, but he could no longer see any sign of the blue bedroom he'd first entered.

In addition to the whispers, he heard echoes of the grief-filled violin music.

He continued to climb until he reached an open door in the wall in front of him. Oliver put his head around the dark wood. With the ceasing of his own footsteps, he heard more clearly the low, keening sound of the violin. The interior of the room was cocooned in darkness.

Oliver's ears filled with the music and the hushed and whispering voices, echoes of the sounds he'd heard as a child. He couldn't make out words, but the whispers were undeniable.

The wall ahead of him glowed with a suggestion of light, but no candle or gas flame was in sight.

For a moment, he wasn't certain what he was looking at, then his eyes adjusted to the dimness of the room. Upon each of the surrounding walls hung portraits in elegant frames. What he thought was light was the white of oil paint against the room's darkness.

Eyes adjusting to the gloom, he turned to glance at the other walls. With a jolt, he realized he stood face to face with his missing portrait, the one taken from his bedroom. Here it stood against a dark wall in an isolated room in the heart of the house.

Isolated, but not unreachable.

Accessible only from his uncle's bedroom.

He stared up at his mother's eyes.

The artist who'd painted her had a gift for capturing expression, for the face in the painting wore a smile Oliver had seen in his mother's happiest days. The smile she'd shown him when she spoke of his father.

How long had it been since Oliver had witnessed that lovely smile?

Here she is, the voices whispered. The notes of the music soared, brittle and aching.

He stood many minutes before his mother's painting before he moved slowly about the room and saw several other portraits, each of a lovely woman.

At first, Oliver didn't find the paintings or the artists' influences familiar, but as he studied the faces, he realized he recognized the subjects. One was a representation of his maternal grandmother, a painting his mother must have had copied, for a small version of the same portrait had hung in his childhood home before his mother died. The woman posed with a gorgeous chestnut mare, her fair hair tangling with the horse's auburn mane in a wind he used to think he could feel. He stepped in front of the painting and wished he could reach out and touch the grandmother he'd never met. His mother's mother. Uncle Arthur's mother.

The next painting was of a radiant, smiling woman holding a honey-colored violin. As he met her eyes, the music in his mind seemed to draw to a close, a note lengthening before it faded to quiet.

Then, on an adjoining wall next to a small cluster of framed drawings, Oliver saw his own features looking out at him from a miniature portrait, one that might have been fashionable fifty years earlier. This wasn't an antique, however. The likeness was too striking. He stared into his own eyes. This was a drawing of Oliver himself. He couldn't doubt it.

Here you are, the voices seemed to whisper. *Here you've always been.*

The drawings surrounding his miniature caught his attention for their own familiarity. He leaned in for a closer look. A childish outline of the dock outside Shadowbrook House hung next to a fanciful pen-and-ink sketch of a large, turreted building. He knew these pictures. He had drawn them. Left them behind when he'd escaped Shadowbrook for school. And now they hung in this strange gallery.

Something rustled at the far side of the room, and Oliver turned to see Uncle Arthur, a stick in his hand and something under his arm. He shuffled out of a shadowy corner, and Oliver saw he was holding a violin's bow.

The whispers fell silent.

Oliver's first instinct was to apologize for intruding on his uncle's privacy. He stepped forward but chose to say nothing. After all, he wasn't sorry to be here, to see this collection of portraits, or to find his uncle. And to begin to understand the mystery of the music wafting through the halls of Shadowbrook.

He turned slowly and continued to inspect the paintings as the two men stood shoulder to shoulder.

When Oliver spoke, he did so in a murmur, much as he would within the walls of a church. The reverent feeling in this dark room felt similar. "What is this place?"

Uncle Arthur shuffled away from the wall and echoed Oliver's movement. "This is what remains of the beating heart of Shadowbrook House. Here I find all those I have lost." He pointed to the familiar painting of the woman and the horse. "My mother. You know this one, don't you?"

Oliver nodded. Would Uncle Arthur speak of her? Tell Oliver a story of the woman's life, as his own mother used to do? He couldn't remember a single detail, only the wistfulness in his mother's voice as she spoke of the grandmother he never knew.

Arthur did not offer anything more about his mother's portrait; instead, he pointed to the next painting: the fashionable lady with the large sleeves and enormous skirts of thirty years before, rings of curls falling beside her face and the violin in her hands. "My wife, Christina. The instrument Pearl plays was once hers."

With a nod, Oliver gestured to the violin the man held beneath his arm. "And you used to play together?"

The lines on Arthur's face softened. "We still do. Do you not hear her playing sometimes in the halls? On the stairs?"

Oliver had, even though he'd tried to convince himself otherwise.

"She was a gifted musician."

Oliver had never heard Uncle Arthur speak of his wife. Looking into the face in the painting, Oliver saw a hint of liveliness around her eyes. It was impossible to believe Uncle Arthur had once been young and vivacious like this woman, but there must have been something that brought the two of them together.

He wanted to ask his uncle a hundred questions, but he wouldn't interrupt this strange tour of the hidden gallery.

Arthur gestured to the painting of Oliver's mother. "My dear sister. There is much of her in you. See the way her eyes shine? I paid the artist handsomely for this likeness. He earned every penny for capturing that look. This was painted before your father died in battle at sea. When she still smiled."

Oliver wanted to hear more. All of it, every story. But Arthur turned to a three-paneled display of a rosy-cheeked baby, a girl holding a toy boat, and a young woman. All three had the same striking eyes. Eyes Oliver knew well.

"This is Maxwell's mother?"

Arthur nodded. "My daughter. Your cousin Bethany. Do you remember the day she came back to Shadowbrook?"

Oliver was sure he'd never met his cousin. She'd left her father's home when Arthur refused to give his permission for her to marry.

As curious as Oliver had been about his cousin, he'd never asked his uncle about her. Arthur Ravenscroft had not invited confidences. But now, Uncle Arthur seemed willing—even eager—to speak about his only child.

"She was in love, she said. He promised to marry her. She pleaded with me to meet him, to welcome him to the house. Of course, I refused. He was a common sailor, a nobody with no past and no future." Arthur scrubbed his hand across his face. "And then he left her. I gave him no reason to stay, so he boarded a ship and disappeared as quietly as he'd arrived."

Oliver forced himself to stand still and listen to the tragedy, told in only the barest of detail. Every word seemed torn from Arthur's throat, leaving him wrecked and wrung out.

"She wrote to a neighbor. Confessed the condition the sailor had left her in. Swore she wouldn't return to this house. When it was time for the baby's arrival, just as you left for school, the neighbor went to be with her. Bethany's body could not bear the birth. She died, and Maxwell barely survived."

The huge hall clock struck from somewhere nearby, each gong reverberating through Oliver's chest.

Arthur's voice was scarcely a whisper. "I couldn't bear to have you at the house when I brought Maxwell to live here. He was so sickly and weak, and I didn't want you to grow fond of him only to endure another loss."

These few words turned a latch in Oliver's mind, forcing him to see his own exclusion from Shadowbrook in a different way. He knew Arthur's reasoning was unfounded, but the old man believed he'd done Oliver a favor.

Oliver and Arthur stood staring at the portraits of Bethany, each considering his own loss. Oliver wished he could think of something to say.

Arthur ran his hand along the back of his neck in a gesture Oliver knew well. The old man closed his eyes.

"Everyone leaves, and I am forced to carry on alone."

At this, Arthur Ravenscroft ran out of words.

Moments stretched between the two men as they stood in a gallery of sorrows.

Oliver folded his arms across his chest and felt the crinkling of paper within his waistcoat pocket. He pulled out Dr. Dunning's letter. "Pearl showed me this."

Arthur glanced toward the paper and then away. More sorrow suffused his wretched face. "Every decision I make seems only to do harm."

Oliver shook his head. "I've gone to London and brought a doctor, one who comes recommended from the school at St. Bartholomew. He's with Max now, and he will continue to care for him. I think Maxwell is in good hands, but there is something else I believe he needs."

Arthur turned to Oliver, grief painted plainly across every feature. "I am willing to try anything that might help the boy."

Oliver nodded. "Come and sit beside him. It may be that what he needs in order to heal is you."

CHAPTER 35

As Dr. Nichols examined Maxwell, he spoke in gentle tones, including Pearl in the conversation through the words he directed to Maxwell. "I'd love to see how strong your grip is. Will you grasp my hand?"

Maxwell remained silent, eyes closed and hands limp.

"When you cough, do you feel the pressure from the inside of your chest or the outside?"

No response. Was he awake? Aware? Conscious? Was he shutting Pearl and the doctor out by choice?

Pearl noticed the doctor's eyes taking in not only every reaction and lack of reaction but also the corners of the room. He looked often toward the weeping wall near the window.

"Has this been your bedroom for long, Maxwell?"

When Max did not open his eyes or give any answer, the doctor glanced at Pearl.

She nodded. "For always."

"When the two of you explore, how does the rest of the house feel to you, Maxwell?"

After a sufficient pause, the doctor looked to Pearl. She answered. "Maxwell is at his best when he's exploring. He has grown so strong in the last while. His legs are getting longer, so he can climb ladders and staircases without tiring."

She would have continued to extol Max's strengths more for the boy's benefit than the doctor's, but she heard a grunt from the bed.

Maxwell squeezed his eyes closed much harder than before, proving by the effort he was no longer sleeping.

She quickly spoke, helping the doctor's conversation along. "What's your favorite room in the house, Max? Of all we've explored, surely you have something you like best."

He grunted again but did not speak.

"Maybe one of the secret rooms with puzzle entrances? Or a parlor where you spend evenings with your grandfather?"

"No. This one."

It wasn't much, but he'd spoken so little since he'd taken ill. She was glad for any communication. She smiled at him, but he kept his eyes closed.

"Naturally, you love your own bedroom best."

Dr. Nichols stepped around the foot of the bed so he could better see the boy's averted face.

"What is it about this room that makes it your favorite?"

Maxwell refused to look at the doctor. "Nothing. Everything."

Pearl wished she had explained Maxwell's tendency to grumble and grouse when he was sleepy.

"Have you ever considered how the room might look and feel different if you asked for a new bedcover? Or if you had the wallpaper changed?"

"Don't touch it." The words had edges.

Pearl put her hand on Maxwell's. "Dearest, please speak kindly to the doctor."

"Don't touch the wall," Max said again, louder this time. "The house will be angry."

A cold shiver ran across Pearl's shoulders.

"Houses don't feel anger, Max." She spoke the words reflexively, but at the same time, she couldn't swear they were true.

"The house is angry when people leave it."

Pearl squeezed Maxwell's hand. She wanted to curb this mood before it escalated. "Your grandfather must have felt sad when people he loved had to go."

Maxwell pulled away from her and curled up into a ball. "Nobody had to go. They abandoned us."

How could she answer such an accusation, especially when she felt so often the same way? Trying not to give in to such thoughts took daily effort, and now she didn't have the energy.

Max's sharp words dulled again. "I'll never leave."

Pearl faced the doctor. "He doesn't usually speak this way. He's tired."

Dr. Nichols glanced at Maxwell and then turned to Pearl. "Is he often tired when he's in this room?"

Pearl felt a slight shift in the air. Maybe a breeze through the cracks in the walls. A humming, shushing sound wafted past her.

"Of course. He comes here to sleep."

"Does he suffer other complaints here? Headache? Stomach upset?"

Pearl nodded. "Sometimes. He rarely complains, but his illness affects him daily."

"Is he more often irritable in this room than in others?"

"Don't talk about me like I can't hear you." Maxwell's voice rose to a higher pitch. "I'm right here and you can ask me."

Pearl wanted to correct the boy's rudeness, but Dr. Nichols turned to Max. "Do you often feel more ill when you're in your bed?"

"I'm in my bed because I'm ill, not the other way round."

She started to interrupt, to stop Max from speaking with disrespect, but the doctor glanced at Pearl and shook his head.

"Maxwell, I'd like your permission to examine your bedroom."

"No." The boy's word was almost a shout.

Dr. Nichols kept his eyes on Max. "Why not?"

"The house doesn't want you poking about." Maxwell's escalating tone shocked Pearl.

She knelt beside the bed and whispered. "Max, dearest. I know you're angry, but it's time to calm down. You'll hurt yourself if you carry on this way."

Maxwell turned on her, his eyes shiny with tears and confusion. "I'm not angry. The house is."

In all the times Maxwell had spoken to her about the whispers he heard in the halls of Shadowbrook House, he'd never sounded frightened. He was frightened now.

The doctor pressed his lips together. "I believe it is time to take him out of this room."

Maxwell shook his head weakly. "No. I need to stay."

Pearl and the doctor exchanged a look. She hated to see the young boy in pain, but she had sworn to do whatever she could to see him well again. She lifted Max from the bed and held him close.

When she reached the door, he began to thrash in her arms. She spoke soft words of comfort, struggling to carry Maxwell without any part of him striking the doorframe.

A few steps from the bottom of the stairs, Pearl heard Oliver's voice call to her. He came running, reaching to take Maxwell's weight from her arms. "What's happened?"

She had no idea how to answer, her heart and mind in a tumult at seeing Maxwell in such distress. She walked with her arm on Oliver's as he carried Max inside the parlor.

Oliver placed Max gently on a couch, and Dr. Nichols stepped forward to rest his hand on the boy's head.

Pearl's thoughts scattered, each trying to become an answer to one of her many unasked questions.

Oliver placed his hand on her arm. "Do you want me to stay with you, or am I in the way?"

Shaking her head, she said, "Please, will you stay?"

The next moment, Mr. Ravenscroft stepped through the door. He looked at the doctor, then Pearl, Maxwell, and Oliver in turn. Without speaking a word, he sat in the chair at Maxwell's side, placing a hand on the boy's ankle.

Pearl stood close and held Maxwell's hand, hoping he would settle.

The boy looked at her with huge, damp eyes. His voice trembled. "I'm afraid."

Tears welled in Pearl's eyes. "I'm here. We are all here for you." She sat on the couch next to Max, and he rested his sweaty head on her shoulder.

Then he reached for his grandfather's hand.

Mr. Ravenscroft leaned forward in his chair and grasped the small hand with his own. "Maxwell, my dear boy, I need you."

His words stopped Pearl's breath. It seemed the most powerful statement a person could say. *I need you.*

Pearl caught Oliver's eye and gestured toward the door. Carefully shifting Maxwell from her arms to Mr. Ravenscroft's care, she followed Oliver into the hallway.

CHAPTER 36

Oliver stepped close to Pearl, and she looked into his eyes. "We need to figure out what's plaguing Maxwell's bedroom. There's something in that room that's hurting him."

She hurried up the stairs, and Oliver was quick to follow. He didn't know what they might be looking for, but he knew he'd search Maxwell's room until he found whatever it was that might be causing Max harm.

Once he stepped into the boy's bedroom, he smelled the sharp aroma Pearl always tried to mask with fire and gathered plants. Acid scratched at the back of his throat and stung his eyes.

Pearl stood in the center of the room, looking around. Her voice, when she spoke, was quiet and forlorn. "I don't know what I'm looking for. I don't know how to help him."

Oliver placed an arm around her back. "Everything you do helps him. This is no different from the puzzles you set for Max."

She gave a humorless laugh. "Except I know the solutions to the puzzles I design."

Oliver moved across the room to the bed, still speaking to Pearl. "You have clues. How does this room affect him?"

"He comes here when he's tired, or he becomes tired when he's here. He'll sleep during the day if he stays, but if he's in a different room, he has more energy to play."

Oliver searched the space beneath Maxwell's bed. He found a

few books tucked in neat piles, a single sock, and very little dust. Someone was careful in the room's cleaning.

As he went to inspect the small bookcase, he watched Pearl move from the window to the table where Maxwell's washbasin sat. She stretched her arms as high as she could reach and touched the ugly wallpaper in the corner. She made a sound of disgust and pulled her hands away.

He hurried to her side. A leak from the near-constant rains had dripped onto Maxwell's wall, and blisters had formed beneath the wallpaper. Oliver pressed against the paper and felt it squish and flatten beneath his fingers.

He glanced at Pearl. "May I?"

She nodded.

Oliver found a corner of the paper, and he pulled. The paper came away from the wall with an audible squelch, the wet wall beneath it a muddy sludge. As he pulled further, the same sharp scent that always lingered in the room increased tenfold. His eyes and nose stung. Oliver turned his face away from the black muck on the wall to catch his breath then turned back and peeled more of the paper away.

Slimy streaks painted the wooden wall behind the paper. Oliver reached for a fireplace poker and levered a corner of the rotting wood away. The board and its nails screeched out in resistance, and Pearl covered her ears with her hands.

Oliver pushed and pulled until the wood tore away. Behind it, the plastered wall ran with black rivulets of acrid-smelling mold.

Pearl picked up a piece of cloth—maybe a small blanket, maybe some piece of Max's clothing—and scrubbed it against the wall. The cloth came away blackened, but the wall still bore thick streams of the nasty substance.

He saw her throat convulse as if she were about to be sick. "This can't be good."

Oliver shook his head. "I don't think you should touch it."

"But we have to remove it. What if this slime is somehow hurting Maxwell?"

"It's certainly not helping him."

Pearl dropped the fouled cloth into the fireplace. Thick, dark smoke billowed up and rose through the chimney. "We have to get it out of here. All of it. Right now."

Oliver reached over and took Pearl's hands. "I don't think Max should come back into this room."

She started to protest. "But it's his favorite space. It's where he feels comfortable."

The stench of acrid smoke began to circle through the room, and Pearl's eyes widened. "I've made it worse, haven't I?"

Oliver led her into the hallway, closing the door behind them. "Whatever that is, Max shouldn't be near it."

He saw tears forming in the corners of Pearl's bright eyes. "It will break his heart to keep him out of there. He loves that room."

"I'm not so sure the room loves him in return."

It was a silly thing to say, and not at all helpful, but before Oliver could apologize for speaking flippantly, Pearl grasped both his hands, a frantic sadness in her eyes.

"This room has made his illness worse, and I brought him here every day and every night." Tears ran down her cheeks. "What if that horror is growing behind *all* the walls?" She shivered. "I don't know what to do."

"None of this is your fault, Pearl."

"It's hard for me to believe that. I am responsible for Maxwell's care."

"Not you alone."

Pearl looked up at him with shining eyes. "For so long, I have felt nothing but alone."

Oliver knew there were far better places for him to speak the words he wished to say, but his heart nearly burst at her statement.

"If you wish it, you'll never need to be alone again. I will be beside you."

She stepped closer, and Oliver's arms wrapped tightly around her. They stood in the dim hallway outside Maxwell's door for several long moments. Oliver felt the beating of Pearl's heart grow steady and slow.

She spoke into his shoulder. "Will your doctor friends know what we need to do?"

Part of Oliver wished for a continuation of the confidences he'd begun to share, but he was satisfied there would be time. Now they needed to help Maxwell.

He released Pearl, but she immediately reached for his hand. They walked down the stairs and into the parlor where Dr. Nichols knelt at Maxwell's side as the boy reclined on the couch.

Oliver stepped toward Dr. Nichols and gestured toward the upper floor. "We've found something awful in the wall."

As the doctor hurried out of the room, Oliver and Pearl knelt at Maxwell's side. Uncle Arthur stood nearby, his hand on Maxwell's shoulder.

In her quiet, gentle voice, Pearl spoke to Max. "You sound so much better. Are you breathing easier? Is there anything you need?"

Max answered in a rough whisper. "Can you stay with me for a while? And Oliver?" He looked from one to the other. He dragged in a breath that seemed to cost him. "I know there are things you need to do, but when you can be with me, I'm glad of it."

Oliver brought a chair for Pearl and sat on the floor at her feet. Maxwell held Pearl's hand and closed his eyes. "I'm not sleepy. Only my eyes are tired. I'd like a story."

Pearl did a remarkable job of sounding unconcerned as she spun a tale for Max. Only the line deepening between her brows showed Oliver the worry she carried.

A few moments into the story, Oliver reached for Pearl's free hand. She curled her fingers into his. Standing over the reclining boy, Arthur trembled as he drew his fingers along Maxwell's hairline.

Oliver attempted to stand without interrupting Pearl's story. He kept his fingers entwined with hers as he shifted over and placed his free hand on his uncle's shoulder to close the circle. Arthur's eyes flickered to Oliver's, and he raised his arm to place it on Oliver's back. A flash of possibility pulsed before Oliver's eyes—this family in this home. Neither were words he'd used before, but maybe the home and the family had been here all the time. He needed only to see them with different eyes.

They stood together as Pearl continued the story, and when footsteps sounded at the door, all heads turned.

Dr. Nichols stepped to the center of the room. "Mr. Ravenscroft, there is black mold in Maxwell's bedroom walls."

In a few careful sentences, Dr. Nichols explained the fairly recent discovery of a fungus that caused dangerous respiratory illness. The weeping section of Maxwell's wall was bursting with it. The longer he stayed in the room with the diseased walls, the sicker he would become.

"I recommend setting up a new bedroom for Max in the driest section of the house. Let us clear the diseased segments of wall away. If we can eliminate the fungus, we'll do so. In any case, Oliver, George, and I will make ourselves useful making a new room perfect for Maxwell as he heals."

Mr. Ravenscroft's brows lowered in a scowl. His voice trembled as he spoke. "Are you saying the house itself is making the boy ill?"

Oliver stepped between the doctor and his uncle. "Not the house. Only something growing in the house. But Uncle, there are many things growing in this house. Not the least, a brilliant boy full of wisdom and laughter, games and ideas. If you protect him from the mold and continue to nurture the love developing here, I'm confident Maxwell has as much chance of healing as anyone else."

Mr. Ravenscroft turned again to Maxwell. "My dear boy, I

fear I've smothered you. In trying to prevent anything from hurting you, I pushed you into the very space that wounded you and caused you pain. Can you forgive a foolish old man?"

Oliver didn't hear Maxwell's answer. He whispered it into his grandfather's ear as he clasped his hands around the old man's neck.

So many questions spun in Oliver's mind, but the most important ones were answered. There was a reason for Maxwell's illness, and there was a solution. Max's suffering would ease.

Pearl's hands trembled with exhaustion. She caught Oliver's eye, and he slipped past the others to slide an arm around her back. He pressed a quick kiss beneath her ear. He didn't care if everyone in the house saw, but he thought each person was busy enough not to care much what was happening between the governess and the heir.

Pearl looked up at Oliver and sighed. "That was lovely, what you said to Mr. Ravenscroft. And now Maxwell is going to be all right?" Pearl seemed to need the comfort of an answer. She gazed at the boy, held tight in his grandfather's arms.

"He will. And he'll have all our help to heal."

Her sigh felt like a release of a great weight.

Oliver leaned in close, her breath tickling his neck in the most delicious way. "No one as exhausted as you are has any right to look as beautiful as you do."

"Mr. Waverley, if that is not a lie, it is certainly a generous extension of the truth." The smile she sent his way sank itself deep into his heart. "I would love nothing more than to make myself presentable before you look at me so carefully. You're bound to discover my flaws, and it's much too soon in our acquaintance for you to know them all."

He shook his head. "I always look this carefully. And if you'll allow it, I'll make it a daily habit."

"Any other habits you intend to develop?" A smile widened across her mouth.

"I have a few ideas." And he showed her.

CHAPTER 37

Shadowbrook House seemed to breathe anew as Christmas Eve dawned. Oliver woke early and leaped from his bed, eager to make final preparations to the gifts he had planned. He hadn't felt this excited to celebrate Christmas in many years. Perhaps not ever.

He gave a gentle tap at George's bedroom door, then at Matthew Nichols's door. Following now-familiar turns, the men headed up the stairs. They emerged several hours later and found the house waking slowly around them. Each man went to his room to clean himself up and erase the evidence of their final hours of labor.

Oliver wished nothing more than to spend days at Pearl's side, but after she'd had a good night's sleep, she'd been recruited by Mrs. Randle and Madame Genevieve to assist with preparations for today's dinner, a meal on a grand scale that quiet and lonely Shadowbrook House had never seen before. The plans were days in the making, and alone time with Pearl would need to wait. He had many ideas for ways to make up for the lost hours.

Not a speck of dust or paint remained on him when he went to Maxwell's temporary room and stepped inside at the boy's invitation. Max sat on the edge of the bed, fiddling with his necktie. It was a duplicate of the one Oliver wore.

"Need a hand with that? The silk is tricky."

"It's slippery," Max said. "And Pearl usually does it."

Oliver hadn't learned the trick of fastening a neckcloth facing someone else, so he stood behind Maxwell and, arms reaching around the boy, tied a perfect knot.

They both moved to the glass at the side of the room. Peering at their reflection, Oliver smiled.

Max echoed the expression. "We look alike, don't you think?"

Oliver nodded seriously. "You are much handsomer than I am, but with a bit of work, I can try to match you."

"If you and Pearl have a boy, do you think he'll look like us?"

A dozen questions flew into Oliver's head. Had Pearl confided in Maxwell? Did she speak to him of a future with Oliver? Had she actually mentioned children? He felt himself blush and brushed his silent questions away.

He chose to give another answer to the first of Max's questions. "We do have a strong family resemblance. See the way our chins square off at the bottom? And my hair curls just like yours when I let it grow long."

"And we like so many of the same things. Adventures. Puzzles. Pearl."

Oliver didn't even try to hide his smile at the list of commonalities. "Speaking of adventures, as soon as you're ready, I have one for you."

Max nodded and clapped his hands. "Now. I'm ready now."

"We need Pearl to join us." As soon as Oliver said the words, he heard her distinctive tap at the frame of Max's open door.

She put her head into the room and said, "Happy Christmas."

"Very nicely done, Oliver," Max said with a playful grin. "All you had to do was state your wish and it came true. Let me try." He cleared his throat and said, "We need a plate of hot scones with raspberry preserves."

Oliver and Pearl laughed. Pearl stepped close and tugged one end of Maxwell's tie to straighten it. "I assure you, there will be more treats than you can eat in a week at the table today."

They moved into the hallway and found George and Matthew waiting for them. Oliver turned to Max. "Captain Ravenscroft, sir, your crew is ready to follow you on this great exploration. We are at your service, as always."

Oliver reached into his pocket and pulled out a folded piece of leather. Max untied the strap around it and lifted out a hand-drawn treasure map. He studied it for a moment, then turned to look at Pearl, wonder on his face. "Did you do this?"

She shook her head. "This was all Oliver and his friends. And from the looks of that map, they're going to put my silly games to shame."

Maxwell executed a smart bow and snapped his heels together. "Right, men. We're off, then."

Oliver let his friends move in close to Max as they followed him along the map's trail through the winding halls of Shadowbrook. Once, there was a slight miscalculation requiring them to backtrack from a dead end, but Max managed to solve all the clues the men had set him, and before long, he was standing in front of the huge old clock in the upstairs hall.

"This map says the clock holds the key to the secret." Maxwell walked from side to side, inspecting the clock. "That could mean anything. Maybe there's a secret code in the numbers. Maybe it's something about springs or gears." He turned a brass knob on the glass door covering the long pendulum, and something small and shiny dropped at his feet.

Maxwell laughed, and Oliver watched Pearl's face break into the kind of smile reserved for the happiest of moments. She truly loved this boy, and Oliver understood why. Max was a delight.

The boy leaned down and picked up the small metal object, holding it high for his crew to witness. "Or maybe it just means there's a key hiding in the clock's cabinet."

Oliver and his friends cheered their captain's cleverness.

As Max turned the key in the lock of the old study's huge

double doors, Oliver couldn't decide whether to watch Maxwell's face or Pearl's. It had taken hours of work, but Oliver and his friends had created a wonderland in the once-forbidden room. One wall was painted like a forest, with cushions like boulders strewn around the floor and a cunning little bookshelf painted to resemble a woodland cottage. The opposite wall contained a mural of the river, and Oliver was pleased how the water in the painting looked like it was flowing across the room. The third wall wasn't merely painted—boards were nailed to the wall to call to mind the inside of a ship, and a child-sized sailor's hammock hung from the ceiling on pulleys and ropes.

The look of absolute joy on Maxwell's face made Oliver wish he could create a thousand rooms just like this one.

"Oliver, did you do this? For me?"

The boy rushed to him without waiting for an answer, threw his arms around Oliver's waist, and squeezed him.

"Not only me. My mates have been working very hard to build this for you. It's just the kind of room we would have loved to have when we were boys."

Maxwell hugged George and Matthew, then he came back to Oliver and embraced him again. "Thank you all. I shall move in to this room tonight and stay here forever."

Oliver watched Pearl's expression go from wonder to gratitude to an echo of Maxwell's joy. She was as thrilled as Oliver was by how much Maxwell loved the room.

He ran from corner to corner, pointing out the features of his fortress and asking Oliver if he knew about this cupboard or that movable wall panel. Oliver nodded and smiled, and he'd never felt such delight in a completed project. He hoped to be on site when Maxwell discovered the dial-lock in the floor's trapdoor.

When Max suggested they remake the entire house just like this room, Oliver wanted nothing more than to tell him, "Your wish is our command."

Instead, he said, "We're all very glad you like your Christmas gift."

At the mention of Christmas, Maxwell clapped his hands again. "Right, men. We've got a party to attend. You're all under my orders to come to dinner in your finest clothes with clean fingernails and combed hair. Oliver and I will accompany Pearl. Don't make Mrs. Randle wait; she won't like it. If you're very well-behaved, there will be lemon cakes and chocolate biscuits."

Oliver's friends each saluted Max, and they marched toward the staircase in formation as Maxwell continued to look behind him at the magical room.

Oliver and Pearl were last to descend the stairs. She took him by the arm. "You've truly created a wonder. Who knew this old place had such enchantment left within its walls?"

Leaning in and placing a kiss on her cheek, Oliver said, "Maybe we shouldn't give up on making a home out of Shadowbrook just yet."

She stopped walking and looked into his eyes. "What do you mean?"

He glanced up toward the space at the top of the house where his uncle kept his gallery of those he'd loved and lost. "There's no hurry to rid ourselves of this place."

She shook her head in confusion. "But what of the Campbell Company's deadline?"

Oliver placed his arm over Pearl's shoulders and pulled her close. "If a sale is meant to be, it will happen in an appropriate timeline. That's what I told Uncle Arthur. He seemed rather happy about it, and if you feel the same, I believe we'll stay. All of us."

Pearl flashed him a brilliant smile. "Nothing could please me more."

"Nothing? Are you certain?"

She put a finger to her chin as if in deep consideration. "Well, maybe one thing . . ." Standing on her toes, she took Oliver's face in her hands and drew him close to her. She pressed her lips to his once, then pulled back and looked into his eyes. She kissed him again, and then—slowly—a third time.

He forgot everything else until they heard Maxwell calling from the lower landing.

"Hurry, you two. It's time for Christmas."

As Oliver and Pearl reached the door of her room, he took both her hands in his. "I have a gift for you, but I'd like to deliver it privately, when our commander isn't hurrying us along."

"Oh, Oliver. I don't need anything more than you've already given me. And I hope you're not disappointed, but I'm not so wonderful as you are at preparing gifts."

He shook his head. "I can't take all the credit for Max's new room. My friends have limitless skills and energy."

She looked up at him through lowered lashes. "My own skills are limited and fairly specific, but I believe you'll grow fond of them."

Oliver laughed. "Doubtless you are right. As for presents, there is only one gift I wish you to give me."

"Name it."

"Say you'll marry me. Say you'll help me make this old place a home. Say we can stay here with my uncle and Max for as long as they'll have us. Say you'll make my life complete by being my wife."

Pearl's bell-like laugh rolled out across the hallway and likely filled the whole house. "That's a lot you'd like me to say. Will you be satisfied with a *yes* that stands for all of it?"

"*Yes* would be perfect."

"Then yes. Yes, my love, to all of it."

He wrapped his arms around her and lifted her off her feet. "Thank you. That is the best gift of all. Now, please allow me to escort you to the largest family dinner this house has ever seen."

"Anything you wish," she said, and he believed all he wished was within her power to grant.

EPILOGUE

1885

Five years later, on a glorious sunny autumn afternoon, an old man stands at the upper balcony of Shadowbrook House while a young boy roams the bricked walkways of a walled garden outside of Shadowbrook Children's Infirmary. The boy's brown curls look auburn in the sunlight, and at thirteen, he's beginning to grow into his elbows and knees.

He pushes a wheelchair around a stand of late-blooming chrysanthemums. He points to the flowers. The old man knows he's explaining to the child in the chair that the late bloomers are his favorites, and that when he was her age, he was ill and weak, but the last few years have brought him a marked improvement. The boy gives Shadowbrook all the credit.

At this distance, the man cannot hear the boy, but he knows the words he's saying: "I grew up in the house beyond this wall. The hospital wasn't even here until two years ago. My family had it built. I used to think it was made just for me, but now I know it was also for you."

It's the same thing he tells all the children he sees when he comes to Shadowbrook between school terms. And he means it every time.

The man watches the boy direct the wheelchair down to the dock, where seats are placed for patients and their families to visit near the water. A couple sits together, a baby in the man's arms and a toddler at the woman's knee.

As the boy wheels the chair beside the woman, she turns and smiles in welcome. The breeze carries the tune of her voice to the old man, and he can guess at the words. "Hello, Max. Clarissa, dear, you're looking very happy this afternoon."

The girl smiles at Pearl, revealing a gap where her front teeth are missing. The man knows Pearl would like to see Clarissa again when the bones in her leg are mended and her new teeth change the shape of her face. Pearl always wants to see the children again.

Pearl's smile reflects the bounty of her life, crammed full of the most joyous blessings: her husband, her daughters, and her boy Max, who is growing into a young man before her eyes.

Oliver shifts the baby to his shoulder and turns her to look up toward the refurbished house. He points up to the balcony, and the baby waves a chubby arm. Arthur waves back.

Arthur Ravenscroft finds new reasons every day to step out into the light, or the rain, or the star-strewn night. He feels the comfort of his home as well as the blessings of the world beyond Shadowbrook's walls. His eyes are drawn to the red-brick facade of the children's hospital where his endowment pays impressive young doctors to discover cures for childhood illnesses.

He thinks of his favorite portrait gallery, the turreted room at the top of the house where he can go to remember and visit the family that has moved on from this world. He still hears ghostly violin music as he gazes into the faces of those he's loved and lost, but the music is more often cheerful than mournful, and the whispers speak of a future filled with happiness.

Now Arthur looks down toward the dock, where he sees a small fist throwing kisses up to him. He throws a kiss back to the baby, locking eyes with the beautiful little girls with their bright eyes and easy laughs. His gaze connects him to the family that will outlive him for many years.

Arthur understands that as with every family, each member of the Shadowbrook household struggles with their own dark moments, but those are small in comparison to the joys they discover every day within the walls of their home. Healing is in the air, and love abounds.

ACKNOWLEDGMENTS

So many people had a part to play in moving this book from my brain into your hands.

To those who write the stories where the creepy and the romantic meet, I salute you. This is a weird place to inhabit, and I love reading it when it's done well.

Thanks to my husband for buying me a treadmill for my standing desk. Because of your kindness, I didn't have to choose between putting words on a page and moving my feet. Miles to go . . .

Many thanks to my writing group and general life-support friends. Salty Bird-Girls, you know who you are. Thank you for a long year of heavy lifts.

A big thanks to the Shadow Mountain publishing team: Lisa Mangum, Heidi Gordon, Callie Hansen, Heather Ward, Bre Anderl, Amy Parker, Ashley Olson, Bri Cornell, and Troy Butcher.

I achieved a lifelong dream to visit Hampshire, and it lived up to all my hopes both in glorious scenery and human kindness. I'd move to the banks of the River Hamble at the slightest provocation.

To all those who asked: Yes, I miss teaching high school kids, but no, I don't miss teaching. Maybe you can understand.

Thanks to all of you who read and sigh and swoon a little and come back for more. You make this lonely exercise worth it.

DISCUSSION QUESTIONS

1. I set this novel in a house on the bend of a river because I've always wanted to live where I could hear water flowing. If you could live anywhere, where would it be?

2. Have you had the pleasure of "found family"—either roommates or neighbors, workplace associates, or someone else entirely? What does it take to create a family out of people who were once strangers?

3. Pearl says she knows a little about a lot of things and that makes her a good governess. What about you? Do you know a lot about a few things? A bit about many things? How does your knowledge serve you?

4. Oliver and Uncle Arthur both live with loss and loneliness, but they don't discuss it. This makes for necessary misunderstandings in a story, but how do you learn to bridge the gap of grief and mourning to repair relationships?

5. If I had to pick a favorite character in this book, Madame Genevieve might be the one. (She has a fascinating backstory that didn't find a place in this story, but maybe, someday . . .) Have you ever seen a performance by a mystic or a psychic? What did you think?

6. The Industrial Revolution changed practically everything in a

family's daily routine. Consider how much of your life would be taken up with sewing and mending and altering if you couldn't purchase ready-made clothes. What other modern developments save you time and effort?

7. Pearl finds herself frustrated and annoyed by Oliver for much of the story. Have you ever had a relationship where your affection and attraction battled with bafflement and exasperation?

8. The story's epilogue suggests something new and beautiful and important has grown up alongside Shadowbrook House. How does this metaphor prove itself true in your own life?

Enjoy this excerpt of

THE ORCHIDS OF ASHTHORNE HALL

REBECCA ANDERSON

Lament

My life, such as it was, ended at the sickbed in London.
Ravaged bones, weakened heart, ruined face. No hope left.
All I knew—gone, destroyed, lost to me.
Now I make my home in the deserted halls of Ashthorne.
The weeping of wind through stone masks my cries
As I await the time until I can, at last, disappear.

Chapter 1

Not until the screeching wind overpowered the sounds of the horses' stomping hooves did Hyacinth Bell pull back the window coverings in the jolting carriage. Though impatient for her arrival, she wondered what a wind so powerful could be doing to the landscape.

As it happened, almost nothing. The moors of central Cornwall were completely barren as far as she could see, and the wind could blow unimpeded across miles of fields without paying any attention to the earth, searching for something—anything—that stood higher than a sheep.

Hyacinth's carriage, for instance. The wind seemed determined to surround it on all sides at once. Nothing else marred the horizon as far as she could see. Not a building in sight. Hardly a tree.

The thought that she was riding in the highest point across the entire countryside made her laugh, a sound made slightly unhinged by nature's accompaniment of wailing wind.

Unsettled by the gale, she hummed to herself. As the noise outside the carriage pressed against her, humming was not enough. She sang. Even at the top of her voice, she was drowned by the volume of the storm. Was this what it felt like to go mad?

The wind roared, screeched, and rattled around her, giving her the feeling that even within the walls of the carriage, the very atmosphere sought to attack her peace. She knew the wind was not whipping her hair about her head like a ghost in a penny dreadful illustration, but she felt as though both her rationality and her hairstyle were holding on by a mere thread. Or a miracle.

Not that anyone but the driver would see her hair, or care if they did. Not until the stop in Suttonsbury village. Not until her meeting with Ashthorne Hall's temporary orchid caretaker, an elderly man who managed a village greenhouse. Hyacinth had agreed to go to his shop to pick up the last packages of soil preparations and instruments that Mr. Whitbeck had ordered.

He would also give Hyacinth any final instructions before she made her way through the gale to Ashthorne Hall and her new position. Her new life.

The horses' whinnies carried on the wind, another layer of shrieking adding to her unease. Hyacinth wondered how the driver fared in this monstrous wind, if he held his perch up on the driver's box by the strength of his will. For a moment, she considered pounding on the wall and calling out to him, but even if she could get his attention, he would not be able to hear her ask after his safety or comfort, so she pulled the window coverings tight and hummed again.

The almost inaudible sound of her own voice was less than reassuring.

She lifted the potted orchid from the seat beside her.

"Eleanor," Hyacinth said to the orchid in a voice of warm confidence, "if you could see outside, you'd not recognize anything growing here. None of our hothouse friends could survive a night like this."

She did not raise the window cover to give Eleanor a peek at the moor; that would be silly.

The roaring autumn wind, she knew, could not last forever.

At least, she thought it could not. In fact, she was aware she knew very little about the weather patterns of Cornwall, to say nothing of its residents or their feelings about visiting botanists.

Once she arrived at Ashthorne Hall, she vowed, she would never again leave. A hundred years would be too soon for another carriage ride like this one. How grateful she was that most of the hundreds of miles she had traveled from Herefordshire had been by train. Only since Plymouth had she been inside this carriage, and only for the last half hour had she felt her excitement turn to anxiety. And that she could mostly blame on the infernal wind, which had alternated in pitch between a roar and a wail.

Hyacinth looked down at the note from Mr. Whitbeck in her right hand. Replacing Eleanor on the carriage seat beside her, she clutched the letter in both hands, the paper grown soft from dozens, perhaps hundreds of openings, followed by careful reading and refolding. After months of seeking employment and waiting, she was finally on her way to Ashthorne Hall.

She envisioned the stone edifice rising out of a grove of trees, chimney pieces streaming warm smoke and window glass reflecting surrounding sunlight. Having never seen the manor where she would soon live, she had created an image of her own devising by compiling the best parts of elegant houses she knew: rooflines and landscaping, trees and ponds and driveways, stones of warm golden hue.

How much of Ashthorne would match her imaginings? And what of the people living inside? She had little more than Mr. Whitbeck's note and seal to recommend her to the housekeeper and the caretaker. And it was possible they would be the only other inmates of the manor. The rest of the staff had either removed to India with the family or been let go to find other employment.

Her imagination gave her comfort, but she realized she might have to let go of her preconception. Her father had taught her that the ability to hold on to an idea was a very important skill for gaining knowledge and understanding, but he emphasized that an even more crucial skill was the ability to let a faulty thought go.

She had trained herself to treat her thoughts like precipitates, the solids that separate from a chemical solution: With a bit of agitation, things settle. Once they do, an observer has something to look at, to study, and to hold on to or reject as evidence suggests.

She hoped the housekeeper at Ashthorne did not hold too tightly to any false ideas about her.

Nothing in Hyacinth's bearing or stature identified her as either an expert botanist or a genius gardener. She looked rather like a tall schoolgirl, if one with a more than usual amount of dirt beneath her fingernails. But Hyacinth Bell was no child, and she had learned from the greatest scientific minds of the day. Her father, a viscount, had early in his peerage grown weary of days filled with receiving complaints and reporting them to the earl. In his leisure time, he gathered to his home men of science, and as he learned of ways to improve farmlands, increase crop productivity, and strengthen plants, he passed on all his understanding to his youngest daughter, who took to the lessons and the experiments with a passion and a consideration he had not expected.

He was delighted.

Hyacinth soon outstripped her father in her understanding, and with his blessing, she continued to study plants and propagation, flowers and seeds, and the maximization of crop yield. Before many years had passed, she had grown from a precocious child with a gardening hobby into a highly respected young lady, eager to share her knowledge and understanding with the farmers in her father's care.

After the death of her dear mother five years prior, Hyacinth took over care of the lady's orchids, and there found a gift and talent she had not anticipated. She soon became masterful in her work with tropical blooms. Many people thought orchids were difficult flowers, but Hyacinth soon realized that they had few needs: soil conditions, water, light, and air. Once you understood these, the care came rather easily.

Hyacinth's father recommended her to all who would listen as one of the greatest orchid experts in the country. She knew he spoke far too highly of her talent but appreciated the acclaim that surrounded her in English botany circles.

Mr. Charles Whitbeck, a magistrate and orchid enthusiast, had written to Hyacinth upon occasion, seeking advice for his impressive orchid collection. Mr. Whitbeck had plans to travel to India, and he invited her to come to his home at Ashthorne Hall and look after his hothouse in his absence. "There is not much I shall miss while I am away, but I will rest easier if my treasured orchids are in your capable care."

Hyacinth had grown more excited by the day about the possibility, and her father believed the adventure would be a wonderful interlude before she settled down as the brilliant wife of some worthy man or other. And now, after months of preparation, Mr. Whitbeck was off in the tropics, and Hyacinth drew near Suttonsbury village, the town nearest to Ashthorne Hall.

Traveling through the ominous and unsettling storm, Hyacinth felt the minutes drag, as though the wind pressed her ever farther from the town. Just as she became certain she'd crawl out of her skin if she had to sit another minute in the jostling coach, she both heard and felt a knocking at the wall of the carriage.

"We're approaching Suttonsbury now, miss," the driver said. At least, that is what Hyacinth thought he said as the wind tore half the words from him and carried them away to crash against the cliffs and rocks of the wild coast.

A few more minutes brought them to the village's greenhouse, and at the horses' halt, Hyacinth threw open the carriage door, eager to escape the tight confines of the vehicle, even if it meant a drenching from the rain. She lifted Eleanor's pot from the seat and stepped down.

The wind had slowed enough that she could stand in front of the garden shop without her hair blowing completely loose from its knot. She looked up at the sign swinging from two metal chains attached to the roof: Gardner's Paradise.

At her knock, a man opened the shop's front door, and Hyacinth's first instinct was to back away. His shirt, covered with an open brown vest, was filthy. He looked at her sideways, squinting an eye, and a muscle jumped near his mouth, pulling his lip into a sneer.

"Closed," he said, as if she did not deserve a complete sentence. He began to shut the door. Was this the man Mr. Whitbeck wanted her to communicate with?

She wondered if she ought to simply get into the carriage and come back another day, but she had her instructions. "There is an order for Ashthorne Hall, I believe."

The man leaned out into the wind and rain as if inspecting her. "You the Whitbeck's new flower girl, then?" he asked with a growl. His breath carried more than a hint of whiskey. His glare, more than a hint of disdain.

His rude behavior made her wish she would never have to return here. But since it was the only garden shop for miles, she knew she'd need to come back. Perhaps she could salvage some of this bad first impression.

"Mr. Gardner?" she asked, holding out her hand and hoping she did not look as much a fool as she felt, standing in the rain.

Ignoring her proffered hand, the man shook his head and huffed in contempt. "I'm James. Gardner is out back in the greenhouse. He has your parcels. Walk on through."

Though relieved that this unpleasant man was not Mr. Gardner, Hyacinth felt James could do with a reminder of basic manners. He spoke to her as he would to a horse. But she chose to say nothing and simply followed him through the shop and out the back door. A glass garden structure glowed with the light of dozens of hanging lamps, warmer and more welcoming than any word from James had been.

The alleyway between the shop and the greenhouse was a throughway for the night's wind, which gusted against Hyacinth's body and practically pushed her sideways. James rapped on the glass door and waited, his hand holding his hat to his head. He muttered something about locked doors that she did not try to hear.

Hyacinth watched through the glass as a figure scuttled toward them, becoming clearer as he approached. By degrees, she could discern his short, round figure, his hurried gait, and his full, white beard. Everything from his posture to his age to his stature spoke of the difference between him and his hired helper. James was large and slouching and sullen. The man hurrying toward her practically bounced as he jogged, and she saw his smile through the glass walls. By the time he opened the door, Hyacinth knew she would be fond of this man.

James muttered, "Whitbeck's new hire," and made a sound of displeasure. "Hope she finds the manor to her liking." He sounded anything but hopeful as he turned back to the shop.

Hyacinth was not sorry to be rid of him.

"Ah, Miss Bell. I'm George Gardner, and very pleased to meet you." With a warm smile on his weathered face, Mr. Gardner reached for Hyacinth's hands and pulled her into the safety of the greenhouse. He chuckled as he looked up into her face, as he was only as tall as her shoulders.

"Welcome, welcome. Come in out of all that weather, dear," he said. "I'm right glad you've found us."

A shock of white hair grew like a cluster of shaggy ink cap mushrooms from beneath his pointed red hat. His brown leather apron did little to hide his bulbous stomach, which seemed to shake as he laughed. With a hand still on her arm, he reached over and locked the hothouse door behind them.

"Can never be too careful," he said when he turned back. With a clap of his hands, he said, "Now. Can I talk you into a cup of tea and a comfortable seat before we get down to business?"

"I really must not keep the Ashthorne housekeeper waiting long," Hyacinth said. "But I hope we can share a cup and a visit on another day. I am sure you have much to teach me."

Mr. Gardner laughed again. Hyacinth believed it might be his natural response to most situations, and she decided she liked it a great deal indeed.

With a wink, Gardner said, "Oh, don't flatter me, young woman. I've nothing like the skill you're known for. Mr. Whitbeck sent word about you."

"Did he?" Hyacinth smiled at that. What might he have said? She was pleased her reputation impressed him enough that he'd spread it through the village before he left for India.

"Oh, aye. You're a right smart touch with the orchids, he tells me. And well you should be, for his collection is a masterwork. Far more than James and I could manage."

"Sir, I'm sure you kept the collection in good order since Mr. Whitbeck left," Hyacinth said.

Mr. Gardner nodded. "It's a beautiful lot he has, indeed. James would have liked to stay up at the manor, for he does fancy life at the big house. As I worked in the hothouses, he took to wandering. I believe he went looking for pirate caves." Mr. Gardner's laugh rolled out of him again.

"But you, Miss Bell, are perfectly suited for the work and the station. Between you and me," Mr. Gardner said, "when I took on the extra work at Ashthorne, I ought to have hired someone who knows more about plants. Or who is more polite to customers. Or who can manage to stay in the place he is supposed to be working." Mr. Gardner laughed again, as if his mistake in hiring his employee was a great joke.

If she knew him better, she might ask one of the many questions filling her mind. Why would Mr. Gardner hire someone so obviously unfit to help him in his work? But even though he led the conversation in that direction, she felt it would be rude to pry.

"Good help is often difficult to find," she said.

Mr. Gardner grinned and nodded, holding the sides of his ample stomach. "Mr. Whitbeck certainly got the best England had to offer when he found you."

Hyacinth began to make a polite denial, but Mr. Gardner gestured to the pot in Hyacinth's hand. "Have you already been to the manor, then?" he asked.

She shook her head. "Oh, no. This is Eleanor. She once belonged to my mother."

The emotion in her voice surprised her. Of course she loved her plant, but the feeling of loss and mourning caught Hyacinth off guard, and she put her free hand to her face as she attempted to steel herself against her grief.

Mr. Gardner seemed able to read her feelings in her face. He nodded gently and said, "And a fine-looking orchid she is. She'll fit right in with the others."

His affirmation was exactly enough to help Hyacinth move past her momentary sorrow.

"Thank you. Having her safe in the orchid house will be a relief to us both, I'm sure."

"We mustn't keep either of you waiting, then," he said, and they made their way to the rear of the greenhouse where he gestured to a stack of crates.

"I'll have my man James load these into your carriage. And perhaps your driver can assist us."

"I'm happy to help as well," Hyacinth said, lifting a small box from the top of the pile to prove her willingness.

Mr. Gardner immediately protested, but Hyacinth didn't give him a chance to stop her from helping. Pulling a crate from the pile, Mr. Gardner led Hyacinth back out of the greenhouse and to the rear of the shop. Mr. Gardner knocked and called out, "James, give us a hand with these parcels, if you please."

As the shop door opened, Hyacinth heard the younger man muttering even over the sound of the wind.

If this was the kind of person working in this village, she felt grateful at the thought of a deserted manor house. She would rather be alone than in the company of men like James.

Returning bearing several of the boxes, he continued to grumble. She pretended not to notice his unsavory language or the comment that may or may not have been about her. As she lifted her crate up to the driver, James came up behind her.

She moved aside half a step to avoid touching him.

He moved closer, standing far too close to Hyacinth's ear. "You'd do well to watch yourself in that old house," he said. "Don't go wandering. Place is haunted by spirits."

Hyacinth chose not to answer, but she stepped away from James and closer to Mr. Gardner. Ghosts? Did this man think her a child, likely to be frightened by silly tales?

She was glad he could not see the fine hairs on her arms rising in response to his warning, unsure if she was more frightened or thrilled by the possibility of a haunted manor.

She stayed between Mr. Gardner and the driver as they moved the garden supplies to the carriage. With all four of them carrying parcels, it only took one more trip to the greenhouse before the packages were loaded. The driver retook his seat and held the reins as the horses stamped in the rain that had become a downpour.

Mr. Gardner handed Hyacinth in to the carriage. "Keep your eyes open up there at the manor. You must know places like that are full of ghosts," he said, still with a grin and a wink, but this time, Hyacinth's shiver was less enjoyable than the first. After that comment from James, Mr. Gardner's jest felt too real. She glanced over Mr. Gardner's shoulder, but James was nowhere in sight.

Mr. Gardner continued, "But that doesn't mean you've anything to fear. Everyone knows old houses are full of haunts. No need to assume the ghosts are of a wicked turn of mind. You might learn a thing from the Ashthorne spirits about making yourself at home."

He grinned, and his whole face folded in wrinkles and the lift of pink cheeks. "Of course, the coast has also been overrun with pirates for hundreds of years, and they are probably a different story. Do stay away from the pirates, Miss Bell. And please come see us when you next make a trip into the village. I owe you a cup of tea."

His silly pirate warning made her feel better; clearly, his stories were all in fun. She gave his hand a squeeze and thanked him for his help. "I would love to come back and visit."

Mr. Gardner nodded and closed the door. Seconds later, the horses were in motion, and once again, carriage full of garden supplies and head full of ghosts, Hyacinth was on the road to Ashthorne.

ABOUT THE AUTHOR

By night (and very early morning), **REBECCA ANDERSON** writes historical romances. By day, she sets aside her pseudonym and resumes her life as Becca Wilhite, who loves hiking, Broadway shows, rainstorms, food, books, and movies. She lives in the mountains and adores the ocean. She dreams of travel but loves staying home. Happiness is dabbling in lots of creative activities, afternoon naps, and cheese. All the cheese.

You can find her online at beccawilhite.com.